THIS IS NOT A LOVE STORY

SUKI FLEET

Harmony Ink

Published by

Harmony Ink Press
5032 Capital Circle SW
Suite 2, PMB# 279
Tallahassee, FL 32305-7886
USA
publisher@harmonyinkpress.com
http://harmonyinkpress.com

This Is Not a Love Story
© 2014 Suki Fleet.

Cover Art
© 2014 Aaron Anderson.
aaronbydesign55@gmail.com
Cover content is for illustrative purposes only
and any person depicted on the cover is a model.

ISBN: 978-1-63216-040-9
Library ISBN: 978-1-63216-041-6
Digital ISBN: 978-1-63216-042-3

Printed in the United States of America
First Edition
May 2014
Adapted from *This Is Not a Love Story* by S. Honunjama, published by CreateSpace, December 2013

Library Edition
August 2014

PART ONE:
WE ARE MEANT TO BE EPHEMERAL

ROMEO

THERE'S THIS boy (isn't there always?), this beautiful, glowing creature who makes me feel alive. Even here, living on the street with all the shit that happens—the cold, the hunger, the terror of spending one more day like this, one more night like this—somehow he makes me want to survive it, despite everything, just to spend another fucking minute in his starry-bright glow.

Even now, *especially now*, as we stand on the embankment next to the busy main road. This is the red-light district for boys like us. This is where we sell ourselves, one piece of our souls at a time.

Four coins rest in the palm of his hand, the rest hidden in the strap beneath his threadbare sleeve.

He holds them out to me, and I am entranced by the warm gold skin of his wrist—people pay a fortune to get a glow like that, for something he just *has* naturally.

"For you," he mouths, fixing his light brown eyes on mine.

Yeah, for me to go and get warm in Joe Brown's stinking cafe while he gets fucked under the railway arches by some dirty creep who doesn't give a shit if he hurts him. I wish Julian didn't act like my big brother. I wish just once he'd trust me to look out for him. I'm not as fragile as he thinks.

But I take the coins, when really what I want to do is throw them into the road and beg him not to go.

He knows, and our gazes lock, the both of us trying to communicate something the other doesn't understand, or doesn't want to.

It's like this every time he gets picked up.

As if on cue, the guy in the car blasts the horn. We both jump.

"Hurry the fuck up," the creep hisses.

Through the steamed-up car window I can't see the face attached to the voice, but the rest of him looks old and thin—hands gnarled as the roots of the trees that line this part of the embankment grip the steering wheel. And though I know that his age doesn't mean he's harmless, I can pretend, I can hope.

Julian tries to smile, his eyes telling me it will be okay. But how will this ever be okay? I can't bear it.

But we have nothing.

We are nothing.

His warm fingers brush my cold ones, and I long to grab his hands and pull him away with me. I want to run along the embankment with him until my lungs burst. Maybe I will anyway.

Alone.

"Twenty minutes," he mouths.

I nod robotically. He gets in the car and watches me from the window as he's driven away. I make a note of the color, model, and registration number. Knowing this makes me feel safer: if anything were to happen, I would have a tether, a proof that this car exists and Julian exists within it.

Nothing is going to happen. I bite back a sob. And run.

JOE BROWN'S cafe is full of wasters. Technically, I guess that includes me.

"Hey, Romeo!"

I ignore the shout. I don't even want to acknowledge Cricket. He's high. But he gets up and comes over to the counter where I'm stood waiting for Cassey to pour my tea.

"Where's Jules?"

I turn around and shrug. It's none of his fucking business. Whatever Cricket's got to sell, I'm not buying.

"Lend us a quid."

He drapes a skinny arm around my shoulder. I hold my breath and shrug him off.

I try not to look at the clock on the wall above the counter, but it's become a sick compulsion. Ten more minutes.

"Pleeease."

I take a clean napkin out of the dispenser and write *fuck off* with the pen from my pocket.

I've been desperate before too, and Cricket took that opportunity to kick me while I was down. Maybe he thinks I've forgotten.

Cassey hands me my tea along with four packets of sugar. She keeps the sugar behind the counter now. She eyes Cricket warily.

"Leave the boy alone. He's never done you any harm."

Cricket backs away, holding his hands up. "Hey, I was just being friendly."

"Aye, course you were," she says, grimacing.

I have this effect on women, especially after they find out there's something wrong with me—when they find out I can't speak, that I'm mute. They want to look out for me, mother me, protect me. Well, apart from my own mother. I never had this effect on her. I wouldn't be here if I had.

"How you doing?" Cassey asks me. And it's not an empty question. She really wants to know.

Got moved on again last night. Tired, I write on the back of the fuck-off napkin.

"Hungry?"

If the rest of them ever found out she was giving me food for free, the place would get trashed.

"Come around the back in five minutes," she says quietly.

MY POCKETS are full of crushed toast that's getting even more pulverized as I run down the embankment toward the railway arches.

Julian's late.

He's been late before but never this late.

As twenty minutes turned into forty, I started to feel sick. So sick Cassey thought I was ill.

Oh God, oh God, please please please let him be okay.

Last week the police found the body of a boy on the heath. The heath is miles from here, but we all knew the boy. He used to hang around the embankment selling himself like Julian.

I knew I should have stopped Julian getting in that car. I had a bad feeling about this from the start. I should have followed them. The thought of him hurt or in pain makes me retch. At the bottom of the embankment, I stop and steady myself against a wall as I stare out toward the railway arches.

Where *is* he?

I wish I could call his name, hear a voice that is mine ringing with it. Instead I scream silently, my heart about to implode in my chest.

Please, I plead to the silence, *let me find him. He's all I have.*

GEM

TWO BATTERED chest freezers and the shredded remains of a car tire litter the roadside, but there is no beige Ford Escort with rust-scoured wings. There are no cars parked up at all.

A swathe of misty rain sweeps in from the river and makes the world a blurry and somehow uncertain gray.

I look at my watch. It's been fifty minutes. Julian said twenty. The police won't start a search for at least twenty-four hours, even given the circumstances.

If he's gone, I've lost him. If he's not here, then he's not anywhere, anymore.

His soft honey-colored hair, his sweet wonky smile (he fractured his palate when he was younger, but the only time you'd notice is when he grins at you full-on). Suddenly it hits me, and I feel light-headed, pain wrings my chest, thoughts spiral… *whatifwhatifwhatif*…? I can't breathe. *Fuck*… I stumble into brickwork that curves in out of nowhere to smack me in the face. The pain is so great I almost pass out… almost… almost…. I kneel on the pavement until… eventually… my breathing deepens, slows down, and I pull myself up.

Ahead of me there are six massive archways. All dark in the depths of them. Perfect for what they're used for.

I hate it here.

Julian would use the last one if he were given a choice. *Was he given a choice?* I bite back a sob.

My ears ring with music as a car races past, subwoofers vibrating the sodden afternoon air.

I inch along the pavement, eyes almost closed.

I'm such a coward, Julian. You would have found me by now. If the situation were reversed, I know you would.

The last archway. I stare up at the greasy black walls for a second as a train clatters overhead. Then I close my eyes completely, as if I can possibly delay the moment.

"Remee?"

Was that pale echo of a desperately familiar voice just my imagination? If it was, I think my heart might stop.

No one else calls me Remee.

Eyes wide, I step into the gloom.

The ground is cluttered with skeletal shopping trolleys, tangled wire, and used rubbers. The air smells weedy and damp. I can't stand to think of him being used in here, his beautiful body, his glowing skin, his sparkly eyes, reduced to… a dark hole in someone else's fantasy… a cheap fuck.

Against the wall in the not-quite dark, I see the threadbare jumper he was wearing. I stoop to pick it up and a thin naked arm shoots out of the gloom and grabs my wrist. *Julian.*

Sometimes relief is sweet and gentle; sometimes it hits you like a truck.

"I'm sorry I didn't come meet you." His voice is small. He doesn't get up.

I don't want him to be sorry. I want him to be okay, but he's not.

I ease myself down next to him. I can't see him properly. There's not enough light. I hand him his jumper and can barely make him out as he pulls it down over his head.

"You smell like toast," he says, softy. "Cassey?"

I nod, and he smiles, not quite a wince, as I hand him the most intact piece I have left.

The notebook and pen I carry around with me are squashed into my pocket too, but everything I want to say hurts a little too much.

Warm fingers brush my forehead, and he frowns.

"You're bleeding." He holds his hand up in front of my eyes, showing me the blood. "What happened?"

How can he worry about my stupid little graze?

I pull the notebook out and scrawl. *Slipped on the embankment and fell over, people were watching and everything.* I draw a diagram of a stick man flying through the air. I draw people laughing. I make them look like us.

Afterward I lean toward him, letting my head rest against his shoulder. He smells of sex—not in a good way.

Want to go to Gem's? I write in tiny little capital letters.

I feel him nod tightly, his cheek against my shorn head. I know his eyes are closed. I know he's trying not to cry. So I don't move until he gently pushes me away.

Gem's is where we go when things get real bad. We can't stay there—she has a kid, and she works as an escort from her flat (it's only one bedroom), not out on the street, and she's always pretty busy—but she never turns us away. She lets us use her bathroom, her kitchen, and if we're desperate, we can sleep for a few hours on her floor. I think she and Julian had a thing once, but I've never quite had the courage to ask.

I help him to stand. I notice he seems to have lost a shoe. He says he doesn't want to look for it, but I don't think we'll get far without it, so I leave him leaning against the wall and start scanning the rubbish-strewn ground. Even though my eyes have adjusted, I can hardly make out anything deeper in this shadow.

"Remee," he calls hoarsely.

I spin around, and he's sobbing. Julian never cries, well, not that he lets anyone see anyway.

"I just want to go," he whispers brokenly.

I nod and slip my arm around his back so he can lean on me, and we stumble out to the road.

GEM IS the epitome of glamour—a glossy television glamour, 1000 watts brighter than real life. Understated is a word she's never heard of.

She opens the door in a long red gown, looking like the star of some old Hollywood movie. Her hair piled up on her head in a beautiful cascade of dark curls, her black skin shimmering and glittery.

But her painted-on flashlight smile drops as soon as she sees us.

"Jesus. What happened to you, Jules?"

Julian looks at her pleadingly, and I tighten my hold on him. I guess he wants to tell her.

After all these months, I still haven't worked out why he never wants to tell me. He tells me everything else.

"Hey, why don't you go and make us a cup of tea?" Gem says to me as she leads Julian into the small living room. "I've got five minutes before the next one's due."

Angrily, I slam the cups down on the counter and shove the kettle under the tap. Does he think I can't see the bloodstains on the back of his trousers? Does he think I didn't notice he can hardly fucking walk? I'm not a fucking kid. I'm only three years younger than him, and I've been on the street for the same amount of time as he has. So I don't pull tricks—it's a bit of a disadvantage when you can't speak, punters think you're somehow retarded when you start writing notes—but I *know* what happens. I know it gets rough sometimes. I understand. Fuck, I *want* to understand.

I grip the edge of the sink until my knuckles turn the color of the bones beneath them.

I'm not angry he won't talk to me about it. I'm angry because someone hurt him.

"Rome-yo!"

Tiny arms wrap around the tops of my legs, hugging me tightly, and I quickly swallow my rage and spin around to scoop up the smiling imp. Gem's son Joel is four and a bit and superclever.

I swing him upside down and tickle him until he begs me to stop, then crouch down to brush against his chest with my hands.

What's got you so happy? I sign.

I enjoy teaching him sign. It amazes me that he picks it up so quickly, second only to Julian.

I love you, he signs back, grinning.

I love you too, Joel, I sign before pulling him against me and hiding my face in his tight braids. I don't know where Gem gets the time to do his hair like this. It's like a work of art. But I do know this kid is her world.

"Why is Jules sad?"

Everyone gets sad sometimes. I sign. *Want to help me make tea?*

I need an excuse to turn away for a moment and wipe my eyes, so I let Joel scamper around finding tea bags and milk.

JULIAN IS buried in Gem's arms as I walk into the living room, burning my knuckles on three cups of tea. They break apart as soon as Julian sees me, and he wraps his arms around a sofa cushion instead, his eyes hollow in a way I can't stand. I'm not jealous that they're close. We hug like that all the time. It's what friends do, isn't it? I just wish he'd let me comfort him too.

This is the last of your milk. I hand the note to Gem as I put the tea down and sit next to Julian on the sofa.

Gem sighs. "Here." She hands me the last coins out of a glass jar on the floor. "Pick some more up for me and run him a bath, yeah?" She inclines her head at Julian.

I nod.

Joel stands in the doorway, staring at Julian's shivering form, worried about him, I guess.

When the doorbell rings, the chime echoes weirdly. It's like those doorbells you get in Victorian mansions. And yet in this bright fourth-floor, tower-block flat, immaculate despite the dodgy windows and the damp seeping in through the exposed outside walls, it seems strangely, perfectly suited.

"Joel, honey, you going to look after these boys while I'm working?" Gem calls, walking to the door.

I take out my notebook and sketch an outline of Joel's face. I show it to him.

Want to come to the shop with me?

It can't be good for him to hear what's going on behind the paper-thin wall to the bedroom. I know Gem's explained something to him, and I know she doesn't trust anyone else in this block to look after him, but still.

We take the lift, even though I hate the lift—Joel finds it thrilling.

I left Julian in the bathroom, unsteadily peeling off his clothes. I think he needed to be alone. Every time now it takes that little bi' longer for the visible warmth to suffuse his being again, for his glo' return. I wish he'd never started this. He thought it would be easy money, enough to maybe get us a room somewhere, something we could build on.

Yeah, easy money and a little bit of your soul.

WE STOP off at the play park on the way back from the shop, so we're gone a while. Gem's still busy when we get back, and Julian is still in the bathroom. I leave Joel in the living room with my notebook and pen, coloring in the sketch of his face, and stand outside the bathroom door.

I don't knock. I hate knocking. People call out when you knock, and I can't answer. So I just slowly open the door and close it again, my heart beating fast.

Though I didn't see much, just a handheld mirror and Julian balanced awkwardly, I'm still glued to the spot a few seconds later when Julian bursts out of the room, water pouring off him and onto the floor, a small towel slung around his hips.

I'm sorry, I sign quickly. Mortified, actually.

You'd think we had no secrets left, living as we do, and I've seen him naked plenty of times, but I've never seen him *exposed* like that, examining himself.

He tugs my arms and pulls me into the bathroom, shutting the door softly behind me.

Raking a hand through his hair, he swallows audibly. "I'm still bleeding."

Oh God. I pat my pockets wildly for my pad, then remember Joel has it in the other room.

What should I do? I sign. *Do you want me to get Gem?*

I'm not even sure he understands me.

"I didn't want you to see me like this," he moans softly, not meeting my eyes, though I'm *pleading* with him to look up. It's so fucking unfair when people won't look at you, especially after they say something like that.

The front door bangs, Gem's client leaving, I guess. I grip the door handle.

And why didn't he want me to see him like this? How is it any different than going skinny-dipping in the lake and wrestling in the freezing water to get warm, or sneaking into the swimming pool showers and sharing the same cubicle, squeezing close, our soapy limbs tangling, deliciously slippy—I had to get out before he noticed how much I liked it.

Doesn't he *get* how I look at him? I can't take my eyes off him. His smile makes me melt. Does he think I'm somehow going to think less of him because some intimate part of his beautiful body is hurt and bleeding? How fucking stupid is that?

Or… or… does he not want me to see him naked at all suddenly? Has something changed in the balance of our friendship?

But….

He sees my mind is crazily spinning out of control and gently picks my hand up off the door handle, shaking his head.

That's not what he means, none of it.

"Remee? Can you check me?" he whispers, his voice full of uncertainty.

With effort, he spreads a towel out on the floor and lies face down. He rolls another towel up and pushes it under his hips so they're raised up.

I can see he's still bleeding redly, not a lot, but the blood is running in a tiny river down his thigh. His skin is still sweetly pink from the heat of the bath, and there are dozens of finger-size bruise marks over his narrow hips. My hands hover over them, too scared to move. He turns his head, and those amber eyes swallow me whole.

I imagine I'm a nurse in a hospital and he is my patient. I'm calm, and I talk myself through what I have to do in my head: I need to place my hands on his buttocks and spread them apart. I need to see why he is bleeding. Is it a cut, a bruise, a tear? Does it look clean? Does it need stitches? But when I place my hand on his lower back to let him prepare for my touch, all these feelings start spinning around inside me, like leaves whirling in the wind, and my mind goes terrifyingly blank. His skin is hot, slightly clammy, and oh so soft. As I brush my hand across the triangle of nerves at the base of his spine, he shivers, goose bumps appear all along his arms, and I snap my hand away, afraid that it's cold. I'm always cold, but when I bring it to my cheek, it's not.

He watches me the whole time. I feel my face start to flush, and I'm too hot in my clothes, uncomfortable in my skin. I need to get this over with. I need to get over my own fear and concentrate on him. This is too important.

Despite his slight frame, his buttocks are full and round and not at all bony. They feel perfect beneath my hands. I struggle to think of his body in abstract anatomical terms. I struggle to slow my racing heart, but it's no use. Gently I spread him apart, careful of the bruises.

I don't know what I imagined, but I feel ashamed I was afraid of this. It's all so… normal-looking, and I've never looked at anyone from this angle before. When I look up to reassure him I'm not freaking out, I see his eyes are squeezed shut, are squeezing tighter shut every second that passes with me peering at this hidden part of him. I grab a piece of tissue to dab away the blood, discovering the graze isn't deep.

The bleeding has almost stopped, and I'm so engrossed in being gentle and thorough that I involuntarily leap up when there is a soft knock on the door. Julian turns over, covering himself self-consciously with a towel.

"Yeah?" he calls out.

The door eases open. Gem's head appears. "Everything okay?"

She frowns when she sees I am nursing tissue after tissue covered in blood.

"You're still bleeding, Julian."

It's not a question. She vanishes and returns half a minute later with a box of those surgical rubber gloves you get in hospitals.

"You can never be too careful," she says to me as she squeezes into the tiny bathroom and kneels down on the floor. "Tell me the fucker used protection."

Julian shrugs and won't meet her eyes. I can tell he doesn't want to talk about this, probably because I'm here.

"Come on," she says, impatiently snapping a glove on each hand. "Let me see."

To his credit, Julian looks like he'd rather crawl under the bath than have another person peering at him.

Gem cocks her head. "It's not like I haven't seen it before."

My eyes catch Julian's.

"How you can still be coy about this I've no idea," she carries on, smiling obliviously.

I look away first.

It's stupid given the circumstances, but I suddenly feel sick and unbalanced, as if someone's whipped the floor away, and I no longer know which way is up. I *knew* they'd had something. A relationship, a fling. Deep down, I knew. You can see from how comfortable they are with one another that they've been close. But having it confirmed... having it confirmed that he's not gay, that all the little things, all the looks, touches, smiles I try to add up to mean something, mean nothing after all.

And I know he's not bi either. Once I overheard him tell Cassey he wished he was. He said it would have made everything easier— whatever that meant.

"Remee?" Julian's hand touches my arm. "What's wrong?"

I scribble in the air, miming that I'm going to get my pad, but as soon as I'm in the living room, I rip out the page for Joel, kiss him on the forehead, and leave the flat.

If I broke down in there, Julian would want to know what had upset me, and I can't tell him, not now. If he knew how I felt about him, I'm certain it would ruin everything.

SKETCHES

THE SKY is an ominous expanse of purple-gray as far as the eye can see, the clouds shot through with shards of silver. So much texture and depth, I wish I could paint it. I've never painted anything… well, apart from in primary school, where I covered sheet after soaking sheet of paper in every color imaginable. Though that wasn't really painting, more just passing the time so I didn't feel like such an inadequate reject, lost in the constant song of other children's voices. I lean back on the swing and let my head touch the ground. Now I can see what I would do with color, how it would *sing* through *me* like—

A can clatters across the road between the play park and the block of flats. Still upside down, I twist my head and see a group is gathering by a silent blacked-up car a few meters away from the entrance to the flats. Slowly, I pull myself upright. I don't want to draw their attention, but I know I'm being watched. As if to confirm this, a second can clatters against the fence around the play park.

Thank God, I think as Julian walks stiffly down the stairs, out the door, and crosses the road toward me.

The ache in my chest becomes almost unbearable as I notice the jacket, jeans, and shoes he's wearing aren't his. They must belong to someone Gem knows. But they suit him, especially the jacket—especially with the collar turned up against the wind. He looks like this guy I saw in a movie once. The guy's jacket was like his signature piece. He wore it the whole film, though in the end it was covered in blood.

The gate to the play park creaks as he opens it, and Julian glances sidelong at the crowd gathered around the car watching us. He turns, and his eyes settle on me. He pretends he hasn't noticed them.

"You okay?" he mouths.

I nod, my head barely moving. I wonder if he notices how swollen and red my eyes are.

We duck in unison as a third can flies through the air and hits the swing bar above our heads with a thunk.

"We should go," he says softly.

IT'S LATE as we head back toward the embankment, the turbulent autumn sky now darkening around us like a shroud.

I don't know where we'll sleep tonight, but the ripped tarpaulin we use to wrap around ourselves is stuffed under the bins at Joe Brown's cafe, so that's where we go first.

While Julian walks around the back of the cafe, I sit on a bench and sketch the river. I'm trying to ignore how cold I am. I get cold easily, and being tired and hungry all the time doesn't help. At least when I'm drawing I can forget all that. I can forget everything and immerse myself in trying to create something beautiful.

Except getting too engrossed in anything is not a good idea. On the streets, keeping at least half your brain alert to your surroundings is pretty essential.

The bin hits me first—sending me sprawling across the concrete—then everything in it as all the disgusting contents are shaken over my shell-shocked body.

Lloyd and his shadow loom over me.

Oh fuck.

I struggle to brush all the crap off me as I scramble up off the ground and prepare to run.

Jack, the shadow, moves around the other side of me to head me off. My choices of escape are now significantly reduced. I can either go through Lloyd, through Jack, in the river, or over the bench.

It's futile, and I know it, but I try and jump the bench anyway.

All the air leaves me body in a violent rush as they pin me down effortlessly before I've run two steps. They're not featherlight or hungry or beyond tired. They're wired for a fight and so much stronger than me. I don't even bother to struggle now. It would be a waste of precious energy. Lloyd sits on my chest, flicking through my pad and crushing my ribs.

Out of the corner of my eye, I see Julian round the corner, and two thoughts occur simultaneously. The first is, I want him to run. I know they'll hurt him—badly, irreparably, and without remorse. The second is not so generous: I want him to see what they're doing and fucking kill them.

Lloyd hates me, and because of me, he hates Julian. Five months ago Lloyd and the gang he hangs around with beat me so badly I couldn't walk afterward. The only reason he didn't kill me is because this fearless kid ran in swinging a metal bar, knocking at least two of them unconscious and nearly taking Lloyd's eye out. *Julian.*

He didn't know me then, and he risked everything to help me. I have no idea why. Afterward, he looked after me, took me to an abandoned open-air swimming pool south of the river, and took care of me until I was healed. It's been like that between us ever since.

"What's a dirty little refugee fag like you doing with this?" Lloyd fans the pages of the book in my face.

I'm panicking so badly I think I might pass out.

I have no idea why he thinks I'm a refugee.

"He's so fucking retarded he can't even answer." Jack laughs and tries to stamp on my hand, which I manage to jerk desperately out of Lloyd's grasp just before Jack's boot hits the ground.

Distantly, I hear glass smashing.

Lloyd holds my pen a few inches from my right eye. He has a nasty scar down his face from Julian.

I can't breathe.

"Where's your boyfriend? A little bird told us we'd find you around here, so where is he?"

My boyfriend. Is that what everyone thinks? And where the fuck *is* Julian? Has he just deserted me?

It occurs to me that I'm going to die here.

All at once a car horn sounds, long and loud. And instantly the whole situation twists a different way. Lloyd glances at the road, then at Jack, and gets off me. The car horn was for them.

"Tell Julian we're coming for him. Tell him he better watch his fucking back," he hisses, taking out a golden lighter and watching the flames lick the pages of my drawing pad before he drops it to the ground.

He mimes firing a gun as they both turn and run toward the waiting car.

Twenty seconds later I'm still lying on the ground, watching the tiny flames destroy everything I've ever been proud of as Julian runs toward me, a baseball bat in his hand. Wild-eyed, he skids to the ground next to my head.

"Are you hurt?"

Blindly, I blink back tears and shake my head. I don't want to get up.

"Where are they?"

GoneGoneGone, I sign over and over until Julian wraps his arms around my body to stop me.

FULL OF EMPTY

WHERE DID you get the bat? I write.

I'm sitting listlessly on the wet ground, leaning against the bench I tried to jump earlier, dragging a stick through the mud to form the words. I'm not sure why I asked that question. I'm not sure I really care about the answer right now.

"I panicked," he says softly. "When I saw them... I didn't have anything to... use. I looked around, but there was nothing. So... I smashed a back window in the cafe." Absently he rubs at the drying blood across his knuckle. "I knew that Cassey kept a baseball bat under the counter in case there was ever any trouble, so I took it."

So that was the glass I heard smashing.

Slowly, I break the stick into tiny frayed pieces. I don't want to have this conversation anymore.

But Julian carries on in a broken whisper. "I thought I was too late. I thought they'd hurt you. I'm sorry I took so long. I'm sorry about your pad." He carefully picks up the worthless charred cover and flicks his thumb through the burned-away pages.

I can't take it. Abruptly, I snatch it out of his hands and fling it away, far away, out of sight.

"I'll get you another."

He's watching me with this tender, concerned look on his face that I just can't stand right now.

Shut up, I want to scream at him. *Just fucking shut up.*

I'm full of empty, useless rage. I want to hurt something.

It starts to rain. Tiny droplets of rain that come in fast on the wind, like blasts of sea spray. Julian gets up and walks away to get the tarpaulin. I think he knows I won't move for anything.

"You're pissed off," he says as he pulls the faded blue sheet around us.

That's a fucking understatement. But I don't glare at him, even though I want to. Instead I glare at my useless hands and pick at the loose stitching holding the corners of the sheet together.

"Is it because… of your pad… or because of… me?"

I shrug.

We've never had an argument before. Normally, I just shut down. But I want… something. I want to sign *you, it's because of you*, even though it's not. It would never be because of him. He's my best friend. But the frustration I feel makes me want to scream, even though I've never screamed in my life. I long for some howling release.

I want a fight.

He gets it, though. He thinks it *is* him—because I didn't let him know it wasn't.

There's this odd smile on his face that's not really a smile at all, just a way to hold his face in a fixed position so he can hide his emotions. He fiddles with the laces of his borrowed shoes.

These feelings inside me—everything that's pissed me off today, all the lurking resentment at the world that I can usually crush—growl to be released. I want to tear the world apart into little pieces and watch the pieces burn.

Did you get paid earlier? I sign.

Earlier, as in when he got fucked. When he got hurt so badly he could barely walk and he bled for an hour after. I have to sign my question twice before he understands me, and my bitter frustration is just about boiling over. I want to sob.

He nods and pulls out a crumpled twenty from his pocket. His hands are shaking. I wish he would just fucking fight me.

You'll have to give the money to Cassey for the window.

He stares at me like I've gone insane.

The window, I sign again, slowly, as though he's stupid.

He's anything but.

I'm being fucking obnoxious, and I know it, but I can't stop. I hate myself, and I hate I'm doing this under the guise of caring for Cassey, and I do care for Cassey, but I couldn't give a fuck about her cafe window; she can claim it back on insurance.

Again, Julian nods.

Stop fucking agreeing with me, I want to scream. *Tell me I'm being fucking horrible, tell me to stop!*

I stand up and throw my share of the tarpaulin at him in anguish.

I walk away to lean against the thick wall that separates the embankment from the water. What the fuck am I doing? Whatever it is, it's destroying me. I dig my nails into the palms of my hands until they bleed and stare out at the dirty gray river, rough and swelling in the rain.

A few minutes later, I feel the tarpaulin being draped over my head, and Julian stands next to me. He doesn't come close enough to touch me. I'm not surprised. I want desperately to close the distance and lean my head against his shoulder. But I don't.

IT'S LATE, and we're wandering. Every so often Julian steals a glance at me, but I'm restless and tearful. I want to apologize, but I don't know how.

We walk past Cricket and Roxy, crouched under a dark concrete staircase leading up to one of the walkway bridges over the river.

Scrap that. I walk past them. Julian, however, stops.

Reluctantly, I follow him over to them.

They're drinking, which means Cricket must have found a buyer for whatever he was selling in Joe Brown's. He's so far gone he offers Julian a can for free, while Roxy lounges against him, half-asleep in his lap. I didn't know they had a thing. Maybe they don't. Sometimes a little easy affection is all we have, and while you can't live on it for long, I guess it eases the loneliness.

Roxy, used to be Robyn, who used to be my friend before I met Julian. He was sweet back then, full of anxiety and wonder, but his big round eyes and smooth caramel skin made him, I don't know... desirable, I guess, and now he just seems so... lost.

I sit on one of the weirdly shaped concrete slabs that tessellate the pavement, out in the rain, away from them. I'm being childish, I know, but sometimes you just can't stop. Sometimes there is no backing down, at least to yourself.

Julian holds out a can for me, but perversely I shake my head. I get soppy when I'm drunk, and it would do me good, shake this helpless black mood, allow me to apologize. Instead I bite the inside of my cheek as I watch them, while pretending to be staring at the ground.

The three of them are sitting close for warmth, even though Cricket stinks and Roxy's skin is covered in sores.

I screw my eyes shut. A while later I feel the tarpaulin hit me. Without looking over I drag the plastic around myself and curl up on the ground.

I've slept wet and shaking with cold many times before, but it's been a long time since I've slept alone.

BOYS KISSING

SOMETIME DURING the night, I wake to find a warm body curled perfectly against mine. We fit together so well I can't imagine we're not somehow part of the same thing. The rain is pooling on the ground around us, and I can't go back to sleep, even though my eyes are aching in their sockets.

Every so often Julian squeezes his arms tighter around me, as though he's checking I'm still there. That he does this while he's sleeping somehow makes it sweeter, just a little nighttime wonder between me and his subconscious self.

I can no longer remember what the past was like without him, what I was like when it was just me and Roxy—Robyn.

I turn my head to look over at him and Cricket, similarly curled under two torn sleeping bags. Julian murmurs in his sleep, and I push myself back against him, closer than close, as close as it's possible to get without admitting that this is more than friends/brothers/whatever he wants to call it.

Robyn and I used to be close too. More than friends once or twice. But it wasn't like this. Nothing in my whole life has ever been like this.

If I tilt my head back, his warm breath drifts against my throat, and I can pretend he's kissing me. I can shift my body so his hands move lower down my stomach... but it makes me hard, and it's frustratingly not right to behave like that with him, not when he doesn't feel the same.

Sometime before dawn I hear Cricket shout. A few minutes later, icy wind and rain whip around us as the tarpaulin is yanked off from around our bodies.

Three police in thick stab vests stand intimidatingly over us. They look like bodybuilders.

A boot presses against Julian's stomach, pushing him farther back onto the wet ground. He looks at me and smiles tightly. Police, eh? Most of them are fucking jerks.

"Didn't we already move you lot on tonight?" one of them asks like he's some sort of teacher questioning pupils over bad behavior, like we have a choice about sleeping out in the fucking rain.

Julian shakes his head. He's looking at the boot. His experience of police is worse than mine.

Cricket and Roxy hang off to the side, watching.

The smallest jerk of the lot crouches down and holds a hand out as if he wants to run it across the smooth shorn cut of my hair. Involuntarily, I shiver. Julian closes his eyes before shoving the boot off his stomach and pulling me up, close to him.

They fold away our tarpaulin.

"Confiscated."

Julian drags a hand through his wet hair. "It's fucking raining," he pleads.

"Maybe it will convince you to get off the streets and into a shelter, then."

A shelter? What a fucking joke. So much violence and dealing go on in shelters, we'd have no chance. But there is no point in arguing this out. Julian glances over at Cricket, and we walk away.

The police talk amongst themselves, their waterproof clothing rustling as they move off to dump our tarpaulin somewhere we won't find it.

CASSEY OPENS the cafe at seven every day. It can't be much earlier now as black-coated commuters are beginning to fill the gray streets in the hundreds. The idea of going there after Lloyd cornered me just outside fills me with dread, but we've got nowhere else to go.

We walk side by side, heads bowed to the wind. Julian steals a sideways glance at me.

"Are you still mad at me?" he asks quietly.

I wait until he turns to face me, and then I shake my head vigorously. No fucking way.

I'm sorry, I sign, because it's easy to say now. *I was upset.*

I wish I could have told him this last night.

Before we get to Cassey's, I tell him about Lloyd and his threat, the fact that he is coming for Julian. With a sickening sense of urgency, I realize we're going to have to find somewhere else to go, somewhere far away, across the river maybe, or maybe just north, up toward the big parks.

He watches me carefully, intently, as I sign. I love having his complete attention like this. When I've finished, he grips my fingers now cold from the rain.

"Okay," he says. "We get warm first, though."

We pay for our tea, but Cassey feeds us a sandwich each for free. She doesn't mention her broken window. If she did, I might die of guilt, especially if Julian then actually offered her his money.

"What happened to your pad, love?" she asks me halfway through the morning, passing me her order book to write on.

I draw all the time. I guess she noticed I wasn't.

I push the book away and look at Julian. He tells her some kids nicked it.

"All your beautiful drawings!" she exclaims.

All gone, I sign before I can stop myself.

I wipe my hand across my eyes and get up to walk around for a bit. Cassey feels sorry enough for me as it is. But Julian grabs my hand and digs around in his pocket. He pulls out a small clear plastic bag. He hands it to me, unwilling to meet my eyes.

Cassey drifts away for a second to deal with another customer, so I sit back down and open the bag curiously. I unfold the paper within and see it's a drawing, my drawing, of two boys kissing on a bus. I drew it when I first ran away, before I met Robyn, even. The boys had been sat in front of me, so the drawing is of the tilted backs of their heads, their mouths.

I had been so amazed that they had done that on a bus, for the whole world to see. They were beautiful.

I thought the drawing had been tucked into the front cover of my pad. Obviously not.

I lay it out on the counter and smooth out the creases. Julian stares at his hands wrapped around his mug of tea. I want to fling my arms around him, but he's retreated inside himself, and I'm too shy to intrude.

"Is that one of yours?" Cassey gently spins the drawing around to look. "It's beautiful," she says thoughtfully.

Carefully, I fold it back up and hand it back to Julian.

"It's yours," he says gently, shaking his head, light catching the gold of it. He is so beautiful.

With a sudden burst of inspiration, I pick the drawing up and hold it out to Cassey. I point up at the near bare walls around the cafe. She smiles, shaking her head.

"It's all you have left," she says softly.

I grab her order book. *I can draw more,* I write determinedly.

It seems so pointless to hide things away like I was, pictures no one will ever see now. If she truly likes it, I want her to have it.

Smiling, she asks me to sign it, promising to frame it and put it up on the cafe wall.

Without even giving our surroundings the grace of a final glance good-bye, we decide to head north, away from the river.

I don't feel so well today, and we walk slowly. It's still raining.

Last night, Cricket told Julian about a squat in Euston not far from the park. He said he heard the bloke who runs it is always on the lookout for new boys. He likes to take pictures, and the squat is part of the deal. We don't have an address, just a snapshot of the house on a card taken from a phone booth.

As always, Julian doesn't say any more and leaves me to fill in the gaps. Pictures means porn, means pictures of Julian, not me. He won't let me be put in a situation like that. I don't know how I know this; I just do, but at least he's not risking his life or sanity in some nightmarish dark archway, dread filling every second that he's gone. At least it's not that.

Snapshots

Oxford Street is some strange masochistic shopping hell. My shoulders are bruised, my feet are bruised, and I just don't want to carry on being pushed and shoved and stepped on as we walk down the busy pavement. *People just don't care.* And unless you push and shove back, you're fucking invisible.

Julian grabs my hand and thankfully pulls me out of the stream of people.

"Close your eyes," he says with this mysterious smile.

When I do, he carefully maneuvers me around until my back is resting against the smooth glass of what I presume is a shop window.

"Wait here."

And he's gone.

The air smells black as tar. At least down by the river the breeze blows the black away. And though the rain has slackened off, I can still feel the occasional drop against my skin.

A few minutes later he returns.

"Hold out your hands.... No, keep your eyes closed."

He's smiling. I can tell by his voice.

He places something weighty and wide in my outstretched hands.

"Okay, you can open your eyes now."

I feel like one of those kids I've seen on TV, kids at birthday parties or sat in front of a Christmas tree, eyes wide with wonder at a pile of presents wrapped just for them. But it's not a pile of presents. It's just one.

It's just, I've never had one before—well, not that someone *chose* for me, anyway.

Quickly I glance up at the name of the shop, seeing it's the same as the name on the bag in my hands.

Julian tilts his head and lowers his eyes, making his dark eyelashes seem impossibly long against his faintly blushing cheek.

"Open it," he says softly.

So I do.

Hesitantly excited, I pull out a sketchpad of beautifully thick paper, hard cover, perfect size for my pocket, and a set of pens, all different thicknesses. He knows I love to draw in pen.

There is also a receipt from the shop, which he whips away before I can see.

This must have cost him all the money he had. I stare at the presents without really seeing them.

Suddenly, I burst into tears.

I'm as shocked as he is by my reaction. And this is not a few gracious tears because I'm grateful to him, oh no—I'm sobbing my heart out uncontrollably, and people are staring.

"Remee?"

Perplexed, he pulls me against his chest and wraps his arms around me tightly.

"Fuck, baby, don't cry," he whispers softly against my ear.

He's never called me baby before. It sounds strange and wonderful. It makes me smile as I cry.

As gently as I can, I push him away. My throat is so choked up it's hard to swallow. I'm so embarrassed.

Thank you, I sign, dragging my sleeve across my eyes. *I'm okay now.*

Julian looks on, utterly bewildered. It would be the perfect excuse to kiss him, just on the cheek, but I'm such a coward.

THE EUSTON Road is not so far away, but I'm beginning to feel a little dizzy from hunger, or maybe I'm a bit sicker than I thought, so we stop to rest, and I take the opportunity to sketch. Just some kids in a park, but I'm fascinated by their movement and how to capture it.

"You're really, really good, you know."

He's sitting so close I can feel the warmth emanating off him.

I shrug, smiling. I like him watching me.

We move on before the daylight starts to go. It's only midafternoon, but already the streetlights are beginning to hum. Sometimes when the darkness comes, it feels like it's going to be dark forever.

Starting at Great Portland Street tube station, we walk the entire length of the Euston Road. There are lots of houses but no squat. It takes us over an hour.

We sit despondently on the curb near King's Cross Railway Station, staring at the small picture on the card. It shows a row of tall white houses, expensive houses; not one of them *looks* like a squat.

There's a telephone number at the bottom.

Reluctantly, Julian pulls out the last of his money. Calling ahead is a last resort. It's easier for them to turn us away without even seeing us, easier for them to lie and deceive us about all sorts of things. And what sort of squat has a phone line anyway?

But we're cold, and we're only going to get colder (and hungrier and more desperate) the longer we stare at the stupid card.

We huddle together inside a phone booth across the road from the station as Julian makes the call. I rest my forehead against his shoulder for solidarity and hold my breath, unable to stand the reek of piss.

All around, the streets are teeming with harassed-looking people going home from work.

I wish we were like them. I wish we were going home. I wish we had one.

It's pretty dark outside now and every light sparkles against the glass. If I squint, it looks like the world is nothing more than a giant burst of starlight, and we're burning brightly at its center.

Julian holds the phone out for me to hear. It's just ringing and ringing. He smiles at me, crooked and tired, a look that doesn't need words to explain it. And then suddenly someone picks up the other end and says, "Hello... hello?" and he shoves it back against his ear.

Said the Spider to the Fly

The voice on the end of the phone gives Julian an address and vague directions on how to get there. It's just five minutes away, apparently. But we're still walking after twenty. I really don't feel so good anymore, and I just want to stop and rest. My vision is swimming.

The directions take us off the Euston Road and into a neglected high-rise estate. Some of the dilapidated buildings are over fifteen stories high, with narrow concrete balconies and gaping black holes for windows. I can't imagine they're as empty as they look, but the estate is ghostly quiet.

Every so often Julian's fingers brush against mine, and I tense at each touch, imagining some crackle of electricity darting between us, a small firework of sparks. But I know it's just me. I know Julian doesn't feel anything like that at all. He probably doesn't even realize we're touching.

We avoid the messy rectangular patches of mud where grass or flowers once grew and keep to the glass-strewn paths, because even though all the lamps are lit along the walkways, it's still somehow dark.

Above us the night sky yawns blackly, the air frozen and still. A strange slow numbness is starting to seep through all my limbs, and my head is beginning to shake uncontrollably. Julian is hunched over beside me, head bowed as though it's raining.

"Fuck, Remee, I think we're lost," Julian whispers into the silence, breaking his stride for a moment to leap atop a wall and look around.

But we quickly carry on, pretending we know where we're going... pretending we don't feel we're being followed at a distance.

In an attempt to lose any possible shadow, we circle each huge building twice until, *finally*, we come to a block with the same number and name as the address we've written on the card.

Vermillion House, Block E, fifth floor.

We take the stairs. So much rubbish lies across the steps I can't even see the floor. At least on the streets it sometimes gets cleaned away.

One flat after another has barred windows and safety doors, but there are no sounds or signs of life within any of them. In Gem's block you're hardly through the entrance before you hear screams or laughter or both.

Without having to check the card, we stop outside Number 49. The door is blue and battered. "Slut" is scrawled across it in bloated red letters. This is not a tall white town house on the Euston Road. This is about as far away from "town house" as you can get and still be in London. We look at one another.

Let's go, I sign. *I don't like it.*

Julian sighs heavily. He's really tired. "I don't like it either, but where are we going to go?"

I shrug. I have a really, really bad feeling about this place, but he's right, where *are* we going to go? If we go back on the streets, Julian is going to let himself be screwed until he's as dead-eyed as Roxy. Maybe he feels like being here is a choice, and we have precious few of those.

I wish I could talk to him about it.

Closing his eyes, he reaches out his hand and rests it cautiously against the door before he knocks. Barely an instant later, a tall Asian guy in loose black pants and no top opens the door a fraction and looks over us. His eyes linger on me, and Julian moves to stand in front.

"You call earlier?" he asks.

Julian nods.

The guy steps back from the door, pulling it wide.

"Come in," he says, giving us an eerily toothless smile. "I'm Malik."

Somewhere inside the flat there's a dog barking continuously. Julian doesn't move. He has a long thin scar on his arm from where he was sewn back together as a kid after a dog attacked him.

"We were told we could get some place to sleep in exchange for… some pictures," he says hesitantly.

Malik looks us over again. I notice how hard and cold his eyes are as they flick from Julian's face to mine.

"How old?" Malik asks, his eyes focused on me.

I hold his gaze as Julian edges his feet closer to mine and says. "Just me, not him. The deal is for me."

Malik shrugs.

"You speak to Vidal tomorrow. You come in and rest now, yes?"

The warmth from the flat floods the cold night air around us, and I lean into Julian, into his solid stance.

I no longer care about the bad feeling swelling in my chest. I no longer care that Malik continues to stare at me. I just want to be warm. I'm so tired. I just want to collapse further against this glowing boy, wrap myself in his warmth. Whatever decision he makes, wherever we go, I feel safe if I'm with him.

"You have a dog...?" Julian begins, but Malik throws his hands in the air like it's a stupid little detail and beckons us inside.

We're led down a dark hallway to a dim square room. Behind us the front door slams shut, and I hear heavy bolts being draw across.

The first thing I notice is the room has no window. The second is the ten or so sleeping bodies lying haphazard across the floor. A few share blankets, but most sleep alone. The whole place smells bitter and musky like old sweat, but at least it's not freezing cold.

"You sleep here." Malik gestures to a corner by the door. "You have blanket?"

We shake our heads.

"Okay, I get you blanket. You want some food?"

Malik doesn't wait for an answer and heads back up the hallway. The dog is still barking sporadically somewhere, the sound slightly more muffled than before. Julian is barely able to suppress a flinch every time he hears it.

We look at one another. Julian swallows and touches my cheek with his knuckle.

"I will look after you," he says softly, his eyes searching mine. "Whatever happens. I will look after you. You are my family."

I let my head fall against his shoulder and breathe in his familiar scent.

I will look after you too, I promise him silently.

Taking my hand, Julian follows Malik to a tiny kitchen right next to the front door. The window is boarded up from the inside with a warped piece of chipboard half-dark with rot. All I can smell is dog.

Two other men are in there, smoking and playing cards at a small round table. We stand in the doorway and watch while Malik flings open filthy cupboard after filthy cupboard, all of them empty. The other men laugh at him. They pay no attention to us.

Eventually Malik finds two pieces of bread and holds them out to us. We're so hungry we don't care that they're stale and tasteless.

With a questioning look on his face, Malik picks a ratty blanket up off the floor and holds that out to us too, but it's a dog's blanket, covered in yellow stains and short black hairs. Julian shakes his head, no way, and pulls me back down the corridor.

Once we've found our spot, we curl on the cold concrete floor, as far away from the other bodies as we can get. Julian takes his jacket off and lays it over us.

"It's going to be okay," he whispers into the dark. "We're going to get off the streets. This is just the start."

It's not long before he drifts to sleep, half on top of me. But despite my overwhelming exhaustion, something stops me from shutting down. It starts off as just slightly panicked thoughts about this enclosed windowless space, about losing Julian somehow, and then it slowly turns into a headache, which gets worse and worse until I begin to feel delirious and sick.

When I try to sit up, Julian stirs in the darkness beside me.

He reaches out a hand, wraps it around my wrist.

"What's wrong?" he whispers.

It's too dark to sign, so I take his hand and hold it against my forehead.

"Your head hurts?"

I nod into his palm.

"Is it bad?"

It's getting worse and worse.

The room is spinning.

And I throw up before I can stop myself or warn him or anything.

I hate sick—being sick, the smell of sick, the idea of it—and I'm covered in it.

Oh God, I feel wretched.

Julian rubs soothing circles all down my back and then helps me to my feet. Everywhere is dark now. The bathroom is opposite the kitchen at the end of the corridor, but before we get that far, the dog starts barking again and a door to the side opens.

A figure that's not Malik appears in the shadow and asks where we're going. He has the dog on a leash at his side, a stocky black thing with a torn ear and snarling mouth.

Without taking his eyes off the dog, Julian says quickly, "My friend's not well. Have you got any paracetamol?"

The figure vanishes for a second, then chucks a mostly empty packet at us before disappearing with a grunt back into his room with the dog and closing the door.

We pretty much stumble into the squalid little bathroom, and Julian tugs my disgusting vomit-covered top over my head. Disappointingly, his new jacket is pretty well covered too.

We rinse our clothes under the tap in the brown bath, throwing a wide-eyed glance at one another as the water starts to run warm.

Julian turns to me. "Hey, do you want a bath?" he asks, grinning.

Of course I want one!

I swallow the tablets and sit on top of the toilet lid while Julian hunts quietly in the kitchen for a cup or mug we can use to cover the plughole to keep the water in.

The bath isn't hot, just warm, and there is no soap or towel, but I don't care. My head feels a thousand times better just looking at it.

Julian sits on the floor in front of the closed door and watches as I trail my hand absently through the water.

"You not getting in? It's not going to get any warmer."

Slowly I peel off the rest of my clothing. It's filthy, it all needs washing. Without giving myself a chance to think about the wisdom of my decision, I dump it all in the bath before I step in.

Then holding my nose, I lie down and slip under the surface. I love the feeling of being completely submerged and enveloped in warmth. I stay under for as long as I can. When I eventually break the surface, Julian is peering over the edge of the bath, a strange faraway expression on his face.

"You always do that," he says softly, his eyes slightly glassy.

I shrug. I know. I can't be bothered to sign.

I've found the best way to deal with being naked with Julian is not to think about the fact that I'm naked with Julian. At least this time he's not naked as well, although he is still watching me intently.

My eyes are drifting shut when I hear the rustle of clothing being removed.

What are you doing? I sign, startled, as Julian strips his T-shirt off and starts unbuttoning his jeans.

The look he gives me as he steps out of his pants is long and complicated.

Of course, it's *obvious* what he's doing. Fuck, so much for him not being naked.

"Do you mind?" he asks as he steps his long, glowy limbs in the bath and sinks down opposite me.

I'm so relaxed it takes a second for my brain to catch up with my body, which is already hyperaware of *his* body's proximity. And, although we're not touching, the more I try not to think about it, the worse it gets. The sweet, sweet ache in the pit of my stomach intensifies, throbs, and my cock stiffens helplessly.

I'm halfway to my knees.

"Don't get out," Julian says hastily, catching my wrist.

I can't look at his face.

Please, I sign, my heart thudding so loud I'm sure he can hear it.

He lets go immediately. I must look desperate.

"Use my T-shirt to dry yourself if you want. It's pretty clean," he says in a voice that's barely audible.

As I crouch shivering by the side of the bath, rubbing my skin with the thin piece of cotton, Julian just stares at his hands.

He doesn't look up for ages.

Afterward, we hang my clothes around the room and share what's left of his. I wear his jeans, and he pulls on the damp T-shirt and pants. It's still too cold, not outside-on-the-street cold, but shivery all the same.

Julian regards the dog blanket on the floor in the kitchen.

I guess warmth wins over everything in the end, and we take it. This time we both sleep, fast and deep, forgetting that time ticks away however much you want it to stop.

SOLACE

I WAKE with a start, shocked to consciousness by all the voices murmuring around me.

This disorientation is common, a hazard of our piss-poor nomadic existence.

Where the fuck am I? is perhaps the most frequent question I ask myself.

Julian blinks away sleep beside me. His *where the fuck am I?* look is almost instantly replaced by resignation as he remembers. His head *thunks* against the concrete floor. Oh.

I look around the room at all the boys with their blankets, whispering and waking.

Entirely without meaning to, I catch someone's eye—a boy about my age, who gets up from his spot on the floor by the wall and comes over to us.

His skin is smooth and dark as Gem's, and he has a beautiful wide smile. He holds out his hand to me, and I notice that he only has one. The other is missing from the wrist. I don't stare. I've seen other people like this on the street. I know it's not a birth defect.

"I'm Phillippe," he says in a voice that is quite high and heavily accented.

I sit up and take his proffered hand. His palm is warm and dry against my cold deadness.

Julian shifts behind me, pressing so close I can feel him breathing, and wraps his arm loosely around my bare waist. If he had any idea what this did to me, well… I doubt he'd still be doing it.

"This is Romeo," he declares, and I smile to myself at the way he says my name, the name he never calls me. "I'm Julian." He never calls himself Jules either, though everyone he gets to know always does. I think he hates it.

Phillippe is fifteen and a refugee from Sierra Leone. He doesn't have a passport. He thinks his family are dead, and he's so obviously lonely it makes my heart ache.

I sketch his face while he and Julian talk.

Malik comes in and passes around bowls of grayish I've-no-idea-what, but at least it's warm, even if it tastes of nothing. He tells us we have to be out in ten minutes.

"Where do we go?" Julian asks Phillippe.

"White house not far from here," Phillippe answers, shoveling food in his mouth. He notices Julian's guarded look at this and thinks for a moment. "They take pictures of you without clothes, that is all. Other boys do other stuff. They ask you when you go in if you want to do other stuff. Sometimes I do, but mostly I say no."

He looks pleased with his decision.

I show him the picture I drew. He seems to like it, so I tear it out of the pad and give it to him. I'd much rather do this than see them all go up in smoke again one day.

He hugs me tightly and for so long that I start to wonder when he's going to let go.

I decide his reaction is better than any satisfaction I would get looking at his picture.

Julian watches me, smiling, then dips his head down, resting his forehead against my upper back between my shoulder blades. I can feel his breath whispering against my skin, down my spine. *Fuck.* It feels so nice.

When Phillippe gets up to collect his belongings, Julian whispers, "Would you draw a picture like that of me one day?"

I try to turn around to look at him, but he presses his head more firmly into my back as though he doesn't want to be seen, as though he doesn't really want to know my answer—or is afraid of it.

Would I draw him? Of course. But I'm scared, because it's easy to draw someone you've just met, or a stranger. You're not drawing them from your heart, you're not sharing your soul, you're not displaying with every fucking fiber of your being how much you're in love with them.

I drop my head back. I need to tell him to stop what he's doing because his breath is so hot it feels like he's kissing me. All too vividly

I imagine it's his tongue flicking against my skin, circling each vertebra with warm wet heat. If I could groan, I know I would. Instead of, oh God, *panting.*

The door opens to the corridor, and we break apart in a rush of cold air. I hope no one noticed the way I just utterly dissolved, and I spin around to see Julian is flushed from his face to his chest. My heart constricts with embarrassment that I've caused *him* embarrassment.

Without looking at one another, we get up.

In the bathroom we find my clothes are still soaked. I completely regret my stupid idea of dropping them in the bath. I don't know what I was thinking.

Julian and I share them between us, even though he is inches taller than me. He takes my T-shirt and jumper, while I take my trousers and wear his T-shirt (immersed wholly and deliciously in his scent) and coat. I realize somewhat desperately that I need to release some of this tension. I look around longingly. Thirty seconds on my own in this bathroom is all I need. I haven't touched myself in over a week. Even when I do, I don't think of Julian. I can't. It would make our interactions way too difficult and awkward. Instead I think in abstracts, a mouth on my mouth, a tongue on my skin, spit slicked on the palm of my hand, and it's enough. But frustratingly Phillippe waits for us by the front door, having a stilted conversation with Malik, who's in the kitchen with the dog. Thankfully the dog is eating.

Julian watches it warily before edging outside. And we leave.

THE ESTATE doesn't look any better in the daylight. All desolate and empty. Each bleak space lined with limp, spindly trees stripped of bark. The only sparks of green come from dandelions forcing their way through the cracks in the concrete. It's as decayed as the Eastern Bloc where my mother grew up. She had few photographs, but the black-eyed girl, so small against those towers of concrete, haunts my thoughts whenever she can.

I press against Julian as we walk along, and he presses back, glancing to see if I'm okay.

And I am. For now.

LIGHT

GRAY LIGHT fills the white sky and does nothing to lift our mood. Since we left the estate, we've given up pretending today is going to be a good day. Maybe it will be better than yesterday, but that's not saying much. At least we've had breakfast. Even if we are wearing each other's cold wet clothes, even if we'd rather be warm than anything, at least we're not so hungry.

Phillippe chatters constantly, endlessly, nervously. Talking about everything and nothing. Carelessly throwing anecdotes of his childhood in a small dust-bound village in with stories of assaults he's witnessed or been subjected to on the street. Julian can't cope. He disappears inside himself when he's anxious, and right now I know he's as anxious as I am—anxious of the street, the day, the next few hours. I know so many things he thinks I don't.

I step between them to give him some space.

I think Phillippe has worked out I can't speak, so he just smiles at me, bright and wide. I haven't the heart to tell him I'm not deaf too.

We turn the corner onto a shabby little street, full of Middle Eastern greengrocers and seedy one-room restaurants. It's as typical and struggling as every other run-down street in this part of London.

At the end of the street is a short row of tall white houses, nothing at all like the terrace in the photograph.

Phillippe stops in front of a house, which he says is actually two houses knocked through into one, though they both have separate front doors. Dirty white curtains hang limply at the windows, and the white paint is peeling off the walls, but it is more like what I expected than the tower block.

Julian squeezes my fingers before standing in front of me, blocking my way up the steps to the front door. It doesn't take a genius to work out what he's going to say.

I shake my head before he even starts. *I'm going in with you*, I sign.

"Remee, please...," he whispers pleadingly as he places warm hands on my shoulders.

I hate the look he's giving me. It cuts me in half.

I can fucking do this. If you're going to do it, I'm doing it with you. It's just my fucking body. We're all naked under our clothes. Whatever they do in there, they can't reach inside me. The only person I'll ever allow to reach inside me is you! I try to convey all that with my eyes.

I don't think it works, but I brush past him anyway and march up the steps after Phillippe.

Julian is right behind me as the black door opens wide and the gloom inside swallows us.

At the back of my mind I had been wondering how this whole deal worked—staying at the squat, the same boys coming back to this house day after day for the same pictures to be taken. It didn't make sense. But now I see as we're led into a dingy hallway that that's not what this is at all.

There are two front doors for a reason: one is for the punters who pay to take the pictures and one is for us.

Damp pervades the air. The smell reminds me of those almost-derelict old houses I stayed in as a kid, walls caving in around us from rot and neglect.

We follow Phillippe down the hall, but before he pushes open the door at the end, a guy with slicked black hair steps out of the shadows and grasps Julian's arm. No one notices his cringing reaction to this but me.

"Who are you?"

Julian looks at him but doesn't say anything. I stand beside him, running my hands nervously across the cold bumpy wall behind me.

"Okay," the man drawls. His accent is similar to Malik's but lighter. "I'm Vidal. Malik sent you, yes?"

Julian makes the barest movement of his head it's possible to perceive in this murky darkness. The light is so dim Vidal appears indistinct and nebulous, a bizarre mix of shadows. I can't work out his features at all, and I don't think he can even see me.

"You come to earn your keep, or you come to earn some money?" he asks and smirks at Julian's nonchalant shrug.

"Julian?" Phillippe whines from the doorway.

But Julian ignores him.

And then, purely by chance, Vidal sees me.

With the same predatory look Malik had yesterday, he creeps closer and studies my face with his hand until Julian pushes me backward with his body harder than he means to, and I crash against the carpet.

Vidal laughs and shoves Julian carelessly aside. His shadow is much more solid than either of ours. He pulls me to my feet, touches my skin again, my cheek, my throat.

"Want to earn some money, kid?"

I hear Julian's muffled shout, but I can no longer see him. I don't want them to hurt him, so I do what Vidal wants me to do and nod my head.

Nothing feels real as I'm taken upstairs. I think I switched off when Vidal's cold hand brushed my face. The wind whips through a broken skylight above us. The sound makes me think of rain hammering against tarpaulin, a warm body curled next to mine. And at least it's not dark up here.

I'm led through a maze of small corridors into a cold, bare room. A double bed is pushed under the eaves. On it lies a naked boy.

It could be me.

I am no longer sure.

IT FEELS like hours later when I walk back down the stairs and out the front door. Julian and Phillippe are sat on the curb sharing a cigarette. Julian looks around when the door behind me bangs shut. He has a black eye, and his top lip is swollen and cut.

No more squat, then, I think apathetically.

But that's where we head, the three of us, in silence.

I'm so scared Julian is disappointed in me. He's barely even looked at me since I came out of the house. But before we get to the squat, he mouths something to Phillippe and pulls me into a shady passage between the buildings. The hug he gives me there is so fiercely tender I can hardly breathe. He touches my face, my neck, my hair almost desperately, and it takes all of my willpower not to graze my fingers against his sore lip.

"Fuck," he says over and over again until it sounds like a sob.

I pull out my pad.

I'm okay, I write. *Nobody hurt me or even touched me.*

It's true. So there's this hollow ache in my chest from what I did do; it doesn't matter. It's nothing. I know I got off lightly. They were just pictures.

When he looks at me like this, I feel like he's looking inside me, seeing so deep he *must* know every star-bright feeling, every truth, every lie.

"We'll stay at the squat tonight, and then we'll leave."

I know the thought of being on the street again is killing him.

We can stay. It wasn't so bad.

And now I do touch his bruised face, because I can't not.

He shakes his head and lets it rest against mine. His hair falls in my eyes.

"They don't want me," he says, so close I can feel his breath against my lips.

What happened?

With slightly shaking hands, he takes my pad and pen and writes in his curvy flowing script, *I couldn't do what they wanted me to do.*

What did they want you to do?

I'm actually surprised the conversation has got this far.

He stares at the paper for ages, pen hovering.

Tell me, I will him, sensing this is somehow one of those bridges we've never crossed, and he must sense it too.

I can't—he pauses for so long I think he's never going to finish the sentence—*get an erection*, he writes eventually.

I almost write *what?* But I manage to control my insensitive hand and write *since when?* instead.

Two/three months.

And what did he start doing two/three months ago? When did he start selling his soul on the streets? It's not fucking surprising, really.

I wish he'd look at me, but when he doesn't, I pull him into my arms, and we stand awkwardly like that for a long time.

It starts to rain. Julian rips the page out of my pad and shreds it into tiny pieces before putting them in his pocket.

"Come on," he whispers softly.

Phillippe is waiting by the doors to the building. I'm not sure what he makes of us, but he smiles like always.

When we knock on the door to the squat, Malik answers, but even though we're standing in the rain, he won't let us in until six. Half a day from now.

Sharing the last money we have, we buy chips and eat them in a bus shelter by the park. I think they might be the most perfect thing I have ever tasted.

I take my pad out and sketch Julian's face. I won't let him see, though, not 'til it's done.

It feels like something has changed between us since his revelation, like we're imperceptibly closer, and my heartbeat speeds up when he looks at me, as though I'm waiting for something to happen.

WAITING FOR SOMETHING TO HAPPEN

IT'S ALREADY dark, and there are quite a few of us waiting out on the cold rainy walkway for Malik to open the door. Julian slips his arm around me as he talks to some of the others, and I melt into his warmth.

Earlier, we told Phillippe I'm mute. We don't tell many people, not after what happened with Lloyd. Even Julian doesn't know the full story. He doesn't know it was Cricket that told Lloyd I couldn't make a sound no matter what was done to me. I don't know why I have never told him. It's certainly not from any loyalty to Cricket.

So now Phillippe talks to me and tries to get me to teach him sign, which is hard because of his missing hand. Julian wants him to be less obvious and shoots him a warning glance, so Phillippe relaxes against the wet railing behind us and whispers almost inaudibly, "Are you two together?"

I shrug. I don't know what he means. Of course we're together; we're always together. I can't ever imagine not being together. My life wouldn't be my life, and, however dire it sounds, I wouldn't want that life, no matter what.

"I was together with a girl once, back home," Phillippe carries on in a hushed voice. He looks down at the pools of blackness forming on the grimy walkway. "I ran away the night they came for her family. I tried to get her to run with me. I should have tried harder…."

I reach out my hand to touch his. It's all I can do without words.

After a while, Phillippe glances up at Julian and mouths almost silently, "He was sweet with me today. They made us get undressed together. Made us touch each other."

I hate the sudden irrational swell of jealousy I feel rising up inside me, and I fight to swallow it back down. I know he's not telling me this to make me feel bad. I suspect it's just the opposite, but fuck, it *hurts*.

"He didn't want to do any of it, but he said he was doing it for you, to take care of you. They made us stop when he got upset."

I feel Julian's arm tighten around me. I know he's listening. I push back into his embrace, into his slight frame, hardly any bigger than mine, and will him to see that it's okay because I did what I did to take care of him too.

Malik opens the door, holding back the dog by her collar. Julian waits until everyone is inside and only when Malik takes the dog into the kitchen does he grab my hand and pull me swiftly down the hall.

Food is handed around on disposable plates, mainly bread, with a bitter savory drink that's barely warm. We all sit on the floor in our loose little groups, shoveling food in our mouths like hungry animals. We don't talk or taste, we just consume, because *we* know food is not something to be taken for granted. Even if most people in this country wouldn't have a fucking clue what it's like to be hungry and not know when you're going to be able to eat again. This is what we're reduced to when everything else is taken away.

After I've eaten I carry on with my drawing. I never take this long over anything I draw, but I want this to be the best thing I've done. For him.

I even draw the bloody cut on his lip, because it's there, and there is beauty in truth so bright and shining it makes everything clear.

I love him because of his flaws, not despite them.

This is what I'm terrified he'll see when he looks at the drawing, and at the same time, this is what I long for him to understand.

Phillippe curls on his side away from us. I think he's trying to give us some privacy.

"Can I see yet?" Julian whispers.

I bite my lip and shake my head.

Hesitantly, he shifts and gently lays his head in my lap, his soft, honey-colored hair falling every which way.

He looks up at me—his face at once so open and vulnerable it makes me want to confess my soul to him, every fucking *thing*—and he lifts his hand as if he's going to touch my face, but for some reason changes his mind and lays it back down.

Fuck, I think helplessly, my heartbeat skitter-scattering.

It uses all my self-control to carry on drawing. I'm so fucking confused. If anyone else were looking at me like this, I know what I'd think: I'd think they were going to take my hand any moment now and lead me away somewhere more private so we could relieve some of this unbearable fucking tension.

I'm so crazy about you, Julian.

With that thought circling desperately round my head, I finish his drawing and tear it out. I get up after I hand it to him and just about run away down the hall, praying the bathroom is empty so I don't have to see what he thinks about it.

Maybe ten minutes later I walk back and see Julian is still just staring at his picture.

The lights are dim now and, even though it's early, all around the room everyone is settling down.

How fucking easy we are, I think hopelessly.

Without looking up, Julian reaches out and pulls me down. He doesn't say a word. He just holds me. I'm grateful. I don't think I could look at him anyway.

We must just fall asleep like that. I have to admit, for me it's strange. I don't sleep easily. It takes me a while to relax, and even then I feel I am half-awake most nights, listening out for trouble.

But this time the sleep is deep, and I am dreaming. A nice dream—a really nice dream. One of those dreams that makes you feel good for hours after. I'm with someone. I can't see their body or their face, but I can feel them all around me, skin against skin, and I know who it is. Who else is there? He tells me I'm beautiful without saying a word, because we have this connection, because he's inside me and his tongue is in my mouth and all I can hear is this one long note of sound....

I blink my eyes against the dark. The sound is still all I can hear. Warm breath humming against my ear. Julian.

And I'm still sort of out of it, but that nice feeling? It's even fucking nicer now.

I don't know how we ended wrapped up in one another on the floor, considering I went to sleep straddling his lap, but now we're spooned on our sides, Julian's front against my back. One of his arms is beneath my T-shirt, locked around my chest and pulling me tight back against him, the other—I'm stroking my hand lightly up and down the other as his palm presses against the fly of my jeans and agonizingly slowly rubs up and down over my aching erection.

Oh God, I must be fucking dreaming still, I think as I gasp.

It feels so good it's almost painful. His fingers brush against my cloth-covered hips, and I can't help but tilt them up and push back into his open hand. The friction is unbearable.

He's still humming against my ear as I choke back gasp after gasp.

Does he even *know* what he's doing?

Each stroke is so unbearably slow I think it might kill me. But I want it to. I want to die like this over and over. I want more. I want skin against skin. I want his hand to reach down inside my pants. I want to be wrapped in his fist. I don't want to last long. I want to come. Oh God, I want to come. *Make me come.*

And then he's not humming. He's whispering and licking my ear.

"It's okay, baby. It's okay," he says over and over, and I press my hands down over his, all of it so tight, and my whole body convulses as I come.

I DON'T remember anything after that. I blink out of existence into a fathomless sleepy dark and am touched by nothing, no dreams, no movement.

AN ICY draft wakes me. I shift backward, searching. But there are no warm arms around me, no warm body next to mine. I am alone. In fact, as I open my eyes and look around the room, I see it's mostly empty. Blankets strewn everywhere. The edge of everything feels… cloudy. Something is wrong.

Phillippe blinks groggily awake a few feet away.

He glances around, looking as puzzled as I am.

Julian must be in the bathroom.

The front door is banging listlessly open and shut in the wind. I can see it's light outside, that blue morning light you get sometimes in winter, but I've no idea what time it is.

There are only two others in the room with us. Last night we were twelve. They both look around, perplexed.

Something is wrong.

I stumble to my feet, feeling sick and shaky before I even get to the bathroom. The door is open, and I know it's going to be empty. I know that Julian isn't there, but I can't believe it. I can't accept it. I don't even recognize the familiar grip of panic locked around my chest, stealing my breath; everything just goes violently black.

LOSS

"ROMEO...?"

My head hurts. I don't want to open my eyes.

"Is he okay?"

"What happened?"

The bathroom floor reeks of piss. The smell disgusts me but not enough to make me move. If I move, I have to accept this is reality. And it's not. It can't be.

Voices fade in and out of the room. Someone closes the front door to stop it banging.

"They've all gone. Even Malik and the dog. All their stuff, everything...."

"Look... the rooms are empty...."

"Is there anything to eat?"

"I think we should get out of here.... Maybe it was a gang thing...."

"I don't feel so good...."

"You feel fuzzy, right? Don't you get it? We were drugged...."

"Last night... that drink...."

I roll painfully onto my back. Oh. That bitter drink.... I didn't feel right.... I don't feel right.

But why? Why would they drug us?

Phillippe steps into the room and crouches down next to me.

"Are you okay?"

I stare up at the yellow stains covering the bloated ceiling. He *must* know I'm not. That can't be....

Where's Julian? I sign desperately, before I can get ahold of myself.

"I don't understand you," he says quietly, helplessly. "I'm sorry."

Please. Where's Julian?

I know if I work myself up, I'm going to have another panic attack. I squeeze my eyes shut. If I think about not seeing him again, about something bad happening to him, about not knowing if something bad has happened to him or just not knowing… not knowing where he is, if he's hurt, what am I going to do? Oh God, what am I going to do?

"Is he okay?"

"Move out of the way. He's hyperventilating. I know what to do. My mum used to have panic attacks like that sometimes."

I feel a pressure like a hand in the middle of my chest. Like a fist.

I can't breathe.

"It's going to be okay…." Someone takes my hand, holds it between both of theirs. "You know why it's going to be okay? Because whatever you feel right now, it's going to pass." The voice pauses as I take in a shuddery breath of stale air, then carries on. "It's not going to last, nothing lasts, one moment always follows another… the good, the bad, the fucking awful. I take it this is one of those fucking awful moments, right?"

I nod. There are tears streaming down my face.

"Well, it's not always so fucking awful, is it? Probably it's mostly just bad with a few bits of good and the occasional fantastic—I mean that's how I see it anyway. And if it's mostly just bad, it makes the fantastic bits better, right? So what if that means the good bits are probably just mediocre really, I don't care…."

The boy babbles on, and I open my eyes, breathing a little easier. He smiles. He has short brown hair and very pale blue eyes. He looks a bit older than me.

"I'm Peter. I saw you come in the other night with your friend. Have you been on the street long?"

I shrug. What's long? A week, a night, an hour?

"He can't talk, he's mute."

Peter glances back at Phillippe.

I mime scribbling in the air, and Phillippe goes to get my pad and pen while I drag myself upright and lean listlessly against the bath.

A horrible cold numbness seeps through me, leaving my limbs uncoordinated and heavy. I just don't want to move.

Peter introduces the other boy hanging around the bathroom door as Nathaniel.

Nathaniel looks nervous and paces backward and forward, in and out of the room. Maybe it should be annoying, but I find I don't really care.

Phillippe hands me the pad, and I write. *I need to find my friend, Julian. What happened? Where did they go?*

I'm not stupid. I *know* Peter doesn't know any more about what happened than me, but there is some bizarre, hollow comfort in asking stupid questions, in talking about Julian—it makes him exist beyond my feelings.

"He didn't tell you he was leaving?"

I shake my head. I can feel my eyes filling up again. Fuck, I'm pathetic.

"I don't know what happened. I came here four nights ago. Malik said I'd have to earn my keep like everyone else, and I've been having my picture taken at that house and then coming back here, like you. I didn't really know any of the other boys, apart from Nathaniel. Different people seemed to come and go. But I've taken enough sleeping tablets to know they drugged us last night. It was probably in the drink—easy enough to crush up a bottle of tablets and mix it in. If I had to guess, I'd say they did it so there was no trouble. I don't know whether everyone went willingly, but there's no sign of any struggling anywhere, I don't think."

Julian wouldn't have just left me, I write shakily. I have to hold on to that.

Peter smiles tiredly and nods before unfolding his legs and standing up.

"We should leave. I doubt this place is going to be empty for long, and I'd rather not be here under anyone else's terms."

I don't want to leave. If Julian comes back, how will he find me? But I don't want to stay either. I hate the filthy flat with its warren of dark rooms and bricked-up windows.

I hover by the front door, so undecided, so unsure. Every decision feels like it's the wrong decision. Every choice left to me doesn't really feel like a choice at all. What do I do?

As Peter collects all the blankets and Nathaniel agitatedly roams the room, Phillippe walks over to me and almost reluctantly hands me a piece of paper—I know it's the drawing I did of Julian. I know it was probably left on the floor in the corner we slept in. I know it's not some sort of sign, but I can't look at it.

Panic flutters through me, but the exhaustion I feel is now so profound, so complete, it's all too much.

The door bangs against the wall as I stumble outside. Somehow I can't believe the fucking sun is shining. The glare of light on the puddles on the walkway is painful.

"I'll stay with you," Phillippe says from the doorway behind me. "You won't have to be alone."

I can't even nod. Something vital has been ripped out from inside me. I'm just an empty husk.

Down below us everything looks exactly the same as it did yesterday, but it's not. It's fucking not.

I want to go to the white house. I pull out my pad and write quickly.

I want to see Vidal. I will do anything to see Vidal, for him to tell me where Julian has been taken. Because that's what they've done, they've taken him. That is the only explanation that fits.

Oh God.

It's like being punched.

Phillippe glances quickly at my scrawl before looking away embarrassed.

"I can't read," he says, shaking his head.

Fuck. I write *fuck fuck fuck* until I have wasted a whole page with obscenities, and I rip it out and throw it over the railing, watching it hover on the wind before spiraling hopelessly to the ground.

A DIFFERENCE THAT MAKES NO DIFFERENCE

PETER STEPS out the front door and hands me three blankets. I take them, but they're heavy, and I don't know what I'm supposed to do with them. I know Phillippe finds it difficult to carry stuff. It's not his fault, but I can't carry all these on my own.

Julian and I used to hide our covers in the daytime, mostly at Cassey's, but where am *I* supposed to hide this? I don't know this area at all. I don't want to.

I force myself to ignore the vision—and all the feelings attached to it—that appears when I think of him. It hurts like hell.

"We're probably going to go up to the heath. We've stayed around there before. Do you want to stick with us for a while?" Peter asks, looking at me more than Phillippe.

I must seem truly pitiful. But I like Peter. He has this understated confidence that makes him seem strong. He's the sort of person who knows what to do when things go wrong, the sort of person I want to trust.

I pull out my pad. *Phillippe can't understand me. He can't read or sign. I need someone to help me speak to Vidal. Come to the white house with us? Please?*

Peter glances at Nathaniel, who's listlessly kicking the doorframe.

"Vidal's not going to help you. I know you want to find your friend, but they're not the sort of people to help anyone."

I have to try, I write, desperately.

Peter solemnly shakes his head. "I want to help you, but I don't want to go back there and get dragged into anything. For all we know, Malik could have been supposed to take all of us."

I stare at him disbelievingly. *So you do think they were taken? Please come with me, Peter. I have to find him. Please.*

I'm not above begging and allowing myself to look as helpless as I feel. I'm not above using him or anyone to find Julian. Although that thought leaves me cold. But it's the truth. I don't care about them, not really. I don't care about anyone, myself included, like I care about Julian. And I feel horrible for thinking like that; I feel like a horrible despicable person. But nothing else matters.

Peter, however, is resolute.

"I'm sorry," he says, and he does look sorry as he and Nathaniel share their blankets out between themselves and then head down the walkway to the stairs.

I'm sorry too as I watch them leave the building and walk slowly across the squares of mud and concrete until they round the corner of the block and vanish.

I fling the stupid blankets over the railing, sink down onto the wet floor, and sob.

Phillippe waits until I've finished, then offers me a sandwich made from two pieces of stale bread shoved together, no filling. I realize dejectedly he's just as lost as I am, and that he wants to stay with me mostly so he doesn't have to be alone.

The sun is on my back as I sit, my head dropped between my knees, and think.

If I go alone to the white house and hand my paltry list of demands over to Vidal, he's going to laugh in my face. Peter's right, he's not going to help me. Why would he?

Even if I allow myself to be fucked and used by every punter who walks into that house, Vidal wouldn't give a toss. He has hundreds of boys willing to do that for less trouble and inconvenience than the answer to a question. *Who's Malik?* he'd say. And what could I do about it?

Because he can't understand me, I realize I'm no longer including Phillippe in any of this, although I am assuming he'll go wherever I go.

Every detail from the night before plays out in my head. Everything I heard Malik say, the taste of the drink, the faces of the other boys I can remember. Julian watching me as I drew his face, that look. Falling asleep with him and… dreaming. Was it a dream? Can I let myself believe it wasn't a dream right now? And even if it wasn't a dream, even if it was real, maybe it was because of the drugs, the sleeping pills. Maybe they dissolved our inhibitions along with our consciousness. But that would mean we had inhibitions to be dissolved, that underneath our fears there were wants and desires. And for me there are, without question, but for him?

Maybe I'll never know now. Maybe the most erotic moment of my short life will slowly blur in its drug-induced haze, remembered only in agonizing fragments. Maybe it will be my undoing. Maybe I am already undone.

"Romeo?" Phillippe touches my shoulder. "Do you think we should maybe go somewhere else? They're not coming back. I'm sorry," he adds when I lift my head and stare at him icily.

No, I don't fucking think we should *maybe go somewhere else.* I don't fucking know what to do, and right now staring at the fucking wet floor seems like a great idea to me.

I'm so frustrated he can't understand me, and I can't snap at him.

Without warning I remember the last argument I had with Julian, which wasn't really an argument at all, just me being fucking obnoxious. The force of it is like an iron fist gripping my chest and then ripping my heart out. I stifle a sob and push myself up off the slippery floor.

Okay, we need to get out of here.

And just like that, I make a decision. Where do we go when things get bad? Who is my only solid connection to Julian?

Gem.

Julian would find me there, I know he would. How have I suddenly switched it around to Julian finding me? And how is he going to do that if they've... if he's....

I dig my fingers into my skull.

I need to move and not think. I glance up at Phillippe. I beckon him to come. And using every last ounce of energy in me, I take the stairs three at a time and run.

It's painfully exhilarating, and Phillippe is doubled over holding his chest as I use the last of the money I earned yesterday to buy two tube tickets. Time is ticking away unbearably fast and walking will take hours. If we were taking overground trains, I'd jump the barriers, but the tube is too well policed these days.

Inside, the station is crowded and disorientating—the last time I used the tube was months and months ago, long before I became officially homeless—and I forget how easy it is to take a wrong turn and end up waiting for the wrong train.

We descend deeper under London, staircase after staircase, escalator after escalator.

Down here the darkness rushes, and the sooty blackness has a sound that echoes off the curved white tiles and mixes with the hundred-year-old scent that permeates the air.

I peer into the blackness of the tunnel, never really sure which direction the train is going to appear from, while Phillippe runs his hand against the dirty white tiles at the back of the busy platform, swirling patterns and drawing pictures.

We get plenty of backward glances, a few unembarrassed stares. And I stare back. If only they knew how easy it is to fall through the gaps—a few unsteady steps and suddenly you're gone.

PHILLIPPE STANDS behind me as I bang frantically on Gem's door. It's a bad move. She thinks it's trouble and won't open unless I tell her who it is. Fuck.

I point at myself and then at Phillippe's mouth. He shrugs, and I put my head in my hands.

Just tell her who it is for fuck's sake, I will him.

Gem shouts again, threatening to call the police, when Phillippe *finally* gets it and stutters my name.

The door swings open.

"Romeo? What the hell?"

A less-glamorous-than-usual Gem looks from me to Phillippe and then down the corridor.

I give a small wave to Joel hiding behind the door to the living room, but I can't bring myself to smile.

"Who are you?" Gem demands, dark eyes fixed on Phillippe. I'd never admit it, but she scares me a little bit. "And where's Jules?"

Phillippe squeaks his name, but I can't look her in the eye. I don't want to break down in front of her. I'm stronger than that.

I lean my pad against the wall and feeling slightly detached, write, *I don't know. He was taken last night by the people we were staying with.*

She stares at my writing as if the words aren't quite right and then ushers us both inside, before just about dragging me into the living room.

"Joel, go play in your room for a minute, yeah?"

"Can't I see Romeo?"

Gem shakes her head firmly. "Not now."

Phillippe hovers in the hall until Joel takes his hand and whispers something. Gem watches warily as they walk toward Joel's bedroom.

"Joel, take Phillippe to the kitchen. Give him a biscuit and a drink," she calls, then turns to me. "Your friend out there had better be trustworthy."

I nod before letting my legs fold under me and collapse back onto the couch. Gem looks different without a mountain of makeup on, more real, less... something I can't quite put my finger on. Slowly she lowers herself down next to me, a grim expression on her face.

"Tell me everything," she says in a flat, dull voice, as if this is somehow what she has been expecting all this time, as if she's resigned to Julian having a less-than-pleasant fate.

All at once I wish I hadn't come here. She's not going to reassure me that he's going to be okay. She's already accepted that he's gone. And I can't deal with that.

But I write everything down anyway, everything I remember, excluding my dream. At first I'm not even sure she's reading. She just seems to be staring at the paper so she doesn't have to look at me. She doesn't say anything for a long, long time.

And when she does speak, "Joel's going to be devastated" is all she says, flatly, quietly.

A sudden painful thought occurs to me, and I write it down without really thinking.

Is Julian Joel's father?

Joel is lighter skinned than Gem. Julian would have been fourteen, maybe fifteen. Gem is older. It's not impossible.

But Gem reads my question with such a look of shock and wonder on her face that I feel stupid and embarrassed. She gasps out a laugh, and I fold my arms protectively across my chest.

"Please tell me you're not as innocent as you look, Romeo. You do know how it works, don't you? A man and a woman... not two...." She sighs, rolling her eyes.

Of course I fucking know. It wasn't such a stupid question, and I can't see why she thought it was.

I stare sullenly at the glass coffee table and the way the sunlight makes colors shine through the surface to pattern the carpet beneath.

"Julian wouldn't have left you, you know that. He would have done anything for you," she says softly. I close my eyes and will her to shut up. I feel her hand on my knee.

Mainly to stop her feeling sorry for me, I pick up my pad and write the first thing that comes into my head.

Yeah, anything except talk to me about how much selling himself was hurting him. He always talked to you, though.

"Are you joking?" she stares at me incredulously. "Honey, Jules is just about the shyest, most verbally reluctant person I've ever met."

He was never shy with me. Except about sex.

"Well, that says a lot about how you make him feel, doesn't it?"

But we always came to you. I thought he wanted to talk to you because he couldn't talk to me.

"We've been friends a long time, and in all that time, we've never once had a conversation about how he felt or was feeling. To be honest, I think he came here because he didn't want you to have to deal with him when he wasn't feeling strong."

That's stupid, I write, but I know it's true.

"You changed him, Romeo. After he helped you when you got attacked by that gang, he was different. He was more himself, more sure of himself. I thought it was drugs or something when he first brought you here. I thought he was high because I'd honestly never seen him so happy. But he was happy because he was taking care of you, and then later on he was happy just because he was *with* you."

She looks down at her long fingers and taps her elaborate nails against the fabric of her jeans, sighing deeply.

"You were always wary of me, and you were right to be, I suppose. I was jealous of you at first." Her deep brown eyes hold mine. I won't look away. She smiles tightly. "I am still jealous, but I wanted him to be happy, and he was."

I grab my pad and not caring that I'm wasting pages by covering them in tears, write, *Stop it, stop talking about him like he's gone, he's not fucking dead. I'm going to find him. I WILL.*

Joel and Phillippe are laughing in the kitchen. Joel has that effect on people, and I know why Gem doesn't trust anyone with him. She goes to see what's going on, and I curl up on the sofa in despair.

I stare out the window at the drifting clouds and the slowly dimming sky, too torn apart to think coherently anymore.

Gem goes to get ready for her next client, and Joel comes and sits on the floor in front of me. He knows I'm sad, but he doesn't know why. I'm holding the picture I did of Julian. Holding but not looking at it. Stupid, really.

"Why isn't Jules with you?"

My pad is on the floor next to us. I let my arm fall limply over the edge of the couch and write, *I wish he was.*

"Why is he gone away?" Joel frowns, looking puzzled.

I look up and see Phillippe watching us from a chair in the kitchen.

Someone took him away. I don't think he wanted to go away. Which is of course the wrong thing to write.

Joel is upset. I hold him as tight as I can in my apathetic arms.

He cries next to my ear. "Are the policemen going to find him? When someone is taken away, the policemen find them and bring them back."

And what am I supposed to say to that? Am I supposed to lie, or am I supposed to tell a four-year-old that we're nothing, that we don't matter, that to everyone else it's better that we don't exist?

IT'S ALWAYS DARKEST BEFORE THE DAWN

WE CAN'T stay at Gem's, and saying good-bye to Joel is awful. It feels as though something has ended, and I'm never going to see him again. Of course Gem hasn't said she doesn't want me to come back. She would never say that, but I know I won't come back unless Julian is with me.

Phillippe follows me out into the freezing night.

Without anything to tether me, I drift back to the streets I know. There is some strange dark comfort in being here again—even the threat of seeing Lloyd here doesn't bother me. As we walk along the black embankment, it occurs to me we could die of this cold tonight. But even though my hands and feet are now completely numb, and Phillippe is shaking uncontrollably beside me, all I feel is emptiness.

Eventually we come to Joe Brown's cafe. Everything is dark and shut up, and we curl up together and sleep around the back of the building our feet in the glass Julian broke.

"Romeo?"

I wake with a start to find Cassey peering over me a deeply concerned look on her face.

"Oh my God, Romeo, I thought you were dead!" she cries, holding her hands over her heart.

It's still dark, and I've no idea of the time as she takes us inside to the dimly lit back room where she used to give me toast to share with Julian. She tells us to sit down in the tatty armchairs and get comfortable, while she grabs every blanket and towel she can find to cover us and make us slowly warm. We don't move but to breathe.

Leaving us briefly to open up the cafe, she returns with hot sweet tea and chocolate biscuits. She doesn't ask about Julian, but she watches Phillippe and me closely, as though she's working something out.

It's so painful warming up after such a long time being cold. So painful I sob as the feeling comes back into my fingertips. I can't walk at first, and the two of us just sit like statues, hoping we'll never have to leave.

Around midday, Cassey gets Phillippe to help clean the tables out front, and when Jodie, the only other member of staff, comes in to start her shift, Cassey closes the door and sits down in the back room with me.

"What's happened, Romeo?" she asks softly. For a moment the light catches in the wispy hair that frames her face before she absently tucks it back in her loose bun.

I wonder if she has children of her own to look after. I wonder why she runs this cafe—it can't make any money. It's perhaps one step up from a soup kitchen.

It must be some sort of self-preservation that kicks in when you dip below the point of survival, when you're on the very brink, but I ask her something I've never asked anyone before—Julian and I were too proud, or too stupid—and I write, *Can we stay here tonight? Please?*

She nods. And for an instant, I can see she's scared for me.

THE NEXT two days are the coldest of the season so far. Frost spreads like fractured glass across the pavements, even though the sun glares down like an icy fire. The nights are full of stars. I don't move from that room except to use the bathroom, and I don't get up except to occasionally stare out the window. Phillippe no longer talks to me, but he continues to stay. I doubt it's for me.

Cassey even sends Cricket and Roxy through to see me when Phillippe is helping with the tables, but I just stare into space and won't talk to them. My mind is paused, stuck in that moment I realized Julian was no longer with me. I want to search the whole of London, but I can't move.

After three days I stop eating the food she brings us, and I start to draw. Obsessively, I search my mind for details.

There's one thing, one thought that's been forming in the cold of my mind, growing like frost across a windowpane. One thing I have become convinced I have to do, even if it's too late, even if I never manage to do anything else.

It started with what Joel said as he cried in my arms, what Joel said about the police....

IT'S MY mother's distrust of authority that I feel as I stand in front of the ugly square building. My mother's distrust of the police. But the thing about not eating for a few days and then not sleeping all night and then getting up at dawn and walking miles and miles is, it makes everything disconnected, and I am dislocated from reality. If I don't really feel like I'm doing this, it makes it so much easier.

At 7:30 a.m. the police station is still pretty quiet.

"Can I help you?" a deep male voice sternly asks before I can even work out where I'm headed to in the reception. I look at him blankly. I fantasize that he's one of the officers that took our tarpaulin away, and it's there hidden under his desk, keeping his feet dry. The look on his face tells me he doesn't really want to help me.

I hand over my prepared speech. I wrote it yesterday while I wasn't feeling so strange. He skims the words and stares at me.

"Is this some sort of joke?"

A joke? I reel backward, floored.

A joke?

It's my fucking life.

I give up. *Fuck it*, I think, *I tried.*

But at that exact moment, a pretty young woman with long dark hair and sparkling eyes like Julian's breezes through the double-lock doors into the waiting area where I'm standing. She has on a long coat, and there is a heavy black leather bag in her hand, and she looks like she's leaving, but for some reason she stops, and she looks at me, really looks. And her eyes are so like his eyes I can't look away. Somehow it's too intimate looking at someone else so deeply like this.

"Is everything alright?" she asks, frowning kindly, still scrutinizing me.

"I've got it, Annie, you get off," the deep-voiced fucker calls to her.

But she shakes her head, ignoring him.

"You look like you could do with a hot drink," she says quietly, almost to herself, still looking at me closely. "Come and sit down through here."

And she leads me through to a small square room just about filled with a metal desk and two chairs.

"I'll be back in just a tick," she says, resting her large bag on the desk and leaving me alone in the room with it.

I look around, feeling I'm undergoing some sort of test. Does she want to see if I'm going to open the bag? Are there cameras filming me? What's in the bag? I blink up at the corners where the walls meet the ceiling. I feel very strange.

Bizarrely, I'm working my way around the sides of the room looking for secret compartments when the woman comes back with a steaming mug and a plate of food, my prepared speech tucked under her arm.

She doesn't bat an eye at my weird behavior or even look to see if her bag has moved. I don't know whether she is just trusting or stupid.

"Here," she says, placing the food and the mug on the table. "I thought you looked hungry, and this was going spare upstairs."

Cautiously, I walk back over to the table.

"Romeo, right?" She waves my speech by way of explanation. "I'm Annie. I'm a forensic medical examiner, police doctor."

I stare at the food. I don't think I can eat anything. But my hand picks up the fork, and before I know it, I'm eating. Ravenously.

"This is what you handed in to Sergeant Moore out there, isn't it?" she asks, showing me my writing again.

I nod.

"Do you mind if I call in a colleague of mine? She's a detective, and I think she'd be really interested in what you've written here."

Feeling slightly more grounded after choking down a few mouthfuls of food, I pull out my pad. *I've done some drawings of Vidal and Malik, and there is one of Julian too.*

She nods, smiling as I show her.

"Okay," she says, before taking out a mobile phone and pressing a few buttons and holding it to her ear. "Are you homeless, Romeo?"

I nod.

"How old are you?"

I shake my head. I can't tell her. They'll put me in a home.

"Romeo, I have a duty of care to call social services if I suspect a person under sixteen is at risk. If you're homeless, you're at risk."

I feel the well of panic starting to build, and I wobble to my feet.

"Hey, hey, listen, it's okay." She holds my gaze, and her voice is calm and commanding like Peter's was. "Just wait a few more minutes with me, okay? Speak to my colleague. If you like, I won't make that call until after she's spoken with you, okay?"

If you put me in a home, I'll run, I write.

"Okay, but you're too young to be looking after yourself. Social services are there to help and protect you. Did you run away from home?" she asks as she puts down the phone.

I shake my head. I don't want to tell her but somehow find I'm writing. *I came back to where my mother and I were staying after school one afternoon, and she was gone.*

"And that was the last time you saw her? You've no idea where she went?" She puts her hand on my arm. It's warm.

Julian looked after me before they took him away. He looked after me better than she ever did.

I don't want to trust her. I don't want to be here anymore.

"Okay, okay," she says soothingly. "It's okay."

She glances at her phone, at the door.

"Okay, I'm going to go upstairs and find my colleague as she's not answering her phone. The case you've outlined here sounds similar to something she is dealing with."

Before she goes, Annie drops a small white card with her name and number on the table. She holds my gaze. She knows I'm going to run. She's disappointed, but she knows. She leaves the door ajar on her way out. I take her card, place the drawings I did on her bag, and run.

I'M NOT sorry I left Phillippe behind at Cassey's. I just want to be on my own. It's strange, but since that desolate afternoon when I came back to an empty room and realized that the woman I have to identify as my mother had just cleared out and left me behind, I've never wanted to be on my own like this.

Never.

Until now.

As I walk down the embankment to the railway arches, I think about what I'll do if I see Lloyd. I know I wouldn't fight it. I think it would be a relief. If he found me and wanted to finish what he started all those months ago, I could accept it now; I could welcome the inevitable. I feel like I'm floating in the icy air.

Find me, Lloyd.

I sit for hours in the grassy wasteland just staring up at the tall, dark archways, just listening to the creak and clatter of the passing trains. Sometimes my eyes unfocus, and I find that everything is a blur, like a long never-ending river of gray, like the real river behind me that I would stare at too if I could be bothered to turn my head.

I'm part of the wasteland now, part of the waste. I'm nothing. I'm no one. Without him.

I've convinced myself he's gone. Without even consciously coming to the conclusion, my subconscious has done it for me. I've always been somewhat pessimistic.

In the late afternoon darkness, I step incautiously across the rubbish that litters the ground, and I aimlessly cross the road. A car swerves to avoid me. I can hear them swearing at me even as they speed off. More car headlights light up the pavement, casting eerie shadows in the gloom.

A car slows behind me, creeps along at walking pace. Are they scoping me? Do they want to drag me into an archway and fuck? I'd probably let them but only if they promised to leave me there too fucked-up to move. Or they paid me in smack or crack or anything to get me out of my head, over the edge… not that I'd know how.

"Romeo?"

My name? I don't stop. The car inches on slowly, behind me. Its headlights light up my way, like spotlights across a stage, all the way to the exit.

"Romeo! Please just stop! I need to talk to you…. It's Julian…." Cassey's voice is raw with tears.

I *cannot* hear her say it. I cannot hear her tell me for certain that he's gone. It's one thing to convince myself, another entirely to find out it's really true.

"Romeo!"

There are other words, but her voice echoes far behind me as I race across the wasteland. I run so far no lights penetrate the dark, and there are no sounds but the whisper of the city talking to itself.

Julian

I'VE NEVER been up here actually *on* the archway, trains whistling a few feet from my back. It's fucking terrifying, and exhilarating, and for one tiny second, it makes me feel so fucking alive. I perch on the ropey brickwork at the very edge. It really feels like the very edge—the dark plunge to the pavement below, the fathomless pitchy black in front of me, those fucking trains speeding along every few minutes behind.

I pull out my pad and, balancing it on my knee, draw one last picture. On the fucking edge. From memory. I draw myself.

When I've finished—it was only a quick sketch—I throw it away into the dark. It actually feels good seeing it vanish into God knows where, like I'm sending a preview out there into the universe.

It makes me laugh. *God,* I think, *that's strange. Am I hysterical?*

What the fuck am I doing?

Slowly, I get down off the edge and lay down amongst the wood and stones in the center of the bumpy track where the trains rush through.

I can feel the whole archway trembling beneath my body, the earth, everything—it's all one big trembling, living, moving, changing, constant, inconsistent, fucked-up, glorious thing.

What the fuck am I doing?

Beside me, the rails begin to whine and hum, and I am bathed in the bright, bright light of an oncoming train.

What the fuck *am I doing?*

Oh God.

I want to get up, but there isn't time. The noise is deafening, the roar upon me.

My body takes over.

I don't think I've made it, I really don't, as I lie in a panting heap by the very fucking edge, my fingers scrabbling at the grimy fucking bricks, at the oily dirt, needing to feel something, to know I'm still here, still real.

Oh fuck. *Fuck.*

Thoughts start flooding my empty brain as though I've been brought suddenly back from the dead in fast-forward.

I rub my hands against my uncared-for hair. It used to be so short it didn't matter. Julian used to shave it for me at Gem's. He asked me once why I didn't grow it. I think he wanted to know what I'd look like. I should grow it. For him.

My skin feels disgustingly unwashed. My clothes need to be binned. There is a clothing exchange every Wednesday at a shelter nearby. We used to go there. I've no idea what day it is, but I will go. I take out the white card with Annie's number from my pocket. I'll ask Cassey to call her for me. I'll go down, I'll do it now.

Oh my God, I think over and over as I clamber down the iron ladder to the ground. My limbs are like jelly. I just lay down on the *fuck*ing train tracks. I'm so glad I'm not dead.

Unsteady and still reeling, I lean against the crumbling brickwork at the bottom of the arches and breathe one deep breath after another.

There is a heavy dawn mist descending, and in the blurred orange glow of the streetlights, I can see another fucking lunatic limping down the middle road a little way off. It must be the night for us. An early-morning ferry sounds its first horn as it reaches the far bank of the river, a sound so familiar I finally realize how cold I am, and I turn to head back to Cassey's, to deal—

I stop.

A sudden, violent shiver courses through my body, and I almost fall to the ground.

I would recognize that silhouette anywhere. Would know it in a crowd of thousands, never mind alone on a deserted road. And now I'm scared. I look back up at that fucking edge on top of the archway. Now I'm terrified I didn't make it out of the way of that train.

But still he limps on, listing to one side as though he can't straighten up.

And then I think he sees me, and he stops.

The wind blasts from every direction all across the road, but still we don't move.

It feel as though I am resisting a magnetic pull, and I know I am going to give in any second, and he knows it too, but just the pull is what I want right now. These few moments of disbelieving anticipation while my brain makes sense of it all.

Julian looks awful.

Something odd has happened to his beautiful hair and one side of his face is completely red and swollen. In fact, every bare patch of skin I can see is covered in cuts and scratches.

He opens his mouth and closes it, but no words come.

Slowly, I begin to walk forward. If I move too fast, he might disappear. He limps to meet me. It's just a few steps, but it takes so long, and we look so hard at one another. And suddenly I'm engulfed in his arms in the middle of the road, held so tight I can't breathe, and I don't want to. I squeeze my arms around him just as tight, so we might hold on to this moment and never have to exist through what we've just existed through, and we'd never be alone again or cold again or needing or longing. I sob so hard my body shakes, and he pulls me backward out of the road as a car hoots to pass. It's not just me shaking, though. And I pull away to look at his face. To really look.

Oh God, what have they done to him?

He closes his puffy eyes as I tentatively trace my fingers over his bruised nose, his sore eyebrows, his tearstained, swollen cheekbones. I don't want to hurt him, but this isn't enough. His lips are torn but so, so soft.

"Remee," he says hoarsely, my name vibrating against my fingertips.

I can feel his heart beating against my chest, and I press closer. There is no way I am going to run from him, even if that night in the flat was just the work of my imagination. I have to let him know how I feel. I have to *feel*.

We are alive.

"Show me you're real," he whispers shakily, his eyes still squeezed shut tight. It almost feels like he's kissing my fingertips as he speaks, and then he does. Oh so hesitantly, he kisses them, and in less than a heartbeat I replace my fingertips with my mouth and press my lips as gently as I can against his.

How have I never dared do this? What did I think was so hard?

We stand unmoving by the side of the windy road, hearts hammering, lips pressed but not really kissing, arms wrapped tight, too terrified to move in case this is all fantasy, all make-believe, all wishful thinking.

Tentatively, I move my mouth against his. I feel so close to him. His breath warm on my face. I open my eyes and pull back a millimeter. I want him to follow me, and he does. He grazes my cheek with his, with the slight stubble that he shaves religiously whenever he can, but he doesn't kiss me.

Does he want this? Does he want me? Does it matter as long as he's here, however miraculous that seems right now?

His hand slides up my back to stroke my neck. I can feel his fingers brushing against my somewhat longer hair, exploring it. Exploring me. Pulling me closer. He opens his eyes, and we press our foreheads together, just breathing each other in. Then, gently cupping the back of my head, he nudges my nose with his, lowers his eyelashes, and suddenly brushes his open mouth against mine, again and again, so almost kissing, so teasing, so close I can taste him.

We're so involved, we don't hear the car pull up beside us, and the sound of the horn makes us both jump apart in shock.

Wide-eyed, Julian grabs me and spins around, away from the headlights, and waves his hand behind him in a gesture I know means *give us a minute*.

"Cassey! Fuck." He lays his head against my shoulder, breathing heavily. "She brought me here from the hospital."

I push away from his tight embrace.

Hospital? Why were you in hospital? I sign, panicked.

Fuck, I'm so stupid, getting carried away in all this want and relief, and he's hurt. I can see he's hurt.

Warm fingers brush away my pathetic, hot tears.

"I'm okay… I just hit my head a bit hard, and I needed a few stitches." Cautiously, he tips his head down so I can see a jagged line of bloody red running an awfully long way over the top of his skull. His hair has been shaved away in haphazard lines. Hesitantly, my fingers hover over the cut. "Here too." And he lifts the bundle of jumpers he's wearing and shows me the dressing wrapped around his chest and stomach, already stained a terrifying dark blackish red. But it's his arm that looks the worst, just above his wrist, the whole shape of it lumpy and distorted with swelling and stiff metal staples.

Holding me must have hurt like hell.

"They need to dress this, and I got a bit of an infection in the bite on my stomach, so I need to have these antibiotics from a drip in my arm for a few hours. I kind of discharged myself when Cassey told me what happened when she found you earlier." Now Julian's voice becomes so quiet I have to lean in close to hear him, and I end up resting my forehead beneath his chin like I always do. "I figured you thought something had happened to me, and I was scared for you. I mean, if it was you, I… I was just so scared, Remee, every awful day I was scared because I wasn't with you. I've missed you so much." He bites back a sob and kisses the top of my head, strokes his hand tenderly up and down my neck. "I've got to talk to the police, and I should go back into hospital for a while, just to get sorted out, but only if you'll come with me? I don't want to go anywhere if I'm not with you."

Where else does he think I'm going to go but with him? I take his good hand and pull him toward the steamed-up car.

Four sets of eyes blink at the sudden light and peer a little anxiously at us as I open the door. Phillippe hops into the front next to Cassey, and Julian and I squeeze in the back next to Gem and a very tired-looking Joel.

And it's me everyone is peering anxiously at, not poor battered Julian, who I'm trying not to crush, when all I desperately want to do is crawl in his lap.

Me.

A little embarrassed, I nod at everyone. *I'm okay.* Really I am. Now.

I smile at Joel, who closes his eyes and leans against Gem's chest.

Cassey gives me a meaningful look but seems satisfied enough to start the engine.

A thin strip of gray lights up the horizon, and I realize I haven't slept in two days. Right now I feel as though I could stay awake forever.

Julian grips my hand tightly in his, lets his head fall against my shoulder, and we go.

THIS WHISPERING CITY

CASSEY DROPS us at the hospital in the pale dawn light, blue-gray shadows washing over everything.

With one arm around Julian's waist to hold him up, I sign *thank you* through the open car window. All four of them look hollow-eyed and exhausted from searching for me all night. I can't really believe they did that.

I promise Cassey I'll get Julian to call her when he's discharged so she can pick us up, and she drives away.

We walk through the hissing doors, looking for reception. The bright, sterile fluorescent lights along the ceiling make me blink and cover my eyes, and at first I'm not really sure which way to go, but the glass-paneled reception booth is hard to miss. Julian leans heavily against me and speaks to the receptionist through a microphone. He's so pained and tired now I'm scared he's going to pass out.

They *must* see that.

But, no, what they see are two desperate homeless kids stumbling drunk-like through reception with nothing to do but hang around the place. And, they dispassionately inform us, Julian lost his bed when he discharged himself, so now we will have to wait in Accident and Emergency for him to be assessed again before he can see a doctor.

I pull him toward a row of uncomfortable-looking plastic chairs in the virtually empty waiting room and shift them around so he can lie with his head in my lap.

Worn out, I lean back, relief running through me like adrenaline at the feel of him, so warm, his body such a perfect solid weight against mine. With splayed fingers I stroke through what's left of his soft golden hair, and I'm filled with so much tenderness I think I might burst apart.

THE WAITING room is beginning to get busy when Julian is finally taken through to a curtain-drawn cubicle and examined. I stay with him and help him as he undresses and puts on the pale hospital gown. He is so thin and terribly bruised from head to foot, but he moves into my touch every time my fingers brush his skin—just his shoulder or his back as I fasten his gown—and I know he's trying to tell me something, something I'm all too willing to hear *now*, something I can't believe I didn't work out before, the way his body is calling to mine.

His eyes never leave me the whole time they're pushing needles into his skin and wrapping his wounds in gauze.

"I'm so tired, Remee," he whispers after the nurses have set up his drip and left.

It's okay, I sign. I kneel on the floor and cup his face between my hands, brushing away stray tears with my thumbs.

I long to ask him what happened, but I know now isn't the right time.

"Could you just…?" he whispers, closing his eyes against the words.

He doesn't need to ask. I climb on the bed next to him and pull him close.

"I'm sorry I'm…," he starts to say, but I hold my fingers against his lips to stop the words.

The painkillers he was given must work quickly as he falls asleep startlingly fast, his chest rising and falling deep and slow under my arm. I know I won't sleep, not yet, not here, the both of us so vulnerable.

Thankfully they don't move him up to a ward, and I stay curled protectively around his sleeping form for hours until the antibiotics have finished draining into him.

When a nurse eventually comes back to check on him, the clamor of the hospital is in full swing. She's busy, she has no time, and with one swift move she whips the IV out and startles Julian awake, causing him to moan in pain.

I glower at her. I understand the hurry, but why the fuck can't she be more considerate?

"There's a detective outside wanting to talk to you. I'll send her in, shall I?"

Julian blinks sleepily and turns in my arms, brows furrowed. *Where the fuck am I?*

And I have to bury my face in his shoulder and grip him tight. *God, I love him.*

The detective is a tall and faintly androgynous woman in a businesslike black trouser suit. She introduces herself as Tessa Sandersen and wants me to step outside for a minute so she can talk to Julian alone. Julian links his fingers through mine and determinedly shakes his head. No.

"Name?" She sighs, reluctantly pulling out a small tape recorder and looking over in my direction.

Julian glances at me, silently checking I'm okay with this, before saying "Romeo Danilov."

I love the way he says my name. It's not right, not the way my mother would spit the word out, but that just makes me love how he says it all the more. Because he tries so hard to get it right for me. He tries so hard to get everything right.

"Can Romeo not speak for himself?"

"No."

I'm mute, I write on my pad and show it to her.

"Oh." And I can see it already, that weird, misplaced, motherly concern.

She certainly wasn't looking at me like this a moment ago.

And then she asks, "Romeo, were you the one who gave us the tip-off about Vidal and Malik?"

I nod and feel Julian's eyes on me. He's probably just shocked I went to the police. I kind of am too.

"Well, Romeo, it's doubtful your friend would be here right now if it wasn't for you. We should get quite a few convictions out of this case if we're lucky."

Now she turns to Julian.

"Your statement is really important, Julian. Shall we start at the beginning?"

Julian nods, and I want to hop back on the bed with him and hold him in my arms. But I just squeeze his hand tightly and stare at the floor.

First he tells her about the squat and what happened in the white house, about Malik and Vidal, stuff I know, stuff I lived through with him.

"So the morning of the fifth, what happened?"

"I can't remember everything clearly. It's hazy. I think they drugged us. I remember being shaken awake and told to come outside. I didn't want to go, but Malik dragged me. He had a dog. It was still dark. There were probably about twelve of us on the walkway, and I don't know how many of *them*, but they all had dogs. They led us out of the block in a line. If anyone stopped, they got hit or kicked. There was a dark-colored van parked near the entrance, and they started to force us inside. I tried to run, but my legs wouldn't work properly. I was punched a few times and thrown in the back with everyone else. They drove for hours. Everything was black in the back of the van, so we couldn't see where we were going or even if it was light outside. We had made a plan to escape when they opened the doors, there were more of us than them, we were going to overwhelm them. But when the van stopped, they threw something in the back that smelled so bad we couldn't breathe and pulled us out one by one. I was dragged into a yard with another kid. The place looked like some sort of factory, and there were caravans everywhere. I didn't feel so groggy anymore, so I managed to take whoever was holding me by surprise and run, and that was when they...."

He pauses, closing his eyes, his breathing suddenly ragged. I pull our linked hands up to my face and rub my lips against his grazed knuckles.

"You're doing really well, Julian," Tessa says gently.

"...that was when they let the dogs go," he says in a rush and releases my hand to pull his gown to the side, exposing the dressing on his stomach and holding out his bandaged arm. Tessa produces a small camera from her pocket and takes a couple of pictures.

"I'm going to have to take some more pictures of your injuries but without the dressings, maybe in a week or so?

"Okay."

"Do you want to take a break for a minute? Or do you want to carry on?"

"I just want to get this over with," he says quietly.

I can't stand not being close to him anymore so I stand up and edge myself onto the bed. The whole side of his body pushes back against mine, and I know I'm not imagining any of this.

Tessa raises her eyebrows but doesn't say anything.

"They tried to get me to work. I don't know what it was they wanted me to do, but I couldn't even make it to the factory door, I was in so much pain. After a day or two, they just left me alone in this stinking caravan. No one brought me food or water or anything. I slept a lot. I wasn't in pain when I was sleeping. The first thing I knew about the police raid was when I heard voices shouting for everyone to get out of the caravans or they would torch them. I don't know how I got out, but when I did, I was grabbed and shoved into a van again and driven away fast. The van was still moving when they pushed me out of it."

Julian leans his head forward and shows her his stitched-up scalp and touches his swollen cheekbone.

Tessa takes another few pictures.

"And this was where the police picked you up from?"

Julian nods.

"Okay. Thank you, Julian, you've been really brave. We have one other boy from the camp willing to give a statement, but if there is anyone else you know from the squat or the white house who you think would come forward, it will only strengthen our case."

I think of Peter and Nathaniel sleeping rough on the heath. I think about finding them.

Before she leaves, Tessa asks for an address, and I'm surprised when Julian gives the cafe as his.

"Cassey said we can stay there until I'm well," he says, leaning against me and sighing deeply once Tessa has gone.

What about Lloyd? I sign, remembering suddenly.

"I don't know. I guess we'll just have to deal with each day as it comes."

I nod distractedly, my brain in overdrive, processing what happened to Julian, how much he's been hurt, weighing it up against the threat of Lloyd coming to look for us. I need to stop thinking.

I concentrate on his breath, steady and warm against my shoulder, how he smells really clean and nice. I smell awful. I stare at the dirt all around my fingernails, ground into the lines all over my hands, and suddenly I feel so filthy sitting on this clean bed with him. And I know it's not the dirt that's the problem, not really. I know it's because I feel overwhelmed by everything he's gone through, and too inadequate to be of any use.

I get off the bed and sink to the floor.

"What are you doing down there?" he asks softly, puzzled.

I shrug. *You're clean. I'm not*, I sign.

Slowly, carefully, he edges his way down the bed until his head lies against the mattress inches from mine.

"Do you really think I give a fuck?"

He reaches out his good arm to turn my face toward him and looks at me searchingly with his warm brown eyes.

He knows what the problem is. He always knows.

With trembling fingers he traces the curve of my cheekbones, the hollow dip either side of my nose, this slow exploration made so much more intimate in the bright hospital light.

"You know what really hurt when I was lying in that caravan?" he says gently, drawing me closer with every touch. "It hurt that if I died there you would never have known. It's stupid, but out of everything, I just couldn't bear you not knowing. It didn't seem right somehow that the one person who was everything to me wouldn't know that I'd gone."

We're so close now; I feel such an incredible tender rush of desire to stop his tears with my lips, to feel the salty skin of his cheek beneath my tongue. I've come to realize it's possible to take away pain with such actions, to show you love someone without saying a word.

He lowers his eyelashes, and I close my eyes. We're so hesitant and shy with one another, the anticipation is painful and… wonderful.

"And I knew if I ever saw you again…." The words are just delicious whispers of breath. "I would…."

He inhales sharply at the first touch of our lips, and I jerk back, afraid that I've caused him pain.

I'm so very scared of hurting him.

His eyes are half lidded, dark, confused.

I don't want to hurt you, I sign rapidly.

He groans shakily. *"Please, Remee."* And his voice is full of a different sort of pain.

I want him so badly I'm aching for contact. And this time, when our lips meet, I open my mouth against his and gasp as his tongue touches mine and sweeps inside. He twists his head against the bed to deepen the kiss, and his moan vibrates inside me when I lean over and kiss him back just as deep.

I clench and unclench my hands in his hair, against the bed sheets, trying to be gentle but losing coherent thought completely. I'm panting and gasping and still barely breathing, high on all the little sounds he makes, his body pleading with mine to be *closer, closer.* I've never kissed anyone like this, lost in some fierce, wild longing that seems impossible to satisfy.

We know each other so well, and we know nothing.

It becomes messy and desperate very quickly, and I pull back to touch our cheeks gently together.

"What's wrong, baby?" he whispers, still clutching me, breathing heavily against my ear.

I can't respond. I can't fucking breathe. That was too nice. I don't want to come like that. I want to come with my body pressed up against him, wrapped up in him, holding me as I fly apart. I don't want to lose control kneeling on the floor next to his hospital bed, the possibility of a nurse or doctor walking in on us.

"Remee?" He turns my face toward his.

His skin is flushed around his neck and the top of his chest, just visible above his gown, and I remember that time in the squat when I thought he was embarrassed after I got carried away. How fucking wrong I was.

Not here, I sign, self-conscious that I am so easy.

He smiles (and even though his face is distorted by bruising, it still makes me melt inside) and then blushes ever so slightly as he catches my gaze wandering down the raised bedclothes and resting with surprise on his evident erection.

Thank God we didn't get any further, I think, as abruptly the curtains are drawn aside and a nurse walks in with a pile of prescriptions and Julian's discharge papers.

These Ordinary Ghosts

THERE'S AN indoor phone booth near the accident and emergency reception. I hand Julian my last coin out of the pocket of my filthy jeans and lean against the wall in an attempt to keep upright. I'm so unbelievably tired I'm seeing weird dancing lights on the edge of my vision.

Julian watches me with concern as he talks to Cassey.

"You okay?" he mouths midconversation.

I nod, even though I'm aware I'm slipping.

He reaches out and grabs my arm, holding the phone to his ear with his shoulder.

"Shit. Remee?"

I feel my head fall back and hit the wall behind me and everything just goes so cold.

Luckily, I'm not out for long, and by the time Julian's somehow sat me on the floor and propped my head between my knees, I'm coming together again.

"I'll be back in a sec," he murmurs, and his comforting warmth disappears from my side.

He returns with a handful of sugar sachets, palmed from the hospital cafe opposite reception.

Opening one with his teeth, he tips the contents onto my hand and holds it up to my mouth.

"When was the last time you ate anything, baby?"

I shrug. I honestly can't remember.

He opens another sachet, tips his head back, and swallows the contents himself. Then one by one we work our way through them. This is why Cassey has to hide the sugar in the cafe—there have been days when we have survived on nothing else but sugar and ketchup sachets.

It doesn't make you feel great; in fact I probably feel more hollow and empty than before, now that my stomach has woken up, but at least the weird lights have gone from my vision, and the brief sugar high means I have a bit of energy.

"You went so fucking pale just then, you know."

Which I know translates as *you scared the shit out of me.*

I push my body against his in reassurance, and we sit like that, leaning into one another, too exhausted to communicate as we wait for Cassey to arrive.

It's dark again by the time Cassey comes in her beat-up car to drive us back to the cafe. We sink into the backseat, and I close my eyes as Julian wraps his warm arms around me. He smells so fucking good, even if it is a bit hospital-y. And I know this is all I need. All I want. Always.

The next time I open my eyes, the car is stopped under the dim orange glow of a streetlight, and Cassey is talking in a low voice to Julian. She hands him a set of keys to the back door.

"Phillippe left with Cricket and Roxy, so you have the place to yourselves. I'm sorry I can't let you stay indefinitely, but if anyone finds out, they'll shut me down. Two or three weeks is the best I can do."

Julian nods gratefully.

"Thank you," he says, squeezing his arm tighter around me and edging toward the door.

Everything is shut up, and the building is dark. I notice the broken window Julian smashed is boarded up with a solid-looking piece of plywood. Secure.

"Gem left you some bits and pieces in the back room," Cassey calls through the car window, remembering, just before she drives away.

"Only out of guilt," Julian mutters darkly as we walk across the yard we've slept in more times than I can count.

My breath is smoky vapor in the freezing air as Julian struggles with the lock, determined to fit and twist the key one-handed in the gloom.

Did you argue with Gem? I sign after we've switched every light switch we can find.

Julian looks away briefly. "You could say that," he says, standing in the doorway between the back room and the hall. "Gem let you go when you went there for help."

Do you still...? I stop. What on earth am I asking him? I *know* he doesn't, of course I know he doesn't still have those feelings for Gem, so why do I want to hear him *say* he doesn't so much?

"What?" he asks softly.

I shake my head a bit too vigorously. Nothing.

Sometimes, when he looks at me like this, I think he can see inside me, right through to all the stupid fears and anxieties written on the walls of my mind.

"It was over a long time ago, baby."

You loved her, though.

Julian cocks his head, eyebrows furrowed.

"Him. I loved him."

Oh.

Realization comes like curtains opening in a dark room to reveal a whole brightly lit world beyond it.

Gem is a guy.

He's Joel's dad.

No wonder he thought my question about Julian being Joel's father stupid. I wonder if he's flattered I didn't know.

"Gem wasn't always as he is now. In the beginning I didn't deal with the whole cross-dressing thing very well. I was a kid. I didn't understand."

I reach out for his hand across the hallway. I can accept his past. Understanding takes effort, but it's an effort I know we are both willing to put in.

WIDE-EYED WITH a kind of sleepy, muted excitement, we make each other cups of sugary tea and round after round of toast slathered with jam.

Cassey said we could use the supplies in the back room's kitchen, as long as we didn't use *all* the supplies in there. I figure she'd give us all the toast we could eat anyway.

I feel a lot better. Weary, but better.

The bits and pieces Gem left us are in a black bin bag by the door. Julian tips it out, and we eagerly sort through the odd assortment of T-shirts and trousers (smelling wonderfully of some flower-scented washing powder) to find something warm to sleep in. There are also a couple of towels, some soap, shampoo, toothpaste, and toothbrushes.

"There's a bath down the hall," Julian says, awkwardly wrapping all the toiletries up in a towel one-handed.

What about your dressings? I sign.

"I can get them wet; you'll just have to help me put new ones on after."

Already my heart is beating erratic and quick.

I kneel beside him and twist the ends of the errant towel together, brushing my fingers against his. The atmosphere between us is all of a sudden heavier somehow, our movements weighted down, drawing us closer.

Slowly, his fingers stroke down my arm, and I turn and press into him, burying my face in his shoulder, breathing in the sharp, familiar scent of him.

I feel him swallow, and his words vibrate through me, urgent with longing. "Come on."

The ancient fan heater up on the wall groans into life as we wash out the grimy bath.

Does it hurt? I sign, gently touching the gauze wrapped around his wrist as he holds it out of the way of the water for now.

He shakes his head in bemused wonderment. "The painkillers they gave me are opiates. Doesn't hurt at all."

His eyes lock with mine, and he brings the fingers of that hand tentatively up to my face, traces the outer edges of my lips until I reach for his fingers and kiss them, and he looks on, lost in some sort of helpless desire.

Emboldened and somehow weak at his reaction, I suck each finger deep into my mouth, feeling my cock stiffen painfully in my jeans. I need *more*. And apparently so does he, as he suddenly reaches out, grips the back of my skull and, in a heartbeat, crushes our mouths together, the both of us struggling frantically to get closer, until we crash, shocked, against the concrete bathroom floor.

"Fuck. You okay?" he gasps.

I nod, my skull still ringing from the impact, even as I pull him down heavily on top of me, searching for his mouth, his skin, at last.

God, his *skin*, warm yet shivering beneath my fingers as I trail them up the long muscles on either side of his spine, under his top, causing him to arch and push his hips down against mine as he kisses me slow and deep.

So much sensation, I lose myself in it, in him. In every grind of his hips, in every rough stroke of his tongue. Our world narrowed to a single bright strip of touch, of taste. Why on earth would we need anything more?

It's only when the bath begins to overflow onto the floor that we come back to ourselves.

Julian laughs as we both grab wildly for the taps, breathless, giddy. *Glowing.*

I try to tell him, but he doesn't understand. Perhaps he just can't see it.

Shyly, we undress, pulling our tops off over our flushed faces and just dumping them carelessly on the wet floor.

Julian hesitates before unbuttoning his trousers, and I just watch him because I'm stupid and hopeless and can't look away.

"It's been a while for me," he whispers, staring at his stilled fingers, so vulnerable it physically hurts to see.

It floors me how much being used for sex was destroying him. I can't bear the thought of him going back out there and selling himself, and I know we will have to find a way to survive without that. But we *will* survive without that.

It's okay, I sign. It's okay if we do no more than hold each other and kiss. It's okay as long as he's here with me. This is all I need.

"I don't mean... I just... *I want you.*" He looks over, and his expression is earnest. "If I don't... can't... it doesn't matter. I don't want you to think that it's you because it isn't. It's me and... I haven't had a hard-on like this in so fucking long," he gasps.

His grin lights me up, and I grin back helplessly as I shove my jeans down and step out of them. I don't even give him time to stand up straight after he has stepped out of his own before I press myself against him, and we fall into the bath.

We lie face to face, his soapy hands on my skin, rubbing slow circles down my back, lower and lower, as he sucks on my ear.

"You're so beautiful, baby," he says, the words whispering down my spine as he speaks, causing my body to arch into him, loving the feel of how my cock lines up perfectly in the deep hollow of his hip, and his erection pokes readily into my stomach. "You feel so good."

His words echo my thoughts, though I'm barely thinking anymore—I'm just a tangle of nerve endings wanting to thrust against his hip and pant openmouthed into his neck as his hand reaches the sensitive skin at the base of my spine and dips lower, his fingers slipping hungrily between.... I push back against him, opening to him, wanting his fingers deep inside me, even though I need him to stop because I'm going to come if he goes much deeper.

His wordless groan as I reach between us, gripping him tight in my fist, is the only sound I ever need to hear. But somehow he shifts our positions. Moves me on top of him, my back against his front, as he leans against the end of the bath and holds me tight.

I twist my head to kiss him as his hand trails lazily down my chest, my stomach, so slow the anticipation makes me blind and... he spreads my thighs, reaching between my legs. I watch with slitted eyes as he grips both our cocks loosely in his hand and jerks his hips, rubbing and sliding against me.

I hold my hand over his to increase the friction, to feel the delicious heat of him, to hear him suck in breath after breath. I feel I'm balancing on the very fucking edge of some glorious abyss, the moment stretching until it stops... and bursts apart as I come in thick spurts. Julian watches me, making this low sound that I know I want to hear again and again, and shudders as I close my palm over the head of him, wanting to feel the pulse as he comes against it and kissing him sloppily when he does.

We slip under the water still kissing, and I wonder dreamily if we could stay like this, locked together in the remnants of an orgasm, feeling as though we are stopping time and creating our own fucking world....

But no matter how hard I try to hold on to the sensation, stay afloat on the fucking *wings* of it, I *know* it's going to pass—the bath will get cold, we will sleep curled round one another on the hard back-room floor, we will fuck 'til we're sore and aching and undone, and all the mornings will dawn colder and icier, and the streets will be waiting but unable to take what we have away... but they will *try*... because we are *meant* to be ephemeral, like the brilliant sparks from a fire shooting up into the dark, we are not meant to last, nothing lasts, one moment always follows another... the good, the bad, the awfully, fantastically ordinary... and in the looping darkness there's only one thing left to hold on to....

PART TWO:
AT THE END OF EVERYTHING

IF WE WERE IN RUSSIA NOW, WE'D BE DEAD

IT IS winter. Or the season of death, as my mother used to call it in her twisted Russian accent. She had names like that for everything; her life dipped in black negativity, her only salvation the prayers she mumbled as she turned the rosary beads.

Draped in old blankets, Julian and I wander down the empty embankment looking for a little shelter and a place to sleep. We must look like ghosts shrouded in the darkness, and in a way we are.

The river drifts on, eerily unfrozen beside us. Icy vapor hangs in the air, making the edge of all things seem indistinct and unfinished.

Half an hour ago, we were moved on from our refuge in a deserted underpass by a near army of police—a bare few hours of blissful contentment, curled in one another's arms is all we get now. It's some sort of crackdown to clean up the city, they said, as though we're rubbish to be sanitized away. Where they think we all go once we've been moved on, I've no idea. Perhaps they'll find a way to really make us vanish one day.

A few weeks ago, we had a brief respite from living on the streets like this—a gift from a friend in a way—we had a room to sleep in, food we could help ourselves to, a bathroom we could use. But however glorious that respite was, it has only made this harder. Made being trapped out here even more hellish than it was before, because now we can taste again the sweetness of each taken-for-granted moment and be tormented by how far it is out of our reach.

The clock on the riverbank tolls three.

If we were in Russia now, we'd be dead.

Out of nowhere, I hear my mother's voice in my head and look down at my hand. I don't know how old I was, but she'd caught me touching myself—there was nowhere to hide in our tiny bedsit—she took my hand and held it up to the flame of the cooker.

If we were in Russia now, they would chop off your disgusting hand, she'd cried.

And I'd cowered before her, cradling my blistered fingers, too afraid to move.

Julian grabs the edge of my blanket and pulls me over toward him.

"Hey, where are you going, baby? Here is fine."

It's just a concrete bench, somewhere people sit on sunny days to stare out at the river, but we can lie tucked away underneath the slatted seat and hopefully no one will bother to disturb us.

"You okay?"

His warm breath whispers against my cheek as we wrap ourselves around each other on the ground, in the perfect dark beneath our blankets. The liquid warmth of his skin, radiating out from under all the layers of clothing, fills me with want, a bone-deep ache to be closer and closer.

"You were miles away."

He doesn't expect a reply. There's no way I *can* reply right now—my pad is tucked away in the worn pocket of my coat. And he is blind to my sign language in the night. So I press my lips to the first bit of skin I can find and hold them there as he breathes me in and grips me tight. We've barely done more than this for a week. Barely more than tangle our hands down each other's pants and kiss each other sloppily for hours on end, holding off from coming for as long as possible. But tonight I feel a different sort of urgency as I trace the contours of his face with my fingertips, a slow deep desire to be his completely. Though I know he won't fuck me out here, I want him to.

I bring his hand up and suck his fingers lazily into my mouth. I smile into the blackness at how, even though he can't see me doing this, it always makes him groan helplessly with need. His hands are warm, and he tastes so completely of himself, so completely familiar… oh God, I need this. I pull him on top of me, my mouth on his mouth as I push my pants down and fumble with the fastening on his jeans.

"Remee…," he whispers hoarsely.

I just want to kiss away his words, and I slip my hands beneath his waistband and cup the smooth, firm muscles of his buttocks as I capture his mouth.

"Baby...."

I kick off my trousers, along with some of the blanket, and wrap my legs around his waist. Right now I don't care if we're hidden, right now I am swept away, I am dust, I am desire.

With certain fingers, I brush the hypersensitive hot skin at the top of his thighs, between his legs, and feel him melt against me. I know without question I can break his resolve, that he *will* fuck me here if I carry on... but, and this is suddenly much more important, do I want to? Do I want to make him do what he'd rather keep sacred, private, out here in the dirt under a bench?

My movements slow, our kisses deepen. I run my fingers up through his shortened hair and arch against him as he strokes my sides.

"It's not because I don't want to, baby...," he whispers, anxiety showing through in his voice.

I shake my head. It's okay. Because what I want is tempered by what he wants. Because love is a promise I won't break.

We end up rubbing against each other, Julian sobbing against my neck as he comes—sometimes he does that, though I don't ask why— my own orgasm triggered by the slick heat of him against my stomach, his voice whispering my name against the shell of my ear.

MY COUGH gets worse the next day. It wakes me up. I think it must be the dirt we slept in. Maybe I breathed it in in the night. I've had this cough on and off for weeks.

Julian watches me with concern as he rolls the blankets neatly together and tucks them under his arm.

His bruises are fading now, the swelling on his face almost gone. It's only his wrist that continues to cause him problems. The hospital took the staples out last week but, although the skin is pink and healing nicely, the mess inside still hurts. It causes him pain every time he moves it, I can tell.

We don't talk about what happened when he was taken by Malik, how terrified he was when he was attacked by the dogs and left in a caravan to die and then thrown out of a moving vehicle when the police raided the illegal work camp. Maybe one day we will. I think it's all just too raw now. And we are still locked in amazed wonderment that we have each other at all. I don't think this feeling will ever fade.

WE HIDE out in Joe Brown's cafe all day, Cassey passing us free cups of tea over the counter when no one is watching. It's somewhere warm, somewhere we know we are welcome.

But by evening when we go outside into the freezing air, I can hardly take a breath without coughing for twenty. My lungs are spasming, my chest aches, and I feel exhausted.

It's only six o'clock, but the light has been gone for hours. I'm beginning to hate this endless dark. We sit on the wooden bench outside the closed cafe doors, and Julian covers me in blankets and holds me in his arms as I shiver uncontrollably and cough on and on and on.

"I think we should take you to see a doctor."

He must be worried. He hates hospitals. Plus he knows that I am a minor—whatever age I say I am, I know I look under sixteen—and if the authorities find out I'm on the street, I will automatically be put under the care of the state until my parents can be found. It doesn't matter what I may want. I have no say whatsoever.

We wait it out a little longer. It's just a cough, after all, isn't it? But by the time I'm coughing in an almost constant loop, hardly breathing normally at all, he leaves the blankets lying haphazardly on the bench and half carries me along the road and across the bridge over the river. The hospital isn't far.

THE CURE

I CAN feel the tension in the hard planes of his body as I press against him. I can feel it bunched in the burning muscles of his arm as he holds me up. I wasn't worried earlier, even though every time I coughed outside the cafe it felt as though my ribs were cracking apart. I've had coughs before, but as we reach the middle of the bridge and struggle against the shards of icy wind, I glance up at Julian's face and see only a clear and desperate anguish.

Julian never makes me panic. He is always the one who takes away the black hole inside me, the one who blocks out the darkness, who stands with no shadow and infects me with his contagious belief that we will be okay, we will always *be okay*.

I don't want to see this. Feel this.

Shivering and barely able to stand still, we lurch into A&E. This is not the hospital Julian was taken to, but I've been here before with Roxy. This place is more central, more packed, and the hurt and injured overflow into the corridors and doorways at this time of day. But even though the place is so busy, there is such a black-eyed watchful silence as we queue for the reception desk—undoubtedly the result of my constant coughing—and we stand uncomfortably in the inescapable channels of freezing wind gusting through the ever-open doors.

I'm doubled over gasping, Julian stroking my back, when I see it. The blood. Dripping out from between my lips to form imperfect red circles on the pale tiled floor.

Oh is all I can think. But the thought has the weight and shape of a stone.

A stone heavy and solid enough to shatter my glass-like indestructibility, if I were to drop it.

I rub the back of my shaking hand across my mouth and smear the pale skin with bright, bright red.

Julian pulls my hand away, takes it between the warmth of his own, and wipes away the blood with his fingertips. He tries to smile, but his eyes are distraught.

"NAME?" THE receptionist doesn't even look up.

"Remee Lavelle." Julian doesn't falter in his lie. The surname is his, not mine. He glances at me, checking to see if I mind.

"Age?"

"Seventeen." Never stretch the lie too far from the truth.

"You're seventeen?"

"What? No, he's seventeen. He's mute. Can't you see he's the one who needs the fucking doctor?" Julian's knuckles are white as they grip against the counter. The receptionist stares.

"*He* needs to see a doctor," he repeats a little more calmly.

"Please step back from the counter," she states icily.

Julian lowers his hands and grits his teeth as I sag against his side. It would be so easy to just slide down to the floor. I wrap my arms around my chest as another wave of coughing hits. I'm so fucking tired. At least we're not outside in that Russian winter, I try to console myself; at least we're together. Even if I'm burning up like a comet, at least he is the cool space that surrounds me.

WE LEAN against the wall between the male and female toilet doors, waiting. I cough into Julian's warm embrace, let his arms envelop me. People shuffle a safe distance away. Someone complains, and I'm handed a packet of tissues. I spit out blood. Julian presses his head against mine and closes his eyes.

I feel so distant from myself, each moment a still from a film, the continuity fucked. And sometimes the sound is gone too, and I am left in such yawning silence I think it might swallow me whole.

HOURS LATER we're no longer waiting. A tired, black-haired doctor pulls back the curtain on our tiny cubicle.

"You have a slight fever but it's just a chest infection. The X-rays have come back clear—no fluid, no shadows. I can give you antibiotics for it."

"What about the blood?" Julian's voice wavers, and he grips my hand as he says this. I feel the strong pulse of his wrist as it presses against mine. The warmth of his skin.

"It's normal. You've been coughing awhile?" The doctor looks at me. I nod. His gown rustles as he sits down on the end of the narrow bed and sighs. "But, if you stay out on the streets, it's only going to get worse." He digs around in his pocket and hands Julian a piece of folded paper. "This is the number of a street shelter in Victoria. They have space for you."

Julian stares at the number scrawled across the paper and then folds it neatly along the creases and passes it back. The both of us must look so young and naive under these glaring hospital lights.

My body is wracked with another coughing fit just as Julian says, "We're not going to any shelter."

"Then your friend is going to suffer with this cough that can easily be cured, and he is going to end up with pneumonia."

Wearily the doctor shakes his head. I can tell he's sick of people like us, people he thinks are refusing to be helped. But it's not as simple as that.

As soon as he leaves, Julian turns around and takes my hands in his. "I don't know what to do," he whispers helplessly.

I lean forward and fall into his arms, trying to breathe in through the rough material of his jumper to stop coughing.

"My mum died of lung disease," he murmurs into my hair, his words making me shiver the way he presses his lips against the feather-soft blackness that now covers my scalp, despite the seriousness of his revelation.

Blindly, I reach for my pad, reluctant to pull away. He's never spoken about his family at all, and because I don't like to talk about my own mother, I've never asked him.

Is that why you left home? I write.

He glances at my words and shakes his head before burying his face against my shoulder.

"I was nine. She used to cough up blood, and I used to hold her and try and stop it. I thought if I could just look after her well enough, she would be okay. But she wasn't."

Lightly, I trace each separate bone of his spine through his jumper, feel him lean into me, his breathing deepen. He likes to be touched like this, slowly stroked and explored.

"I'm scared they're going to take you away from me if we go to the shelter," he whispers. "But I can't go back out there with you and make you sicker."

SHELTER

JULIAN LEAVES me to steal some blankets from the laundry deep in the cellars under the hospital. He always seems to know where to find places like this—as though some sort of urban survival manual has been uploaded into his brain.

I wait nervously on the cellar steps, smothering my mouth with my sleeve to silence my cough, and listening out for his quiet footfalls.

The hospital is a huge Victorian monolith, and although brightly lit and painted shiny yellowing white, I can smell the damp, blackened bricks a paint's thickness away from my fingertips. I can feel the freezing Russian wind as it forces its way through the thin windowpanes and howls down the corridors and stairwells like a wolf… or a ghost.

A whisper, and my name hangs in the air. I glance around behind me, shivering. The door at the top of the cellar steps bangs lightly against the wall in the breeze.

There is no one there.

"Hey, baby."

Julian's voice has me near jumping out of my skin. I didn't hear his approach at all.

His gentle hand steadies me.

"You look spooked. You okay?"

Fuck.

Oh, I'm fine, I think. *I'm just hearing things.*

People say you can hallucinate with a fever, though I no longer feel particularly feverish.

I try to smile at him. He leans in and softly kisses the side of my mouth. And I do smile, genuinely, my mouth against his for a fraction of a second before I need to cough again.

"Sorry I took so long. I had to search to find the clean blankets."

He reaches down to the pile at his feet and hands me a couple.

They're so much heavier and thicker than the ones we left behind on the bench.

"Didn't want to pick ones people might have died in or anything."

I shake my head, *no*, because that would be bad, like an omen or something.

How do we get out? I sign, after I've pulled the blankets around my shoulders and settled under their weight.

"Well, we can go this way."

He points up the cellar steps, back the way we came.

"Though people might wonder where we're going with these."

His fingers tug at the blanket around my shoulders.

"Or we can get out this way."

I watch him incline his head briefly toward the dimly lit cellar and instantly think, *no fucking way*.

"It's not far," he says softly, his eyes catching the low shine of the lights and glowing warmly. That way he has of looking at me, as though there is nothing else on this earth he would rather rest his eyes on, it sometimes makes me wonder if I could ever have felt like this about anyone else, whether I would have lived, but my life would have been forever incomplete without him in it.

IT'S NOT so cold down here wrapped up, but I'd rather be wandering the freezing streets. I don't like it. At all.

There is a central corridor that runs through the cellar, doors coming off either side leading to rooms full of equipment or rubbish. There doesn't seem to be an end to it, despite Julian's reassurance that it wasn't far.

We see a porter in one of the side rooms moving trolleys. I stop. Trolleys with mounds of something other than blankets on. Oh God.

This is where they take the dead! I sign hurriedly.

Cautiously, Julian steps back toward the doorway and takes a closer took. He nods, he looks a little pale.

How far? I sign as he takes my hand.

After maybe a quarter of a mile of corridor, we come to a short flight of stone stairs, at the top of which is a door with an emergency release bar that I suspect leads to the street outside.

I'm ready to run up those stairs to get out of here, but Julian stops, lets go of my hand, and edges toward a small dark anteroom to one side. He disappears inside. After a moment he leans in the doorway and says, awkwardly without really meeting my eyes, "Hey, why don't we stop in here for the night?"

He's never done this before, planned something, planned to *do* something he knew I wouldn't be overjoyed about. He's usually so straightforward, so *clear*, the truth shining through him like sunlight through glass.

And I can see now he's unsure of my reaction.

Reluctantly, I peer past him into the room. It's small and empty—concrete floor, concrete walls, door on the back wall leading to God-knows-where. I know he only wants to find shelter. I know he's scared.

I nod without enthusiasm, because I'm scared too, of this place.

The door on the far wall is locked. We huddle in the corner farthest away from it and cover ourselves in blankets. Julian leans against the wall, and I sit between his legs with my back resting against him. His arms envelop me. One hand rests against the cool skin of my chest beneath my top and strokes soothing circles across my ribs when I cough.

It feels nice, and it's starting to turn me on, especially when he brushes his fingers over my nipple like that—almost, but not quite carelessly. My breath hitches, and I shift uncomfortably, feeling myself grow hard in my jeans.

"When do you have to take your medicines, baby?"

Warm breath whispers against my neck, and I lean my head back to feel more of him, to tell him without words where I want to feel his lips, his tongue.

He's so good at distracting me.

I wish I could forget about this fucking cough, though.

"Remee… baby…," he whispers, and a rough wetness licks the ridge of my ear.

Fuck, I think weakly as I melt against him. I am his. Completely.

I spread my bent legs open against his, push my hips back and up, the tight friction of my jeans almost painful as I rub against them.

I start to cough. And we slow it down. Julian's fingers trail slow delicate lines along my ribs, all the way from the back to the front, and then he's dipping down beneath them, ghosting his hand across my stomach, causing me to suck in breath after breath as he goes lower and lower until I'm coughing uncontrollably again and ready to cry with frustration.

"Baby," he whispers as he presses soft kisses down my neck. "I just wanna do this for you. I just want you to lie back against me and relax, okay?"

Okay, I sign into the darkness.

I'm malleable as clay right now.

He kisses my neck and hair while his gentle fingers trace the outline of my erection through my jeans. Nothing compares to this feeling of being so completely surrounded.

With one hand still stroking my chest, he deftly undoes my button and zip and slips his hand beneath my pants. I arch up into his touch as his fingers tangle in the hair at the base of my erection, the side of his hand rubbing firmly up and down its length. He likes to touch me everywhere, reaching lower between my thighs, cupping my balls, feeling their weight in his hand. I'm so supersensitized and wide open, I lean my head right back, let my eyes close, and gasp when his mouth sucks on the tender skin between my neck and my shoulder.

"Come for me," he groans as he grips me tight and pumps my cock in his fist.

MORNING ARRIVES, and we are woken early by the whirring hum of a milk float dropping crates off somewhere nearby. Julian pulls me tight against him, breathing deeply.

The room is still dark, and my body craves the lighting dawn, the way the sky cracks brightly along the horizon and spills over.

I tug at him, and sleepily we gather the blankets and make our way up the steps and out into the icy backstreet. Almost immediately I'm bent in two, my lungs convulsing, and I'm coughing and coughing and coughing. Julian pulls me against him, my head to his chest so I can breathe in through the warm fabric of his jumper.

"That shelter was in Victoria, right?" he says softly. "Let's go."

CHANCES I

THE SHELTER is in an old factory building, the accommodation set out over four huge floors. Each massive factory window is made up of smaller panes of obscured glass, so you can't see in or out. In between bouts of coughing, I lean my head back and try and take in the enormity of the place. Above the roof I can see the dawning sky is going to be bluer than it's been for weeks, the air clear and colder than ice.

Julian slips his hand around my elbow and tugs me gently.

"Come on," he whispers.

The double doors are hard to push open, and Julian lets go of me to place both hands on the glass and push. A cloud of warm chemical air engulfs us as we step inside the reception area. There are posters everywhere, papering the walls: faces, help lines, drug advice. I don't look at them. They make me feel hopeless. They don't reflect the truth at all. Not one of them can help us. No one can help us. Not in the way we need to be helped.

Even though it's early, early morning, the reception is manned by a middle-aged man in a tracksuit. He looks more like some sort of night guard than a receptionist. Overweight and hard faced, his demeanor suggests we don't want to fuck with him.

Julian walks over to talk to him, leaving me by the door to avoid staring at the walls.

This place is bigger than any we've been in before, and we've both stayed in shelters, albeit separately.

Bigger and more organized.

There is space for 256 in need, and there is always need. It is always full.

The man doesn't care that we're together—he gives us beds on different floors.

I don't know what I was expecting. I guess it wasn't this.

I walk with wavering steps to sit on the metal stairs a short corridor away and cough miserably into my thin coat.

"These are the only beds available right now."

"He needs me with him! He's sick, and he can't fucking call out for help if he needs it! Do you understand sign? No?"

I don't want to listen, but I can't help it.

"If he's sick, he can't stay here."

"The hospital sent us here!"

"I have to think of the other residents. I'll have to call the hospital."

Quietly the guard makes the call while Julian paces. He stops at the end of the corridor and catches my eyes. He blinks slowly, once. My heart swells with the meaning—our secret language.

I close my eyes and blink back, slower. Because I love him more than he can ever know.

"Okay, it's fine. The hospital confirmed it's okay. But it will be the beds you've been offered."

"Don't you understand anything I'm trying to tell you? He's mute, he's... he shouldn't be on his own. Look, I've been in shelters before. I know what goes on. You can't put him on a floor on his own."

"He wouldn't *be* on his own. There are CCTV cameras in every room for all residents' safety and—"

"And it's too late by the time you catch anything on fucking camera."

"We've never had a prob—"

"You haven't got a clue. Fuck you," Julian hisses.

He's going to get himself kicked out. He knows he is. I hear him walk away and suck in one deep breath after another.

"I can sleep on the floor next to his bed," he says quietly after a while.

But I don't hear the reply as I cough uncontrollably into my sleeve. My throat now so raw I can taste the blood.

AFTER WE have signed ourselves in and accounted for our possessions—the exact details of my medicines are recorded in a little blue book hung on the wall with string—we are shown to the first-floor communal bathroom.

Posters display the benefits of keeping clean and the malignant harm of not. I try not to look at them. The pictures are horrible: grotesque malformations of skin, weeping sores. Things that happen after you've been on the street for years. Things I don't want to think about.

We drift in and out of the bright empty spaces, following the guard. I stare up at the maze of pipework that runs overhead—tracing a map through toilet cubicles, urinals, changing areas. I imagine I hear them creaking icily as the water expands and contracts, moving through them in tidal ebbs like a sea.

The huge echoey shower room is freezing but clean, and I can't wait to stand under the showerhead, the warm water blissfully washing away my thoughts, letting them drain away into that dark oblivion beneath the streets.

The night guard watches us as we awkwardly look around, and Julian slips his arm around me as I try to stifle my cough. He wants the guard to see that we're together. It's almost like a challenge. The guard either ignores it, or he doesn't notice.

"You can take a shower here, and there is a common room on this floor at the end of the corridor you can use. But you can't go into the communal sleeping areas until after ten o'clock this morning."

I wonder absently if it would be against the rules to stay in the shower until then.

Finally, the night guard leaves us alone, and Julian lets his head rest against mine.

"Fuck."

We don't have to stay, I sign without turning around, knowing somehow that he is watching me. *We could go back to Cassey's.*

"No. She's done too much for us already."

I wonder at which point you begin to lose your pride. At which point you will beg for any help you can get. At which point you will lie down in the street and hope that someone will stop instead of step over you. It's a place I can't imagine Julian ever reaching. That he would rather die in a silence greater than the one I exist in, that he would step into the void with his head held high, only intensifies my love. And maybe that is a mistake.

There are clean towels in a huge gray plastic cabinet next to the showers. We search through the piles to find the ones that aren't so thin and worn—there aren't many.

Julian strips off his clothes and leaves them in a messy heap on the floor. He inclines his head shyly toward the shower room.

"Before everyone else gets up."

I've been breathing in so shallowly, trying not to cough, that I feel a little light-headed as I bend down to strip off my trousers. Cool fingers trace along the length of my spine, making me shiver, and my movements falter. We're still so new to each other that every small exposure of skin draws us closer, just wanting to touch one another. Affection more than arousal, devotion more than desire.

He leads me nakedly, my hand in his, and pushes me under the steady stream of lukewarm water (it doesn't get any warmer) until my back is pressed against the gaspingly cold tiles.

"If the water was hotter, the steam would help your chest," he mumbles, his mouth open against my shoulder as the water runs over our faces and spills down our entwined bodies.

We stand there just holding on to one another, just needing to be close. Somehow scared we won't have this chance again.

LOUIS

FOR TWO days we just exist—not leaving the confines of the shelter for any reason—wandering from one room to another, from one floor to the next, avoiding everyone but each other. We are entitled to a meal a day in the common room, to free soup and tea and water. Every few hours I take the medicines and stare listlessly into space as I feel their drowsy effects. My cough becomes better, then worse, then better again.

The inertia is suffocating.

I can't even see a clear impression of the sky through the shelter's floor-to-ceiling windows. The days just trail from black to gray to white to gray to black again.

AFTER OUR one meal on the third day, we organize the chairs in a far corner of the common room and sit facing one other. Julian runs the back of his left hand meditatively up and down the dark fabric covering the armchair, and I lose myself sketching the hunched shadow of a man, an almost formless black against the brightness of the window.

"Do you know him?" Julian says in a low voice, inclining his head, not at the figure I'm sketching, but to the left, behind me.

We are being watched.

I pull out the paper we've been using to write on and scrawl, *Five beds down from me.*

We don't sign. Not here. And although the guard knows I'm mute, we don't want anyone else to know. People have taken advantage of my silence before, taken advantage of the fact I can't scream or cry out for help.

Julian's fingers touch mine as he takes the pencil, and I close my eyes briefly at the contact.

Does he watch you? he writes.

How can I lie? They *all* watch me.

I nod.

For the past two nights, Julian has crept (under the ignorant gaze of the CCTV) into the cold room I sleep in and lain down on the floor next to my bed, leaving again before the traffic starts up outside. But he *knows* he can't be there all the time, and he doesn't trust any of them.

I don't want to ask him if his lack of trust is a formless feeling, a worry just because he loves me, intensified because of the things that have happened recently, or if it's based on a definite thing, something that has happened to him in one of these places, because I think right now, looking into the amber depths of his eyes, the truth might break me.

Louis, I write. His name. *He never takes off the black knitted hat he wears. He sleeps in his clothes. He is strange.*

I hesitate over writing the last bit, because aren't we all, a little? And just because he doesn't speak (like me) doesn't make him suspicious. Does it? I stare off at the window, into the brightness, my eyes obscure as the glass.

Ten years, twenty years, it could be me. Still on the street or stuck in a soulless shelter, so lonely and silent—so completely lost without my love. Maybe he can see what we have, maybe he had that once. Maybe he just wants to remember.

But instinctively I know that's not all there *is* to it. I know Louis really is strange. I just can't put my finger on why.

I put my hand over my mouth and cough agonizingly deeply again before turning back to Julian.

It's okay. He never comes near me.

I hold out the pad, but Julian doesn't take it immediately; for a second he just looks haunted. I want more than anything to just crawl onto his lap and take that look away, to pull him into my arms. I want him to say it will be okay, like he always does. I want him to believe it. But something has changed. I don't know when exactly it happened, though I can guess why. I guess he lost his trust in life a few weeks ago when he was taken from me. When he was kidnapped and thought he was going to die alone and out of sight, and that I wouldn't know. That's what he said scared him most—that he would have died and I would never have known, could never have said good-bye. A desperate unfinishing, our love collapsed from the sky like a dead star.

I can't bear the thought of leaving you every night, he writes eventually.

IT *IS* night and I am alone, lying on the lumpy mattress and staring up at the map of shadows the streetlights cast on the ceiling. I won't sleep until Julian is here beside me. I *can't* sleep unless I can hear his slow deep breaths, scent his warm skin, *feel* his glow as though he is radiating heat like a sun. I thought he'd be here a while ago, though I'm not sure how much time has passed. It's just that waiting has started to become painful, and I've started to convince myself he's late—even though he probably isn't—and the endless unanswerable questions as to why that might be are circling like my own private vultures above me.

Shelters remind me of hospitals and those communal rooming houses I lived in with my mother before she left me. Yeah, they may shelter you from the elements, from the icy wind and rain, but not from other things. Not from the constant noise all around me, the tangled webs of other people living very different lives in close proximity. Not from the constant reminder I am more alone for all of that.

And the men in here don't care if you hear them masturbating or whispering eerily into the dark all night. They don't care if they wake you when they stumble drunkenly against your bed. In fact they'd rather wake you, rather fuck up your night's sleep as much as their own, because being dropped by society makes you grasp every little thing you can for yourself, makes you grip your own thoughts tight as the skin around your bones, because no one else cares about you, so why the fuck should you even *consider* anyone else? Like her. My mother. That was the rationale she used, I'm sure. She didn't give a fuck about me, her son. She lived so close in her own skin, she was suffocated by it, blind to everything else.

But I don't want to be like that, I think desperately. I don't want to close myself off, shut myself down.

I'd rather be out in that cold Russian winter. I'd rather be dead.

I count to sixty and decide enough is enough; I'm not waiting. Slowly, I push off the heavy blanket and ease myself gently onto my side before rolling off the bed. I hate the way the springs creak noisily with every movement like some sort of antiquated alarm system, and it's only because I'm trying so hard to be quiet that I end up holding my breath, making the urge to cough overwhelming and impossible to ignore.

Quickly plastering my hands over my mouth, I crouch down and smother the sounds as best I can, coughing into the hard unforgiving floor—and I know now that if I had never coughed, I would never have looked down through the spaces under the beds, and I would never have seen him, lying there. Louis. Eyes open, watching me.

Carefully, I stand up. I convince myself he's just lying on the floor, asleep with his eyes open, or turned in my direction because I woke him. But he's not.

His movements are slow as he lifts his heavy body off the floor and stands in the space between his bed and the next, a few meters away, still watching me. The thick, dark clothing he wears makes his body look bulky and misshapen. He never changes them, and I can smell the reek from here.

For a second I feel paralyzed and unreal. I don't know whether this is a threatening situation or not. I'm scared, but I also think I'm being irrational. There are thirty other bodies sleeping in this room, and there is a CCTV monitor (albeit useless) in the far corner. The rational part of me *knows* he could have come for me anytime he wanted when I was lying on the bed, but the rest of me just wants to run. Awkwardly, I press my arm across my face and cough into the rough cotton of my sleeve.

We stare at one another. Two rabbits? Or a rabbit and fox?

The door isn't far. I don't even have to pass him.

Julian, where the fuck are you?

My heart is thudding in my ears, the panic beginning within me.

Not now, I think. *Please not now!*

I look over to the window. He follows my gaze. It gives me an edge—and I run.

DESPAIR

THE DOUBLE doors crash loudly against the wall as I stumble through them and bolt toward the stairs. There is no way Louis would be able to run as fast as me with his body so heavy and slow-looking, but the terror has taken on a sickening momentum, building itself into a frenzied black panic.

Julian is my destination.

But what if he's not there? I think in a rush as I career along the corridor and burst into his dorm room. *What if he's gone?*

The thought is blinding, like a torchlight thrust into a sleeping face. And I know this sort of panic is a hurricane, picking up the debris of my mind, swallowing the tiny rational voice that asks *where would he go? Why would he go?* But I can't help it.

And where and why indeed, because his blankets are thrown back and his bed is empty.

Angry grunts are coming from every direction at my coughing inconsiderate self as I touch his sheets searching for warmth, for knowledge that he *was* here, not so long ago.

Fuck.

A sudden prickling sensation flows over my skin like an icy whisper. I imagine it's my *name* on the wind again—even though that's impossible—and I spin around, half expecting, no, *mostly* expecting, Louis to be silhouetted in the doorway like the stalker in a horror film. But he's not, and as I peer down it, the corridor behind is thankfully empty as well.

Now the surge of adrenaline has passed, I feel sick, and I stagger out of the dark room and into the bright of the corridor once more.

Where the fuck is he? Bathroom?

I stop and listen for the slightest of sounds before inching my way, thief-like, back down the stairs. The bathroom is at the end of my corridor. I think my heart might stop if I see Louis waiting for me. But again, he's not. The dorm door is closed, and all I can hear is the deep, almost palpable hush of sleep.

Slowly and with more caution than I've ever possessed, I push open the heavy bathroom door.

The soft water hiss of the shower echoes around me, the air lightly misted with vapor. It makes me wonder if the thing is broken, the hot water hammering emptily against the tiles.

I cover my mouth to smother my sudden coughing and creep within. A large pile of clothing is heaped unfolded on the floor by the entrance to the shower room, a trail of wet footprints looping an infinite figure of eight around it.

Now I'm closer I can hear staggered breathing, strangled gasps for air, the groan of bodies searching for release. Embarrassed, I start to back away; the lack of privacy in this place is painful enough as it is without me leering in the darkness.

Since that first day here, when we held one another in the shower, all we've managed are a few stolen kisses, hugs taken on the wing as we walk from one room to another—touches that qualify our existence, that prove we are real, we are here.

And then it happens, so quickly, before I'm even conscious of why. The world tilts and all the air is sucked out of my lungs. I can't cough. I can't fucking breathe. Or even see straight. My legs give way. Because, oh God, tangled in the pile of clothing is the jumper Julian was wearing earlier. I would recognize it anywhere. And his jeans… pants… all mixed up with someone else's, and now every sound they make cuts into me, flays me raw, and I spread my palms wide on the concrete and heave.

I *know* without doubt he's not doing it for pleasure. There is no question of his being unfaithful to me like that. I *know* there will be a reason. But as I sob, coughing into my arms, and lay my head against the cool concrete, I can't imagine anything hurting worse.

I used to be able to ignore the fact that he was letting people fuck him. It was just a word, because I didn't *see* it or *hear* it. And because the whole sordid operation was carried out far away from my sight, it was abstract and unreal.

Without warning I throw up. And crawl away from the mess, disgusted.

I move as far away from the shower room as I can. What else can I do but sit back against the lockers and wait for it to be over?

I'm so deep in despair, I don't even notice the bathroom door swing wide and an awkward figure move in front of me. When Louis crouches down, I don't even care—I'm not scared, I'm in pieces. Distantly, I notice how sad his eyes are, how lost his whole expression is when he looks at me. He holds out his hand, reaches for mine—my limp and useless arm offers no resistance—and places a many-times-folded piece of paper in my palm. Gently closing my fingers around it, he then gets up and leaves, as if this was all he wanted all along, to give me something, a message, a letter, a blank folded sheet—I don't care. Yet I keep my palm folded tightly around it and stare at the wet sheen glossing the surface of everything as the shower runs on and on.

Time hisses away. It could be a little, it could be a lot. I think of how far I thought we'd come. How far away from Julian doing this I thought we were. But in reality we hadn't even moved, or if we had, it was in a great pointless circle right back here again. Back to where I only want to run from.

If I'm honest, I can't stand the thought of anyone else touching him. Touching him in places only I should be allowed. It's despicable, but I want him to be mine and mine alone. I recognize the tightness of my skin around *my* bones, but I have nothing else. I'm only asking for one thing. Him.

And if he feels any meager pleasure out of the act, then it's my pleasure that's being taken away, my heart that's being ripped out.

Voices emerge out of the shower room. The water is switched off.

And suddenly I can't know. I can't face him. And, not daring to breathe, I dart silently out of the shower room and out into the bright of the corridor to the quiet of the dorm. Where I lie coughing and sobbing and completely not caring about anyone else around me.

Our Time Like This Is Temporary

It's the first night he doesn't come to me. I doze off, but every so often I wake and turn my head and notice he's not there. The emptiness beside the bed is like the emptiness inside me and I close my eyes, chanting excuses for him, reasons why he isn't here, make believe, fairy tales, stupid lies. The unbelievable anxiety that swept me away last night has been surpassed by this futile game.

With a sense of bleak fatality, I watch the cold dawn light inch up the walls and lengthen the shadows in the room. Shattered with tiredness and hurt as to where Julian has spent the night, I smother my cough and creep out of the room.

Strangely, it's only as I reach out to push open the door to Julian's dorm that I realize I'm still clasping that folded piece of paper Louis gave me last night. The hard corners have left numb red marks in my palm from where I have been holding on to it so tightly. For a second I debate unfolding it before I go in, but it can wait; this can't.

The door creaks, the room hushed. I release the breath I was unconsciously holding when I see Julian sat on the bed leaning listlessly against the headboard. A mound of ripped paper is piled on the sheet beneath his fingers. He doesn't seem to be aware of me as I walk across the room. But as soon as he sees me, he comes alive, his expression stark, his eyes desolate.

"I'm going to explain everything" is the first thing he says, fixing me desperately in his gaze, as though he thinks I'm not going to listen, not going to want to stay long enough to hear what he has to say.

Scraps of paper scatter as I sit down, and I shake my head. Right now I just want to be near him, be with him, close. I want to settle the relief I feel that he is here, and I have found him.

I don't notice the blood smeared on his fingertips and wrist until it's too late, until he's sobbing into his hands in front of me.

I've never seen him cry. Not like this.

Unsure of what to do, but wanting to do it in private, I encircle his wrist with my hand and gently tug him to his feet. All the hurt I felt is vanished, evaporated in the warmth, the reality of him, here with me. Even if I have no explanation, my trust is a shining beacon of light that will not falter.

Looking back as we stumble across the room, I can see the dirty white sheet is marked with bloody fingerprints, and everything I thought I knew about last night is now unknown and assumed.

It's nearly 7:00 a.m., but no one is around. I stand at the functional metal sink in the kitchen and watch as Julian methodically washes the blood off his hands and every so often wipes his eyes on his sleeve.

I stroke his side with my fingertips, lovingly brush the sharp ridge of his hip, visible even through his jumper, and feel torn apart when he flinches away.

"I'm sorry," he whispers brokenly as he leans over the sink and splashes his face with the cold water.

It's okay, I sign, even though it's not.

And I know I'm failing to hide the hurt I feel at his reaction to my touch.

I don't want to stay here anymore, I sign as he dries his wet skin on a paper towel.

Always so aware of me, he watches the movements I make and stays my hand, opening my fingers with his and gently taking out the paper I have been gripping so tightly.

"What's this?"

I shrug and watch with trepidation as he unfolds it.

He holds it titled away from me, almost as though he wants to hide it. I have to lean over to see.

At first I can't take it in as I stare at the boy pictured in his hands. At first I don't recognize him, and then with an icy shiver I suddenly realize what all the ripped paper on his bed was. Me. Pictures of me. Missing. *Please call this number. Please call....* My mother's voice, missing me.

My throat works dryly. I can't swallow. I stumble backward into the row of chairs.

"Who gave this to you?"

Why didn't you tell me? I sign, flushed with anger and bizarrely fear. *Last night you let someone fuck you! I heard. I was there in the shower room!*

I refuse to be the first to look away, and Julian isn't answering me. It feels as if everything I had left is swirling away from me like water running down the drain. I have nothing. There is nothing for me to hold on to. And with startling clarity I realize the fear I feel is of her finding me, and of all this, everything I have with Julian, vanishing away like a dream when she takes me. And I can't let that happen. But some part of me knows that it will.

"He threatened me with these." Julian's eyes are full of so much pain.

The flyer waves lifelessly in his hand, and I keep looking at my face in the picture—so different and yet exactly the same, so much younger, so naïve. I can even remember the photograph being taken.

"Leon, the guy on reception the day we came. He threatened to call the number. You're underage, and he knew they would take you. I had to… I'm sorry…." He reaches out to touch me, and I back away. "I can't lose you!"

So why didn't we just leave? Go to another shelter, I try to sign, but I'm doubled over coughing, crouched down.

He gets it anyway. He always does.

"Why do you think?" he says gently. "You need to get better. Going back out there right now is… it's suicide, Remee! And your picture will be in other shelters too! And I just thought if I could stop Leon, if I could just… until you were better, we would be alright."

He kneels down on the floor in front of me, screws the flyer up, and takes my face in his hands.

"Who gave this to you? Who else knows?"

Louis. I want to go back to Cassey's, I mouth.

He nods. "Okay."

Now.

"Now? Okay."

I collapse into him, my head thudding against his shoulder so hard it must hurt. And in a way I want it to.

But I know he doesn't care. I could hurt him in a thousand ways, maybe I already do, and he would just fold his arms around me and stroke my hair.

After a while I pull back and sign, *You made your fingers bleed tearing those flyers up.*

He shows me his hands. They look okay now, not bloody, though his knuckles look a little sore. I trail my fingers lightly over his skin, making him shiver when I catch his eye.

"Found out Leon had a stash of them. I punched the wall. It hurt." He smiles wryly. "Should have punched Leon, but then I know he would have called for sure."

I would never let them take me, you know.

Awkwardly I reach up, trace his jaw with my thumb, anxious lest he pull away from me when I'm so open like this, my feelings so naked.

I want you, I mouth. I want him to take away all I heard last night. I want him in the most basic way to show that he's still mine. But he sighs sadly and takes my hand between his, kisses the palm.

"I'm scared, Remee. Because if they took you, it wouldn't be like this for you. You'd have a home. You'd have a chance. That's what I'm terrified of. I'm terrified I'm being so fucking selfish keeping you with me, because I love you above everything, and I want you to have more than this—"

I don't want more than you.

I pull my hand away and cup the back of his head, my fingers threading through his hair.

"Well, you should. I've got nothing. I am nothing."

In one swift movement he stands up, backs away.

Don't talk like that, please!

"It's the truth."

I pull out my pad and scrawl. *You think my mother cares about me? She doesn't give a fuck. There'll be a reason she's done this, be it for money or for a place to live. She can't give me what you give me; she can't look after me like you do. I never want to see her again. Never. And she will never find me.*

Julian looks on, his warm eyes dark and suddenly unknowable to me.

The double doors at the end of the room open and a few people start to come in, waiting for the drinks and toast that will be served for breakfast soon.

We make our way out in silence, Julian walking in front of me.

In the corridor I see Louis. I stop and hold out my hand to him. I feel stupid and guilty about last night, about how I overreacted when he just wanted to warn me. His grip is gentle, and he nods, as though he understands, smiling sadly for a moment as he moves away.

And I realize I've learned things aren't always as they appear, and more than anything, nothing can stay the same, nothing will stay the same, and our time together like this is temporary unless we find a way out.

NOTHING BUT A SHELL

UNSURPRISINGLY, LEON isn't on reception as we leave the building. Julian must have known he wouldn't be there—he wouldn't have wanted to face him, not with me.

I convince him we don't need to stop and get my medicine; it would mean calling through. It would mean someone knowing we had left, and that would mean leaving a trace, however vaporous. I convince him I'm okay, and it's only by sheer force of will that I don't cough as soon as we get out of that claustrophobic warmth.

The huge graying space of sky above us feels wonderful, feels free, even if it is cold as fuck. Like tourists in a foreign land, we stop in the middle of the pavement and take it all in: the Technicolor traffic, all exhaust fumes and noise, the consuming crush of people hurrying to work down this busy thoroughfare, pushing past or trying to ignore us. All of it.

Julian glances over at me and, of all things, I smile. What fools we are. What fucking bleakly glorious streets.

By eight, we regret skipping breakfast—but we weren't feeling as rational *then* as we are now, shuffling along the freezing embankment, hunger gnawing a hole inside us so deep it's painful.

Funny how rational being hungry and cold can make you feel. Funny what becomes important when you have nothing solid to tether yourself here, no home, no constancy. Funny that, however bad the shelter was for so many fucking reasons, right now I wish I was back there, sat in that soulless common room. I want to be warm; I want to be fed. I want this fucking cough to give up the ghost. I don't want to think about consequences, about tomorrow or tonight (I might not live that long). I am only certain of this moment, here with Julian. And if I thought he was any sort of tether, I was wrong because we are both adrift, and although hanging on to one another will not bring us back down to earth, it *will* keep us alive—I know it will. It has to. I have nothing else but hope.

Funny that it's times like these I think about things like this.

An icy mist hangs above the river, hiding the far bank from view. Even the city's tall buildings are shrouded, made beautifully indistinct, like a pencil drawing unfinished and lost before now. The world recreated in grayscale. All things stretched, like gossamer, between white and black.

This is what I will sketch when we get to Cassey's and I can feel my fingers again. This empty world. The pad deep inside the pocket of my coat swings against my ribs with every step. A weight, a reminder, an escape.

The sky is now the deep heavy gray of dirty snow, and I hope to God it doesn't, because being wet and cold out here tonight will kill us. I hope Cassey has some boxes or something we can use as shelter. More deeply, and secretly, I hope that she will take pity on us, as she has before, and let us stay at the cafe. Even though she now rents out the rooms we used, we would sleep on the hard cafe floor without complaint. But I can't let such desperation, or such hope, rise up to the surface in me.

But long before we reach Cassey's, we can see something is wrong. We must be around 750 meters away down the embankment when we see there is a blackness about the place that is unfamiliar. Even in the dull morning light that refuses to give substance to anything, the edges of the building that once seemed so solid now seem smudged and insubstantial, the roof whisked away, swallowed by the nights we have been gone. It's definitely not the mist. Not a dream.

I blink and glance over at Julian, my fingers brushing the hem of his worn-through jumper as he turns toward me, his face as anxious as mine.

Cassey's, I mouth.

And we run, skidding on the frost that glitters menacingly in the glare of the street lamps—running until I have to stop and cough so hard I throw up, bile burning my throat. I hit the frozen ground with my hand, frustrated. There is a little blood, which I shift to hide. I tell myself it's just a reaction to the cold.

Julian crouches down beside me and rubs my upper back with one hand and places his other arm around me. It's times like these he feels so much bigger than me, so much stronger, even though there's not much difference, even in our height, anymore.

My body just wants to cough, on and on, until I am spilled out and diminished with every wracking contraction.

"Relax," he whispers soothingly, then places his lips closer to my ear so his warm breath ghosts across the base of my throat. "I'm sorry, Remee, I'm sorry, baby, we shouldn't have run."

The grass looks black beneath my splayed fingers. The color of everything dulled, deadened.

He takes a deep breath—I feel it shudder through him—lets his head fall against my shoulder, his soft hair brushes the back of my neck, and I know he's seen it, seen the burned-out shell of Joe Brown's cafe—*Cassey's* cafe—that's on the very edge of my vision, though I'm trying hard not to look.

WE SLIP inside the boarded-up entrance. By the looks of it, we are not the first to have done so.

It might be my imagination, but I can still smell the acrid black smoke that must have darkened the sky. I can still taste it at the back of my throat as we pick our way across the ruin. Water drips on us from the few skeletal beams left above, forming large black puddles that cover the floor, their dark edges paralyzed by ice.

Tables and chairs lie mostly intact but scattered and overturned, their legs bowed and buckled, as though dropped from a height. The till is broken open and empty.

On the floor behind the counter, under the mess of broken cups and plates, is the picture I drew of two boys kissing, the lines all blurred and faint, the heavy paper soaked to near transparency.

I pretend I don't see it. It's easier that way.

There is a bare bit of shelter in the back room. The roof in here still holds tight, and though the room is wet, the walls black with smoke, Julian picks up two sturdyish chairs and urges me to sit down on one of them.

He cradles his head in his hands briefly, then takes a deep breath and looks up.

"What do you think happened?"

I shrug, clueless, and not actually wanting to think about it really. I'm half-aware, avoiding the screaming truth. I'm still only looking with the corner of my eye. I can't face it full on.

"Cassey will be okay." He touches my hand. If I could say the words back to him, I would. As it is, I just nod. But it's not enough.

"What are we gonna do?" His voice breaks horribly over the whisper. I can hear the anguish in it.

I wish I could pull him into my arms. I wish I was strong enough, but I'm not right now. I'm too brittle, I'm made of glass, and I don't.

This place was always our shelter, countless days we spent warm within these walls. This place was our hope. Cassey was our hope.

Where are we going to go now?

We shouldn't stay here, I sign.

"Why not?" There is an edge to his voice I don't usually hear.

I'm struggling to find words, reasons.

We could go to Gem's.

"No." He shakes his head. "We'll be okay here for a while. It's sheltered."

He's being blind. And I know just beneath the surface he's distraught, but I push it.

Is it, though? I write quickly on the back page of my pad. The page already half-full of our scribbled conversations, stupid doodles, I-love-yous. *Yeah it's sheltered from the streets, but we're not the first to find our way in, and we won't be the last and....* I stop writing. It hurts to see the place reduced like this to a cinder, and I can't stay.

And now I reach out, touch the still-bruised skin on the side of his face, feel his hair fall against my fingers. There is so little light, and the room is so dark we are but shadows. So dark that when he snaps, I don't see it, but I feel the tension jolt through him, sudden and electric as he stand up and kicks over the chair.

"You look to me like I know what to do *all the time*. And I don't, Remee, I don't have a fucking clue. I don't know what to do to make this okay. I don't know what to do now. I'm *trying* to make the right decision!"

Spinning around, he vanishes farther into the gloom, pacing back and forth across the debris-strewn floor.

He stops in front of the boarded-up window, hits the frame with his fist, and then collapses against it.

Unsure of how I feel, I go to him. Wrap my arms around his shoulders. Sign *it's okay* against his chest.

I think he's going to push me away, but he turns in my arms, hugs me back, and sobs, "It's not okay. None of this is okay. I can't do it anymore… I can't, Remee… I can't."

I search his face with my lips, kissing his closed eyes, his nose, his cheeks. Suddenly he spins me—I feel glass crush beneath the thin soles of our shoes—pushes me against the sheet of plywood covering the window, and finds my lips with his, crushes all the air out of my lungs, so I can't cough, can't do anything but kiss him back, suck his tongue into my mouth, and hear him groan helplessly.

We are lost.

I never want to be anything else.

He holds my hands high above my head and leans against me, pinning me in place. His teeth nip my jaw, then pull at the neck of my jumper to expose more skin to his mouth.

The pressure hurts me, and I want it to. I want him to leave a mark.

I'm stretched so tight I'm panting as he pushes my jumper up to expose my stomach. His teeth grazing my ribs send me beyond coherent thought.

I don't remember taking off my trousers or wrapping my legs around Julian's waist as he lifts me. I don't remember the sharp sting as the plywood grazes my spine, or the pressure and sudden pain as his fingers push inside me, causing me to sob into his neck. I don't remember him spitting into his hand, the wet heat of him as the head of his cock rests against the back of my thigh, and I don't remember begging him in my mind to just push inside.

I don't remember any of it until he stops and says, his words slow, his breath heavy with the exertion of holding me up and holding himself back, "We shouldn't do this. We should use a condom."

I shake my head. Fuck me. Just fuck me and make everything but this stop.

This need overrides everything. I take his hand and guide him, push my body down, feel the way it burns and the pressure builds as I take him inside me.

He mumbles wordlessly into my hair, kisses me, strokes my back, my neck, my cock. I feel him everywhere. He steadies himself on the window frame until he is sheathed so deep inside me I can't breathe. It hurts. But the pain is good, thrilling, necessary.

For a moment we cling to one another in perfect stillness. The constant drip of dirty water, the distant rush of traffic, the voices in the street outside, are nothing, are not connected.

Everything stops.

And moves on.

In the tight crush of his arms, I can feel the faint tremor of his body as he cries silently into my hair. The wordless mumble becomes more coherent, and I feel the pressure build up behind my eyes too. I don't want to fucking cry. I want to be fucked, and I want to forget.

"I'm sorry, baby," he whispers over and over as he strokes me, his body barely moving against mine, barely pulling out, but it's enough. "I'm sorry."

And he feels so close, so fragile, I'm afraid I will feel him breaking apart inside me.

After, we curl into one another on the floor, away from the glass. We stay like that for hours until I can't stand it anymore and I drag him up, ignoring the sharp pain in my chest, because now when I cough, it hurts.

We have to move. If we move, we're still alive. If we stay here like this, it feels like we're lying down and taking it, letting the shit pile on top of us and not fighting anymore. This place is gone. We'll deal with it; we'll find somewhere else.

Julian makes no protest. And while it's easier for now, I know that ultimately it's worse.

WASTED

THE STREETS are too crowded now. It must be lunchtime already. We seem to be heading toward the financial district, toward the blank-eyed divide we usually avoid. I don't know why I've come this way, making the both of us struggle through a tide of fucking beige-gray people all wrapped up in their fucking beige-gray little lives, pushing and glaring and just about fucking stepping on us as if we shouldn't exist, as if our passage through the streets is somehow less important than theirs.

And it should all be bright sensory overload, the way cities are meant to be, but the fumes and the rain grind everything down to dull shades of gray. I drag Julian onward, my fingers twisted in the sleeve of his top, walking recklessly across busy road after busy road, stopping the traffic, daring the stupid cars to hit us. The rain picks up, and it might as well be snow, it's so fucking cold. I need to stop and rest, I'm coughing so hard, but I know if I let go of Julian right now, he'll sink down where we are, and I don't have the strength to drag him up again. The emptiness in his expression is scaring me, and Gem is the only one I have to trust right now, the only one who might know what to do to help us.

But I'm not walking to Gem's.

The rain becomes heavier, a gray mist obscuring our vision, soaking us to the skin. I search street after street before dragging us into a graffitied and drafty bus shelter, the sort with the red plastic seats that tip you off so you don't get too comfortable and want to stick around too long. For an area so full of moneymaking businesses, it's surprisingly rundown.

Without thinking I hold Julian close to me, slipping one arm around his waist, keeping the other still gripping his sleeve. Even as skinny as he's become, he still feels solid to me. And all my anger drains out of me as the warmth of him touches me—warmth that colors the filthy streets with brightness, lightens the ashen sky—his body takes my weight and makes everything bearable. Almost.

I let myself have this moment, however brief. I don't look at his face. I can't accept the desolation laid out like a wasteland in his eyes. My mind flees from the truth of our situation, from the fact that Julian is barely even there with me. I need him so fucking much, but I can't dwell on that. He is already crushed beneath some great weight, something he thinks he has got to face alone. And maybe he has, because I'm not sure I can be strong enough for both of us for long.

Eventually the rain eases, and I drag our sorry selves onward, guessing the direction I move in from the ragged gray skyline I can barely make out.

I'm not in good shape. I must have dragged us over half of fucking east London. I will myself to be angry, pissed off, anything to keep going, but I don't know how much longer I can. Julian is just a shadow, trailing listless behind me.

What am I fucking doing?

Running, a voice whispers hauntingly, filling the streets. I stop and turn suddenly at the imaginary sound. *Running blind.*

And maybe I am.

Above us the clouds start to thicken and darken, but not from the threat of a storm; suddenly it is late afternoon. We haven't eaten or rested all day. We're dizzily running on air. I have no idea where we are going to spend the night, and I need to find somewhere dry. If I give up on these crucial things, I might as well give up entirely.

We come to a market in some filthy unknown corner of the city. A woman wearing layer upon layer of fleeces packing away a fruit and veg stall takes pity on us and gives us a bag of bruised fruit that will be inedible by the morning.

It's this sudden kindness more than my near passed-out exhaustion or Julian's anguished expression that finally lets me stop.

We huddle in the doorway of an empty shop. She watches us out of the corner of her eye as she packs up the rest of her stall into a battered old van. Maybe she thinks I don't notice the way she looks at us, a mixture of pity and dread. I don't mind. I can tell she has her own kids at home. And who would want this for their own?

There are a lot of empty shops down the street, all boarded up and inaccessible. Shabby markets like this one are making a sudden resurgence in their wake. I wish I had the impulse to draw the scenes around me. I wish I could draw something beautiful, because I know it's there, it's everywhere, but my inspiration has gone, fled like the whispers on the wind.

Maybe for good, I think darkly.

I hold out the bag of fruit to Julian, but he shakes his hanging head. I feel like flinging it across the street, but I'm too hungry to waste food on frustration, and instead I reach inside, take out an apple, and start to eat it. After a few bites, Julian reaches and takes a piece of fruit too. The market woman waves as she leaves. I nod. I have no energy to lift my hand any farther than my mouth. Across the wet street the lights of a cafe glow warmly. A few people sit chatting happily at the tables. I can't stand it. Hastily I pick up the bag of fruit, my fingers find Julian's jumper, and without having to pull him, we get up and leave.

It's night before we find ourselves in familiar territory. I can smell the river, almost feel the way the waters rush like a pulse through a vein.

Light-headed, I stumble, fall. I feel as though I am hopelessly trying to hold myself together, but I'm so weak I'm separating into pieces, falling through the net. Between bouts of coughing into the pavement, I hear drunken laughter I recognize. I hear swearing, a shout, Julian's name called from across the street, and it brings me back. Julian crouches low and unresponsive behind me. I wish his arms were around me, holding me together, away from the edge, soothing the pain, like this morning. I wish someone would take this awful day back, destroy it, obliterate it. I would gladly have taken my chances at the shelter.

Looking around under the sparkling glare of the street lamp, I see Roxy staggering toward us, his arms around a boy, a much younger boy, who looks just about as far gone as he is. Roxy and I were on the streets together for a while, before he got swallowed up and consumed by them. He sells himself as Julian did, but I still find it in myself to be shocked to see how hollow he has become.

"Jules!" he shouts again.

I can't decide whether or not I want him to go away. I'm not sure I can cope with other people right now. He looks awful, his hair sticking up rakish and unwashed, his clothes dirty. Our ages are similar, and he still has an innocence that will make him desirable, to some, whatever his state of dress, but *fuck* it hurts to see him like this, his eyes flat as though there's nothing left inside.

Where's Cricket? I sign, when he is close enough to see my movements.

Sinking down onto the wet pavement, he slings an arm around my shoulder and reaches out for Julian.

"My best friends!" he slurringly informs the boy hanging back behind him, ignoring my question to grin at us all in turn.

I move away on hands and knees and cough into the gutter. I know I'm bringing up more blood now; I can taste it.

When I crawl back, Julian is drinking deeply from some label-less plastic bottle the boy was carrying. It could be anything. *And Julian couldn't care less*, I think bitterly. We don't look at one another, or rather he doesn't look at me. If he did, *I* would be looking away.

Roxy holds the bottle out for me, but I hit his hand away, and he moves swiftly out of my reach so as not to spill a drop.

Silently, between them they finish it. The boy's name is Pasha, and from his perch against the wall he stares at me. Roxy talks and talks and doesn't seem to notice no one else is joining in. Pasha's dark eyes on me are beginning to make me uncomfortable. And I stare back, noticing how similar our coloring is, our appearance—black hair, black eyes, pale skin, oval faces.

What? I sign, doubting he can understand me but needing to show my frustration.

"You can't talk?" he says in Russian. His voice is light, young.

It's only after I've understood him that I realize the language difference.

I shake my head.

In one great stride he invades my space, boldly runs his finger against my cheek. He is freezing.

"I *know* you," he says with sudden clarity, again in Russian.

I'm so shocked by his hand on me, I can't respond.

He drops down to his knees, so we're eye to eye, so close.

"I've seen you," he whispers. "At the train station."

Behind him, I become aware of Julian watching the both of us, but his expression is so pained I can't tell what he is thinking, and he doesn't come and haul Pasha away.

Before I can ask Pasha what he means, what station, when—because apart from the tube, I haven't been to a train station for months—Roxy waves the bottle around.

"We've got more back at the Bank, come on," he shouts and starts to haul Julian to his feet. He holds out his hand to me, and Pasha melts away into the background, the sudden fervor and clearness gone from the boy's eyes, and he looks wasted once again.

"Come on, Romeo. Come back with us. Have you heard about Cassey's? Fucking destroyed, wasn't it…?" Roxy chatters on inanely, not realizing how fucking devastated we are, how fucking past the brink.

"But Cassey's okay, though?" Julian asks roughly the first words he's spoken in hours.

Roxy nods, fleetingly looking like the boy I once knew, the boy who was affected by things before that part of him shrank away to nothing so he could survive.

"She was taken to hospital. But they didn't keep her in for long. Her sister has a cafe near the Bank. I've seen her there."

The relief takes me for a moment, and I close my eyes. When I open them, everyone has moved off.

Julian glances back, our eyes meeting for half a second before he walks away with Roxy.

I don't know what that means, I want to shout. I don't know what to do!

Was he asking my consent to go back with them? Was he just making me aware that's what he was doing? Because I don't want to go across the river to the underpasses under the South Embankment. It's just about the worst place to be sleeping rough in London unless you've got some sort of status, unless you have friends with knives or some other sort of weapon who will defend you. I don't want to go there, and I don't want to get wasted. I just want Julian to turn around and stop. I want his care, his warmth, but right now Pasha is the only one who is hanging back for me.

HEROIN

PASHA'S HANDS are pale and cold, and yet he looks at me intently and takes both my hands in his, as if I am the one half frozen to death. And maybe I am—the sensation of his fingers on my skin now barely registers.

Emptily I stumble along behind him as he follows the others, now so far ahead they are only visible as they pass under the streetlights. I can barely walk for coughing. I wait for Julian to turn around, to hear me, to fucking feel something and remember, but he keeps walking, Roxy's arm draped over his shoulder, his body swaying at Julian's side. An irrational surge of jealousy sweeps through me. I feel too weak to fight against it.

Dark water rushes beneath us as we cross the bridge, and even though I can't see it, I can feel its power… hear it calling me.

"Hurry up," Pasha says, his Russian breathless, slurred.

But I can't. I hang back, gripping the railing—though it's as painful as gripping onto a piece of ice, the pain shooting through my fingers like an electric shock—and I stare into the blackness, trying to make out the formless ripples of the water, its ever-changing shape.

He comes to stand next to me. I'm surprised to find he is a little taller than I am, but he leans forward so our shoulders are the same height.

Everything blurs along the Southbank. The lights hurt my eyes.

"It will be okay," he says softly, pressing our arms together, but I wish he wouldn't touch me. It's not him I want to be standing beside me, telling me that.

Angrily I wipe my tears away.

It's not fucking okay, I sign, knowing full well he doesn't understand. I want to shout the words. I want to know how it feels. I want to let the anguish out, and for some sound to tear out of me, so everyone will know how much this hurts, but all I do is cough.

WHEN WE reach the underpass, there is no sign of Julian or Roxy. Hunched dark shapes are mostly camouflaged against the walls of the tunnel, but I can hear the low murmur of their voices, and I can feel the watchful gaze of their eyes on our bodies. For a second Pasha looks around, eyes wide like a lost child, but then he schools his expression back to that of some wasted streetwise kid, and we stagger on.

Ahead of us a few fires flicker, the vastness of the space we've come to all but invisible in the darkness. It's as icily cold as the street in here, but at least we are protected from the rain, and the ice won't form like garlands of frozen flowers over our exposed skin. Pasha makes his way to the far corner, stepping over bodies—shapes that could be drunk, passed out, sleeping, or dead—we don't stop to check. From a distance, I spot Julian's light hair. I could pick him out from a crowd of thousands, my eyes drawn to him, only him. Cricket is there too, his face lit up in front of a small fire. He looks old, his skin patchy and wrinkled, even though he can barely be twenty-five. A small pile of foil wraps and what I take to be a pack of needles sit on the floor next to him. Even in the minute it takes before we reach that side of the room, he has another customer, the exchange so open and casual, I wonder if he cares. Maybe he doesn't have to—on either side of him are two large silent forms, as imposing as guardians of the gates, the hoods of their coats pulled down, covering their faces.

As soon as we reach them, Roxy drags Pasha away, and the boy laughs, the sound high and fake, like the drunken act he puts on.

I take the last few steps and am ready to drop to my knees in front of Julian, ready to fall into his arms, ready to do anything it takes to just be close to him again. But I stop. I see the way his body is slumped down against the wall, his head fallen forward against his chest, his sleeve rolled up his arm. And with a sickening realization of what he's done, I turn. In a breathless panic I search him out—I know whose fault this is. I know who gave Julian the drug. I know who's fucked things up for me and who will keep fucking things up for me, ever since he told some thug I couldn't scream however much they beat me. I'm so fucking angry and afraid and lost—and all these feelings concentrate into a pure spear of hate, and with every last bit of strength I have left in my body I launch myself at Cricket and pull him into the fire.

The pain is wailing and raw. A blinding white heat sears my skin, and I can't breathe. I'm struggling wildly. I feel Cricket bite me, punch my neck before I'm suddenly dragged roughly across the floor and dumped beyond the crowd that has quickly gathered. Distantly I make out Pasha's voice, a quiet mumble beneath Roxy's screaming. The whole of me is hurting, my arms and hands are burned, the pain now becoming overwhelming.

I curl up, sob once, and realize this is it, this is the low I reached once before, except that time I had a spark, I had a tiny hope to live for, a tiny hope that Julian was still alive somewhere and that I was going to find him. But how can I find him right now? How can he find me? Right now he's gone completely, and I need him! I need him so much, but however hard I search, however hard I try, I can't give him what the drugs can. I can't take the pain away. I can't make him forget. What chance have I got against this?

Ever since we met, we had an unwritten rule, an unspoken promise we wouldn't let ourselves be reduced to this, that we would fight as hard as we could, because once you start taking drugs out here, there is no way back.

Oh God, it hurts. I let my lungs empty out on the concrete beside me, and when it comes, I welcome the blackness.

SLEEP

A WARM hand brushes lightly across my forehead. The gesture is absentminded maybe but not uncaring. The touch is what has woken me.

For a moment I feel okay. Wherever I am it is quiet, and I am warm, and the warm hand, Julian's hand, is protecting me from all harm. As long as he is here, it will be okay, everything will be okay. But it's just a moment, just the time it takes for air to fill my lungs, and when I open my eyes, the world is not how I want it to be, and it hurts. It is hell.

Everything is dark, but gradually I begin to make out the low walls that surround me. I am not warm. I am shaking with cold. My burned hands are curled into fists that can't open. I gasp with the pain.

It is Pasha and not Julian who leans over me, concerned. His movements and his voice are calm, but his eyes are terrified.

"They dragged you here," he says.

This time he speaks in broken English. Maybe he thinks I am too far gone to cope with deciphering anything else. Maybe he is right. In any other situation, I would be transfixed by the heavy accent he has, the lilt and song of it, the way he masks the rough harshness with the lightness of his voice.

We are in a narrow drain that leads out to the river. I can hear the water as it touches the concrete below us. It is freezing.

"Are you in pain?" he asks me and places both hands on my head to feel my answer.

He tells me he is going to get help.

Julian, I mouth, but he can't see to understand me in the dark, and I'm not even sure he knows Julian's name. Or mine.

Belatedly, I reach for him, but he is gone, and all I can feel is the numbing ice of the tunnel floor through the sleeve of my jumper.

Drunken yells, the never-ending sound of cars, the dark water that laps against the concrete that entombs me—these are what my world is made of. I feel the familiar tightness of panic stirring deep in my chest.

Desperately, I try to remember something happy. I need something to hold on to. I have nothing else but this. I don't think of Julian. It is too painful right now, and even though I believe he is all the good I've ever had, I must have something other, somewhere....

The crush of lips, so sudden and secret, of my first kiss—the memory sweet and fleeting and not enough. My first night sleeping on the street, in a doorway, my arms around a warm body, Robyn/Roxy, feeling safe for the first time in a long time, even though we weren't safe. How could we be, alone out here? Thinking it was all going to be alright, *I* was going to be alright, because I had somebody to hold on to. Only it wasn't the right somebody, but we used one another for a while. We pretended.

I wonder vaguely if Cricket is the right somebody for Roxy, and if so, how is that possible? How can Cricket be the right somebody for anyone? He doesn't care enough. He gave up so long ago he's probably forgotten. He is grasping only for himself. And every single one of us needs more than that. We all need someone to hold on to who will hold on to us back.

Julian holds on to me back. I don't know what has gone wrong, but I can't accept it. *I can't think of Julian right now*, I plead. I slide further back in time... my mother... it hurts to think of her too. I hate her for abandoning me—walking out to buy bread one morning and never coming back. I blame her for all this now, for all the bad that has happened. It is all her fault. My anger is more use than despair. My tears are hot against my cheeks. I would wipe them away if I could. But I had loved her; I can't pretend I didn't. That's why it hurts so badly. I want to lie. I want to have always hated her for the things she did to me, for the shame that I felt, but I loved her so openly, so trustingly that when she left, it obliterated some bright hopeful part of me. And I know I can't take that kind of abandonment again.

When she spoke of home, of my *babushka* and *dedushka*—her parents—she was different. She was gentle when she told me how much they would love me when we met, but we never did. She missed them, but she never told me why she had left to come here, why she couldn't return home with me, and those are not the questions a child ever thinks to ask. A child just accepts the way things are—that tomorrow always follows today, that some people live not knowing whether or not they are going to be hungry today because that's the way they live. Some people are rich, some people poor; it goes no further than that in a child's mind. There is no blame, no why.

I remember she smelled sweet. Her cheap hairspray filled our room with clouds of sticky vapor. Even now out on the street, if I passed someone, their hair molded and held in place with the same stuff, it would remind me, and I would have to suppress it. If I didn't, I would go crazy.

Now, I let the scent come. I let myself remember the feel of the brittle strands of hair against my cheek as I threw my arms around her neck. I was young, five or six, and awake with nightmares. I remember her arms. She felt so strong to me then, as though she would protect me forever. *How could she leave me?* I choke back a sob. I remember how safe I felt. I remember feeling at peace completely. I feel it now, and I let myself go, knowing it could destroy me.

When they come for me, they are people from a dream, all made of light. From below the surface of the dream, I hear Julian scream himself hoarse, but he is so far away, and the arms of a darkness deeper than sleep hold me.

REALITY FLICKERS

REALITY FLICKERS. There is no pain, no sensation, no thought, but this wavering thread, this filament of disappearing light that is my life.

These people are taking me home.

I scream silently when they touch my hands, because *this* is where the pain lives, this blistering agony I cannot breathe through. I have no strength to cough—my breath bubbles, drowns in my throat. The darkness comes again and I do not think I will ever wake....

A familiar melody weaves its way into my dream: a Russian lullaby my mother used to sing about a boy who is lost in a forest and his mother's song guides him home. This part of the lullaby is her call to him. She believes her love will guide him back to her. She never loses faith.

Feeling as though they have been stuck down with glue, I try to open my eyes. I can see nothing but the odd blurry shape of everything, hear nothing familiar but the song that is woven in the air. I can't move any of my limbs, and when I try to open my mouth, it feels as though something alien has crawled inside me. My brain starts to panic, but my body is a heavy bag of sand sinking to the bottom of an ocean, and it drags me under again...

...a machine beeps solidly...

...This time my awakening is sudden, my consciousness shot through to the surface like a bullet. I try to gasp and see, leaning over me, are two nurses or maybe doctors, I don't know. They tell me to breathe out as the tube down my throat is withdrawn. They say it makes it less uncomfortable. They ask me to nod when I'm ready. It's all so sudden, such a shock, I just nod, and they pull, and it feels like I am throwing up in one long, continuous heave.

Afterward, they ask if I feel okay. They watch the machine that beeps beside me and settle me back down on the bed in a more upright position.

I glance beyond their concerned faces and see the pale curtains around my bed are drawn. It's all a little claustrophobic. But I don't want them to draw the curtains back. I want to remain in this insular sectioned-off little area. I feel too unsure and exposed to be stared at. And more importantly, I feel as though I have forgotten something, something incredibly important. I don't push it, but as I lie back testing how it feels to swallow again, how sore my throat is, I'm wondering.

Sleep claims me in the time it takes to draw a breath.

"Here, he is here!" calls an excited voice so very close to me.

His accent is from far away, across the sea.

Do I know him?

"Shhh… he's sleeping."

My heart stutters. This voice I recognize. This voice I know. Every cadence. Every pause. He sounds sad somehow, and even through the haze that is stopping me remembering, I know that I love him. But that is all I know.

"We only have half hour!"

"It doesn't matter."

My eyelids are weighted down, my lashes made of lead, but I know his eyes are beautiful, some unusual light shade of brown I have never noticed on anyone else. I know he is skinny but strong, and I know how his body fits against mine. I know the weight of it in my arms. But forgetting is a strange sensation…. I don't know his name (I don't know mine). If only I could open my eyes, see him before me, then I am sure I would know, the haze would lift like morning mist… but I'm gone again before I can think any further.

Was it a dream?

Remee.

I open my eyes and blink. The ward is dimly lit. The sky beyond the windows as black as it ever gets in London.

Julian….

I remember.

A whole day passes. Every minute of every hour weighs on my heart, because he doesn't come. I don't have the strength to move, never mind leave. I am immobile, on a hospital ward full of other immobile, depressed-looking people. I am a prisoner in my own head.

No one comes to explain the extent of my injury, and I am left staring at my heavily bandaged hands, unable to feel my fingers.

I cough, but it is no longer painful or unstoppable. There is no blood on the bandages as I lift my arms to cover my mouth.

I don't give up, but I no longer expect to see him walking down the corridor toward me. Visiting hours are almost over anyway.

But suddenly, out the corner of my eye, I see a dirty gray coat. I turn my head, and Pasha's elfin face is pressed up against the glass in the doors. He holds one hand up in greeting.

Anxiously, I search for Julian standing somewhere behind him in the swell of ever-emerging people, but he is gone before I can even blink.

"Romeo?"

I jump and turn away from the doors to see a woman standing beside my bed, her wide blue eyes watching me. She looks out of place. She should be standing outside surrounded by nature, in a field or on a beach. She gives off an aroma of fresh air and flowers. Her red hair is wildly flyaway, and the low sunlight coming in through the windows gives her an aura of fire. She smiles openly and touches my arm.

"I'm sorry I'm late. I'm Estella King, your social worker."

I don't want to like her, I really don't, but the ache in my heart is making me weak. And she's being too fucking nice, too kind, and I'm literally unraveling before her as she talks to me, tells me that I am under her care until I am ready to help her piece together the story of what has happened to me. She tells me it is okay. There will be someone to care for me. I'm not on my own.

She goes away to ask the doctors what the situation with my hands is, and I curl up and sob silently into the pillow until she returns. She introduces a doctor who looks barely older than me, who peels away my bandages and tells me that although my burns are extensive, I should have full functionality back within a few weeks. I take a deep grateful breath as I slowly move my blistered fingers. But the relief quickly evaporates when I think who I want to share this news with, who is not with me right now, who I would go to if I could get out of this bed and even just fucking crawl.

"This is great news, Romeo!" Estella looks radiant as she watches the nurse carefully bandage my hands back up. "The foster family that I have found for you will be over the moon!"

I STARE at the ceiling for hours, planning my escape and imagining increasingly far-fetched ways of how Julian is going to come and rescue me, until I finally drift off to sleep.

Pasha is there when I wake—sat low in the uncomfortable plastic chair next to my bed. Outside the early-morning rush hour is just beginning, the slow roar of traffic, the yawn of commuters conscious long before the sun.

We are the only souls awake on the ward.

"I promise him I check on you," he whispers conspiratorially.

I have no idea how Pasha managed to sneak past all the nurses. He carries an air of quickness with him, an innate catlike agility, but he is not invisible.

Where is he? I mouth, spreading my arms helplessly. I want to reach inside him and pluck out the truth.

He studies my face for what feels like an eternity.

"I tell him you look better," he says eventually before getting up to leave.

Vigorously, I shake my head. I am so frustrated by his apparent lack of understanding, willful or not.

I am not better, I mouth—even though I am. *Tell him I am dying!* I don't care if he doesn't get it.

Pasha smiles kindly.

"He would come," he says as he looks up and down the corridor.

I know he is going to disappear any moment.

I flail my arms to grab his attention.

Why? I mouth. Suddenly this is important. *Why are you helping me?* He hardly knows me, yet he saved my life, and now he's risking arrest creeping in and out of this hospital to check if I am all right. And something tells me being arrested is the last thing he needs.

With abrupt intensity, Pasha sits down on the bed so close to me I can feel the warmth of his skin. His pale fingers hover next to my jaw, but he stops himself from touching me. Perhaps he can see how uncomfortable it makes me. His Russian is breathless when he speaks, and it takes me a moment to translate it.

"When I got off the train in London, the first face I saw was yours. Your posters were everywhere along the platform. I thought about you. I wondered who you were, what had happened to you. And then I met you, and I knew we had this connection, our paths were meant to cross. There has to be a reason."

WOOD FOR THE TREES

THE SUN streams in through the tall windows opposite, glares blindingly across the wet rooftops below, and lights up Estella, who stands smiling at the end of my bed.

I still think she looks too otherworldly to be anything as mundane as a social worker. She should be casting fantastic sculptures in some ruined cottage by the sea or playing the harp to an audience of open fields. I stare too long, and she smiles even wider as I look away, embarrassed.

I've never met anyone so easy to be with, and after I work out she lip-reads pretty well, we talk about my drawing. Shyly, I show her the sketches in my pad.

She studies each one with great care, as though they are delicate pieces of art, her expression thoughtful. I expect her to comment on some of them, on what they depict—I have grown bold in my subject matter—but she doesn't. Afterward she looks me in the eye with wild intensity and says I have a gift, I must use it. She says people would buy my work. I tell myself she's just being polite. I tell myself it's her job to be like this, but how can you fake this glowing enthusiasm for everything?

I tell myself that even though she doesn't mention the fostering or ask me any questions about my life, about what I'm throwing away living the way I do, she doesn't have to. The words are there, the questions unasked but looming darkly over us and every frivolous thing we say.

Every few minutes I find my eyes are wandering toward the corridor, looking out for Pasha—*for Julian*—as if my brain has been rewired to follow a compulsive new pattern.

Estella notices. How could she not? She asks me if I'm expecting someone. I wish I were. But no, I shake my head. I'm not *expecting* him. I'm just clinging on to my stupid lonely hope that he'll come.

She stays the full visiting hour. She says she will come back this evening.

Does she never go home? I think. But I'm grateful, even if I don't want to be.

When she leaves I wonder how I'm going to make it through the afternoon.

AFTER LUNCH my bandages are removed for a while—for as long as I can bear it. My skin feels tender against the blankets covering me; the rawness of it looks unreal. My hands start to hurt if I stare at them too long; if I move them, it feels as though the skin is tearing along the crease lines.

Why doesn't he come? Why?

I keep stretching my fingers. I torment myself with the pain. It stops me thinking.

Visiting hour starts again at two. I watch the ward fill with other people's friends, other people's relatives, and I curl up, the pillow in my arms, my face buried in the stiff, scentless cotton. I feel so fucking unwanted and I can't keep it up, the pretense that I don't.

IT'S LATE.

"Romeo? Is that you?"

Amid all the chatter, I hear my name.

Oh God, I think, *Cassey!*

I push the pillow behind me and wipe my bandaged hands across my puffy eyes. It's so good to see her. Her wispy, pinned-back hair, her kind smile, remind me how much I've missed her. It's as though I can pretend everything is back to normal and that big fucking nothing inside me can be ignored and forgotten for a moment.

Glancing at my hands, she hugs me as though I am made of glass. Her warm arms hold me for much longer than she perhaps intended, but I don't want to let her go.

I make her sit on the bed so she can see me as I try to form my words clearly.

She concentrates so hard I want to cry.

I'm so happy to see you! We saw the cafe. I was so worried! So completely crushed and devastated I couldn't breathe, the dawn folding like a blanket of ice around us, Julian's arms holding me…. I press my hand into the bed painfully. No.

"Could do with a paint job, couldn't it?" She smiles, sighs. "No one was hurt, and really that's what matters. Sometimes these things happen, and we just have to deal with them as best we can, don't we?"

And I don't think she's just talking about the cafe any longer.

"I'm helping my sister out in her cafe across the river while they sort out how much insurance they're going to pay out, which will determine whether or not the place is going to be rebuilt. I didn't own the place, Romeo. I just leased it. Ever since it happened, I've been looking out for you two, you know. Every morning, every evening, all along on the embankment. I wanted to let you know that even if my cafe is gone, there is somewhere else you can come to. My sister would welcome you."

I nod, staring out at the winter blue sky.

You two. Us two.

Yet right here, right now, it's just me.

And somewhere out there, it's just him.

Cassey touches my arm. "I spoke to one of the nurses, and he said you're going to be okay."

I nod again, distractedly.

She must sense my enthusiasm. "Can I tell you something?" she asks, her expression becoming wistful. "Something I think about when everything seems too much to bear?"

Okay, I mouth.

"When I was your age, my parents split up, and while they fought out who was going to have custody of Deonne and I, we went to stay with our aunt in Cornwall. It was summer. It was beautiful, though it rained every other day. After living in London, being in the countryside was like learning another language, and at first we understood nothing. For weeks we'd wander about those fields and woods, sometimes not seeing another person all day, until one day we saw this guy. Well, actually we saw his caravan first, and we were going closer to explore it—we thought it would be empty. It was on the edge of a copse, miles from any road. I still don't know how he got it there, or whether he just found it. His name was Caius. He was young and friendly. At first we thought he was as young as us, but he wasn't. We spent every day after that with him, either at his caravan or down by this secret cove he took us to or helping him to collect the food he ate. He lived entirely off the land. He had no money to speak of and anything he needed that he couldn't find in the woods or fields, like fuel or clothes, he would offer himself as a laborer to one of the local farms and trade for. His existence was idyllic to us. He had no one to answer to. We had to go back to London at the end of the summer, of course, school and all that. We were devastated. We'd all gotten so close." Cassey smiles sadly. "This is what you do, Romeo, as you get older. You become nostalgic and wish for what could have been. I've often thought about him, and the way he lived, so freely. I've dreamed of doing the same, and it's got me through some hard times, the thought of that caravan, of living like that. You need to have a dream, something to hold on to."

She looks away for a moment, and I wonder what it would be like to have somewhere like that, to be someone who could live in that way, surviving off the land. I've only ever lived in this city. Curiously, I think of Pasha. Is he someone who could do that?

Am I?

I think of how we struggle through each day on the streets; would it be easier? Harder? Is it just having nothing in a different environment? But I don't think it is; somehow it seems a more forgiving environment, or at least a more noble and satisfying one. I think of my mother trying to find me if I disappeared into the wilderness. I could be dead, and she wouldn't know. No one would know.

Did you ever go back and see him?

"We tried many times. But although the caravan was still there, it was full of debris and didn't look like it had been lived in for a long time. We've never found Caius. We even asked at the local farms, but no one had any recollection of him."

Caius could be dead, and Cassey and her sister would never know.

I need to change the subject, so I tell Cassey about the posters, about my mother's search. I'm relieved to finally tell someone, someone who cares for me that way.

"How would you feel about seeing her again?" she asks after I've finished.

Anger flashes through me like a spear of lightning, and I'm going to say I don't want to see her ever again in my life. After what she's done, she has no right to come back into my life. All this is her fault, but... I stop. I'm angry at her, of course, but that anger is just a mask for all the other feelings I have. If I let myself feel them, if she was stood at the end of the ward right now, what I'd feel after all this time, after all this hurt, all this pretending-it-doesn't-matter, is, perplexingly, relief.

Confused, I mouth eventually.

Cassey nods, and I know she understands.

She reaches into her purse and pulls out a piece of paper, which she hands to me.

"I wasn't sure it was you at first. But you're right, Romeo, these posters are everywhere. There are thousands of them. It must have cost someone a fortune."

I stare at my face. I can't even remember when this picture was taken, but I'm not so thin, or my eyes so hollow. It must have been a few years ago. I wish I could screw the stupid fucking thing up. What a fucking pointless waste of money! I think of all the ways it could have been better spent.

"Someone really wants to find you."

But I don't want to be found. By her, anyway.

The nurse calls out only five minutes left before visiting time is over.

My heart sinks. It's now been two days. What fucking momentous thing happened to us that I wasn't aware of? How can he suddenly not fucking care? I sweep the poster onto the floor. For the first time, I feel so angry at him and not just grief stricken that he's abandoned me. Outside the blackness reflects my face, the window a ghostly sepia mirror.

My fingers twist together inside my bandages. I have to know. *Have you seen Julian?*

"Yes," she says, and even though her expression doesn't change, I know by her voice that something is wrong.

Dreams

ALL I think about after Cassey leaves is how I'm going to get out of here. But there is no question of me leaving tonight. I'd have no chance on my own out there. I'm too weak, my hands incapable of even getting my hospital gown off. I feel at the mercy of everything. I am powerless. I have no control, no choice. I'm trapped here.

It takes all my willpower not to think of Cassey's tight smile as she told me she would look out for Julian on her way home. She didn't expect to find him. And she left too quickly after that for me to ask her anything else.

I try not to notice people coming into the ward shaking ice off their boots. The moon and all the fucking stars will be visible tonight, it's so clear and cold. People die out there on nights like this. Alone and unnoticed, their frozen bodies discovered by some disgusted passer-by walking to work. I feel sick.

Pasha will look out for him, I tell myself. But who will look out for Pasha? And how can I trust him?

How? How do people survive this?

I don't know what to do.

The evening visiting hour comes and goes. No Estella. I don't know what I expected. I don't know why I let myself trust her, even just a little bit. People let you down. It's just what they do.

When everyone is gone, the duty nurse gives me a sleeping tablet. She strokes my hair and tells me it will be okay. I stare listlessly into the space between the beds, waiting for oblivion.

Sometime later, I'm woken. I feel groggy and swollen, as if my brain is pressing uncomfortably against the inside of my skull. Disorientated, I half expect the boy I love to be lying warm next to me. And when he's not, I think I'm dreaming and I want to wake up.

Estella, her eyes downcast, helps me into a wheelchair and pushes me out of the ward. The clock on the wall reads 12:15.

She wheels me down the corridor to a small consulting room with a couple of soft chairs in it. She pushes me opposite one and sits down in front of me.

I glance around the blank little room. A couple of generic pictures of fields, nothing too adventurous, beige carpet, beige walls.

"I'm sorry I had to wake you, Romeo." It strikes me then that these are the first words she has spoken to me tonight. "I'm in Leeds tomorrow and maybe for the rest of the week, and I wanted to speak with you before I went." She sighs, and I feel my breathing start to go.

She's arranged the foster home. I know she has. Maybe she's taking me there tonight. I look at my bandaged hands and imagine myself shut in some tiny bedroom somewhere far away, unable to get out, unable to communicate, a house full of people I don't know watching my every move.

What else could be so important she has to wake me up in the middle of the night?

"Romeo, it's about your mother…." She runs a hand through her hair. She looks tired. This woman who has seemed so full of energy suddenly looks as though she's had it all siphoned off.

My hands are beginning to throb from how tensely I'm holding them.

"I've just spent the evening down at the police station. The last place you told me you were living with your mother, I cross-referenced it with any significant events in the area for the approximate time period of her disappearance."

I can't believe I've been so stupid. Why did I tell her all that stuff earlier? And now she's put it all into some fucking police computer. I think of how I'd run if Julian was here, how we'd escape all this. She'll never find me.

"From what you've told me, it struck me as out of character. She'd never left you before, even for a short period."

God, I long for him. I need him here with me. I need his fucking arms around me, holding me together. The tightness in my chest constricts my throat.

"Romeo?"

Reluctantly, I open my eyes and look at her.

"I'm so sorry… but there was an accident. Your mother was crossing the road when she was hit by a motorcyclist. She had no identification; no one knew her. No one knew she had a child waiting at home for her to return. She never woke up. She died in hospital."

They should take the pictures down and paint the room white, because it is too fucking small. There are too many things inside it, not enough space to even breathe.

Absently, I wipe my face. Why the fuck am I crying anyway?

Tentatively, Estella reaches out and touches my arm. When I don't flinch or pull away, she puts her arms around me and hugs me, but I am too numb and spilling over to hug her back and just lie limply against her, giving up to the current and letting myself be washed downstream.

If she had no ID, how do you know it was my mother? I mouth after pulling away at last.

"I did a DNA test. Your mother's DNA was kept on file because she was unidentified."

Oh.

I nod.

Can I go back to bed now?

"I'm so sorry, Romeo. I really am," she says as she gets up and carefully pushes me through the doorway and out into the corridor.

I watch the strip lights above us blur into enormous starlike brightness. There is no use in pretending the tears aren't streaming down my cheeks, no use trying to hide them, but I can't connect to them, I can't feel anything—I'm not sobbing, it's not sadness or grief welling up inside me, it's not anything.

So why does it hurt so much?

It is not yet morning. It is that almost time between night and day where the clock hands tick slower and the minutes grow fat and lazy with sleep. The birds aren't singing, but they will be. The sky is whispering.

Pasha is watching me sleep. Except I'm not. I'm watching him through the haze of my eyelashes, thinking I'm dreaming and not wanting to chase my dream away. Right now he is the only connection I have to Julian.

He is like the picture of a boy on the cover of a book I had as a child. Ragged and elfin, his nose and cheeks pink from the cold. I didn't have many books, and the ones I did have were decrepit and watermarked, their spines cracked from use. My mother had brought what she could carry with her to England and no more.

Baba Yaga, it was called. The witch in the woods.

"Turn your back to the forest and your front to me," my mother would say with mock authority, holding me in her arms and letting me turn the pages for her to read.

She used to read to me a lot. Stories were all we had to keep the dark and the damp away.

We were all each other had.

Funny how after spending so long trying to forget, now everything reminds me.

"I know you not sleep," Pasha whispers. "Come. I take you to him."

My eyes fly open.

"Come," he urges, holding out his hand to me. "We do not have much time."

Determined I can walk unaided, I follow Pasha slowly down the ward. The nurse's station is empty, though I can hear their voices echoing from the brightly lit corridor nearby.

As we pass a laundry cupboard, Pasha grabs a couple of blankets and drapes the heavy things around my shoulders. With every step, the urge to cast them off and run builds and builds.

"You need them out here," he mumbles, opening a barred exit onto a long, narrow, flat roof.

The soft rose of the sky gives the illusion of warmth when really it is unbelievably fucking cold. I cough lightly before bringing the blankets up over my nose to breathe. But if I'm shivering, it's not just from the temperature.

Pasha glances around, whistles, and my stomach drops. I can't believe I'm this nervous. It's only been a few days.

A sudden doubt creeps into my mind. Pasha just said "he." He didn't say "Julian." Maybe whoever is out here is not the one person my heartbeat is thudding in my ears for. Maybe it's Roxy, Cricket, fucking anyone else I don't want to see. But that doubt is forgotten as he steps out of the shadows a few feet from me.

Julian.

I've seen him damaged and bloody before, but it shocks me now how different he looks. How that bright spark, that glow that shines from within him, is dulled to an ember. I can't take my eyes off him as he walks toward me. He moves as though he is in pain.

I know he will not cry, but he falls to his knees, wraps an arm around my stomach, and buries his face in the rough blankets that cover me.

I sink onto the coarse roof, cradling his head. *He is here... he came for me....*

His blond hair is matted and unwashed, suddenly grown so long, and his dirty clothing gives off the bitter smell of smoke. I try to ignore the cuts and the dark patches of blood that cover him. I have to—it hurts too much.

I reach to stroke his hair, to touch him after what feels like eternity, but I forget my hands are bandaged and how weak I have become, how hard it is to move.

He nuzzles my side, and I close my eyes, trying to curl against him. We end up cuddling awkwardly, Julian pulling me back against the wall.

Pasha keeps lookout next to the doorway, doing his best to ignore us.

"Don't cry, baby," Julian says softly. Even his voice is tired, worn out, thin.

But I'm not upset. This is just the closest I've been to feeling safe and okay in days now.

With the greatest care, he brushes my tears away with his thumb, his fingers tracing my jaw. I lean into his touch. I want to reach out to him.

I don't understand why he looks so sad.

Fuck, I sign in frustration, my fists together. I want to grip him tightly and never let go. I want him to never leave me again. I want this not to be a dream.

I want to ask him where he's been, why he didn't come for me, but I feel too vulnerable and exposed out here on the roof, too uncertain of what's changed between us.

But before I can gather my courage to say anything, he says quietly, "I have to go away for a bit."

What? I mouth, panicked, but he's not even looking at me.

I wriggle out of his grip, the blankets falling. All of my fucking wishing and longing and his not being there, all the fucking grief that I can't face, all of it ripping me apart.

Breathe.

How can he fucking go? How can he come here and tell me that? After all we've been through, everything. He doesn't come for me and now he tells me he's got to fucking go like it's the most okay thing in the world. For a blindingly painful second, I think I hate him.

"Breathe, Remee."

A hand brushes across my shoulder. I flinch, angrily shrugging it off.

"I'm sorry."

Sorry? Sorry doesn't fucking cover it.

Fuck off. I gesture, selfishly. *Go.* I want to hurt him.

How did we grow so far apart?

"You've got to stay here, Remee. You've got to get better."

I'm not a fucking child. It's my life. I want to shake him, make him understand. I should be the one to decide whether or not I stay.

Is Pasha going with you? I mouth. I will not fucking cry, and I will not make it easy for him.

Glancing quickly at Pasha, he shrugs like he doesn't want to give me the answer. And I don't think there is anything between them. I'm not jealous of Pasha. I'm not. I just want to be with him. That's all I ever wanted.

Why? Why do you have to go? They're going to put me in a foster home, and you'll never find me.

With shaky hands he caresses my cheek. The dark rings around his eyes make him look wasted. I close my eyes.

He puts his arms around me, pulls me close.

"Baby, I *will* find you," he whispers, his voice choked. "I'm not leaving you. I've just got to go. It's better for you this way."

For a second I let myself lean into him, bury my face in his neck, let my lips brush against the warmth of his skin. I don't want this moment, this heartbeat of time, to ever end. *This* is what's better for me, this touch, this feeling.

Why can't you go to Gem's?

He shakes his head, slowly, sadly, all the time moving away, getting to his feet.

Where will you go?

His eyes never leave mine, but he doesn't answer.

What's going on? Is it Cricket? The drugs? I grip his arm between my bandaged hands, ignoring the agony it causes me.

He doesn't deny it.

And it makes so much fucking sense. The way he looks, how he's acting. I feel betrayed.

Gem told me once Julian started using, years ago, to escape stuff that was going on at home. But things got so fucked up, and he got clean, swore he would never touch anything ever again. We swore to each other we would always find another way to cope. We had each other. And now? And now I guess he just couldn't take it. I guess what we had wasn't enough, and he's not as indestructible as I thought.

Pasha watches us from the doorway. "We should go," he says.

Julian looks down at me one last time.

Don't, I mouth, hunched up on the floor. But he looks away as though he can't take it and vanishes into the shadows, suddenly dropping out of sight. Distantly I hear the gravel crunch and know he has jumped to the ground.

Pasha hangs back. He crouches next to me and says earnestly, "We come back. I promise. It's not safe right now for him, but we come back. I watch you."

He turns to leave too. But I reach out.

Look after him.

I FEEL so utterly bereft, I could just sit out here in the cold all night, staring into the blackness, staring at the one spot I saw him last. And for a long time I do. For a long time I just sit and think, about everything. Beginnings, endings, how wrong I've been about lots of things.

I'm scared too. If my mother is gone, who is looking for me? Putting a lot of effort into looking for me. Without Julian, I'm on my own.

I can't touch even the edge of the darkness surrounding my feelings for her, not yet.

But maybe I am stronger than I think. Maybe I can be strong enough for both of us. I realize I've been scared, and I've not trusted myself since Lloyd and his gang beat me, months and months ago. Julian saved me then, and he's been saving me ever since. But maybe I don't need saving anymore. Maybe I've got to be the one to save him now. If I ever find him, I think hopelessly.

No.

I'm *going* to find him. I can't let myself doubt that.

I think about what Cassey said, about needing hope, needing something to hold on to, and I begin to question deeply what I really want. When each day is a struggle to survive, you don't think too much about the future. It's no sure thing. Everyone wants to get off the streets, get a job, *be* one of them, cross the divide. We just don't know how to do it. That life is separated from us by a wall of glass we're not strong enough to break through and we can't get a purchase on to climb over.

But maybe that isn't the answer anyway. Maybe there is another way for us. Maybe we just have to step back, ignore the glass wall completely.

I think about Julian, glowing, alive, with me always. I think about green fields and quiet woods. And I let myself dream….

CHOICES

TOO MANY days pass.

I don't look for Pasha, because I know he will only come when I am not looking for him—I don't turn my head if dark hair flits at the edge of my vision. I don't let my heart pick up speed at the sound of running footsteps, lilting whispers. I don't look, and yet still he doesn't come.

I try not to think of Julian at all because it kills me. But obviously I do, and maybe that's what love is, maybe dying inside when you're not together is how it has to be.

Because, believe me, I'm dying.

JULIAN.

So beautiful and serious. I can't take my eyes off him as he walks toward me, lighting up the darkness.

His arms fold around me quicker than a heartbeat, and we fall like flicker-book figures onto the bed.

But in his diminishing glow, I begin to notice things aren't quite right. As he moves his head, clumps of his beautiful hair are left stranded on the pillow, the side of his neck is black and bruised, and when he looks at me his eyes are the hollow eyes of a memory, or a ghost.

What have you done? I ask in horror.

He pulls up his sleeve, his arm just skin and bone covered in hundreds of needle marks.

And as I look, the marks shift to form two words. Help me, they say.

I wake up, shaking, my breath coming in painful gasps. I have to get out of here.

FOR THE past few days, Cassey has been my only visitor, although Estella has phoned and left messages, which the nurses pass on to me, saying she wants to introduce me to my foster family at the end of the week. She must really believe I'm going to let her ship me out to some holier-than-thou couple ready to pour the prerequisite amount of sympathy onto another difficult kid the state has handed them. The idea doesn't appeal on any level. I won't let it. The streets are where I live now. They are where I'll be until I find Julian and we make it off them together. What the last year has taught me is that I have a punishing will to survive. I am not some helpless, scared kid anymore. And I know it's easy to think these things sitting in my warm hospital bed, eating regular hot meals and not curled up frozen in a doorway, but still I believe it's true.

Yesterday, in uninterrupted silence, I told Cassey about my mother, and she held me until I finally pretended to let go and cry. She said the whole thing breaks her heart into pieces. But I'm still not sure what I feel, and I don't know how to deal with it on my own—I don't *want* to deal with it without Julian, so I lock it all up in my heart, where its dark weight bides its time, and I know one day it will consume me.

Finally the cold dawn light brightens the horizon. I've been lying here waiting for the day to begin for hours. It's Thursday, and though I'm still weak, and my chest is still tight in the cold air, I have to leave tonight before Estella comes back tomorrow ready to send me off to my foster family like a good little package. After the nurses have finished their breakfast rounds, I get up and wander the corridor, building up my stamina and thinking about what I'll need when I leave later on.

Except when I get back to my bed and start to get everything together and prepare myself, I find my clothes are gone. The plastic bag that rests on top of the cabinet next to my bed, containing the only possessions I have in the whole world—my jeans, top, jacket, and my pad and pens—is no longer there. My pad is the most valuable thing I've ever owned. Julian bought it for me. And I filled it with pictures of him. They are the only pictures I have of him. Panic flutters like a bird trapped inside my chest. I should have been more careful. I only went for a short walk up the corridor, but I should have hidden it, or taken it with me, or… something. I look around the ward at all the immobile patients lying in their beds, then over at the duty nurse wheeling around the trolley of drugs.

Who would steal from me?

Suddenly light-headed, I stumble over toward the nurse's station through the double doors. The world is unclear at the edges. I just want my drawings back. I'm not looking where I'm going, and I crash blindly into someone who gasps and catches me, but I'm so shocked I can do nothing but stare at her openmouthed and think *you shouldn't be here, you can't be here, and please don't take me away anywhere tonight.*

"Romeo?" Estella frowns in concern. "Is everything alright?"

No, nothing is fucking alright! I think, riding a sudden rising wave of shock and hating how fucking perfect her world must be. How, if her boyfriend or husband or relative went missing, she'd have the resources, the money, to find them. How, if her possessions got stolen, the police would commit themselves to reacquiring them. How, if she collapsed out there on the street, people would stop to help. How, if she wanted to leave this hospital right now, she could just walk out the fucking door get into a taxi and go *home.*

I shift out of her grasp and notice there is a tall, brown-haired boy a little older than me standing behind her, looking at me anxiously. When I catch his eye, he smiles shyly.

Hello, he signs with the fluidity of someone who has spoken sign for a long time, and closes his eyes for a second as if surprised by his own boldness.

His dark eyelashes fan out against his cheek, so long they look to be false, but I know they're not.

I look away.

This isn't part of the plan.

I need to hold on to my anger, stop panicking, and figure out a way to get out of here, now.

Glancing quickly between us, Estella says, "Romeo, this is Crash. Crash, this is Romeo."

She smiles, and I hope she's not going to leave us alone.

"Crash is deaf. He lives with the foster family I want to place you with. He's been with them for two years now."

Oh.

"You were going somewhere with a purpose, Romeo. Do you need something? Can I help?"

I shake my head, then change my mind and mouth, *My bag has gone. All my stuff. Everything!*

Too calmly she places a hand on my shoulder, and all at once I realize I've underestimated Estella and her freeness. She may possess some seemingly wild elemental force inside her, but she's been herding me straight down this path since the beginning.

"It's okay. I'll go and speak to the nurses. It's probably been placed somewhere for safe keeping."

Fuckfuckfuck.

She knew I was going to run, and she got the nurses to move my things. She knows she can't physically stop me leaving, but she also knows how much those drawings mean to me after our stupid conversation the other day. Angrily, I watch as she disappears back through the doors, then I storm back to bed, uncomfortably aware that Crash is just standing there biting his lip and looking one way then another, probably wishing he'd never agreed to come.

Just because I can't speak doesn't mean I can't live with normal people, I think, knowing I'm being an obnoxious prick.

I can feel Crash watching me, but I don't care. I don't want to know his story or be his friend. I just want to get out of here and go… where? My plan never got further than just leaving and somehow finding Julian—mostly banking on luck and intuition.

Crash's hands are shaking a little by his side as he stands at the end of the bed. I don't care that he's nervous. I don't, but I do look up.

Romeo? he signs carefully.

He's shy, and I can tell talking to me is hard for him. But I don't know why he would want to try.

Estella told me a lot about you. She said you were living on the street.

I nod distractedly. Could I leave without my pictures? Clothes, I could steal, but could I leave my drawings? What if I never found him? What if they were all I had left?

I lived on the street for a while too. He mouths the words as he signs them. I don't know whether it's a habit or a push to be clearer.

He looks like he's about to say something else, but at that moment Estella walks back, smiling. It only serves to make me angrier. It's so fucking unfair!

"Romeo, the nurses have your bag. They'll make sure it's kept safe."

I want it back.

"It's locked away right now, but I'm sure we can get it back for you tomorrow."

You can't force me to go with you.

"It's my job to protect you, Romeo. If I don't make sure you are being appropriately cared for and living in a safe environment, I'm not doing my job."

I roll away onto my side.

"I brought Crash to talk to you. He's been through a lot of similar experiences. I want to show you other people do understand what you're going through."

Yeah, but I bet he's not lost the one fucking person he loves more than anything. I bet he's only here because he's been manipulated somehow.

"Romeo, will you just listen to us for a moment? Please? I'm not trying to take away your freedom, that's the last thing I want to do. I'm trying to show you things can be better for you. I'm giving you a choice. If you go back out there, you could end up spending your life living like that, and there are better ways to live. You've got so much potential. Crash is an artist too, of a sort…."

It's about this point that I tune out because she doesn't understand the choice she's giving me. She doesn't understand the implications. If I go with her, I lose him. Simple as that. There would be too much separating us. I would be on the other side of the uncrossable divide.

I've already made my choice.

LATER THAT night I leave. I steal someone else's clothes from the laundry on the lower ground floor and then slip back along the corridors and stairwells, just like the thief that I am. I no longer hear the whispers. I no longer feel so haunted. An incredible loneliness sweeps around me like a suffocating mist instead. The night is a deep starless black, the hospital grounds eerie and full of shadows. I crunch through the gravel lining the narrow hospital roads and pathways until I come to the spot I last saw Julian when he jumped off the roof. I wish I could reach out and feel some tangible link to him, follow the secret connection between us like a boy following a trail of breadcrumbs. I pull the blanket I stole tighter around me, feeling only cold, and somehow lost.

At first I head toward Cassey's. I know I need help, and I know she will help me—I have come to trust Cassey deeply—but I change my mind. If Julian has gone into hiding, if he is running from something, there is only one person who might have a clue as to where he would run to. Gem. And, though it is not something either of us would ever mention, Gem owes me.

I take it slow, forcing myself to walk as though I have all the time in the world. I need to remain okay. I pass Victoria train station, the station where Pasha said he saw all the missing posters of me plastered along a platform. I stop outside for a moment. It's too early for the trains to start running, and heavy latticework gates bar the entrance onto the concourse. Without thinking too much about what I'm doing, I slip down a back street, over a low wall, and out onto the empty tracks. The mouth of the station devours the tracks darkly, and in its shadow I am terribly small. I don't really know why I'm putting myself through this. I just want to see. But as I approach the platforms, stumbling noisily over the uneven ballast between the rails, I see I'm not the only one wandering around the deserted station. A hooded figure moves soundlessly between the pillars, stopping every now and then to stick something to the walls. All at once, the figure turns, and I'm sure I've been seen. Dread fills me, and it's hard to catch my breath. I crouch down beneath the lip of the platform, my heart beating too loud, wondering desperately if it's too late to run.

NEAR MISSES

THE OVERHANG on the platform is so shallow, I'm sure whoever is out there will see me. I try to calm the white panic rushing through my veins so I can listen out for footsteps echoing nearer. But I can hear nothing but the high-pitched wheeze of air as it forces its way in and out of my lungs, the dramatic thud of my heart. I know I'm fast, but right now I'm not sure I can run. I can barely breathe.

So I wait, cowering on the train tracks, willing myself not to cough, not to make a fucking sound. Though what I'm waiting for, I do not know.

I try to picture the figure I saw, but I can remember nothing distinguishing—dark hooded top, dark trousers. Tall enough for me to assume it's a man rather than a woman. But really it doesn't matter. I'm not going to confront them. I convince myself I've no idea what they were doing really, and that whatever it was it has nothing to do with me. They just looked like they didn't wanted to be disturbed. When you've been on the streets this long, you know when people don't want to be disturbed with what they're doing. You develop a sixth sense.

I shiver and pull the blanket tighter around myself as a cold wind blows down the worn-down tracks and into the station like a ghost train. I am so conspicuous. Anyone else walking down these tracks would spot me a mile off. I feel caught out in open fields, birds of prey wheeling the sky above me. Vulnerable as fuck. And this is not how I saw my first night out of the hospital going. I told myself I could do this. But this is the first time I've been truly on my own out here, and it is fucking terrifying.

Sometime before dawn, I get the courage to take a quick look along the platform. Birds are screeching loudly in the skeletal rafters above. I haven't heard another sound since I crouched down here, and it feels like I've been stuck in the same hunched-up position for hours; my legs are stiff, my fingers frozen.

I peer around. Everything is as grainy as the picture on a black-and-white television set in the gray morning light, and it makes it hard to see even with the low station lighting still on.

Beneath my feet the ground starts to vibrate, and I know the first trains are going to be coming in soon. I'm going to have to get up off the tracks even if there is someone else still around. A horn sounds. A train horn. I spin around and see the sudden immediate glare of lights advancing quickly along the track toward me.

Fuck.

I sling my body forward and slither ungracefully up over the edge and onto the platform, the train missing me by seconds. My blood thunders. I didn't expect that at all.

And this isn't the first time I've had a narrow miss with a train. I let my head rest against the filthy concrete for a moment. But this is completely different. Well, maybe not completely—I was without Julian then too. But back then I was a little lost, and now I have a purpose. And even though my situation is no less hopeless, I have hope.

In the main part of the station, beyond the platform, I can hear people arriving for work, doors being unlocked, shutters drawn up. The minute shift from nighttime to daytime, the shreds of safety it brings. I look around. Whoever was here is most likely long gone. But... for a moment the posters, pasted to every pillar and wall, take my breath away. There must be hundreds of them. It's like Pasha said—I'm everywhere. The platform is an eerie hall of mirrors reflecting my face. *This* is what they were doing. I can see where the posters have been torn down and others stuck over the top, as though they are replaced whenever the previous ones are cleared off. At the bottom of each one is a telephone number. I look away and shudder, utterly spooked.

I scan the concourse anxiously. I need to get away from here. I don't care who they are or why they're doing this, I really don't. This is too creepy. The sort of creepy that could have me ending up in small pieces in a bin bag dumped in the river.

I can't go back out on the tracks with the trains now running, so I shoot toward the barriers that divide the platforms from the main part of the station. Someone behind me yells. A train driver with a perplexed look on his face points in my direction, but I turn away and carry on walking quickly. If I can just manage to get over the barriers and slip outside, I will be okay. I can vanish into the streets, and no one will be able to find me. But he shouts to a guard on the concourse who starts running toward me, and I don't manage two steps before I'm tackled to the floor from behind. I hit the concrete with a painful thump and try and scramble away from the heavy weight pinning me down, but I just can't. I don't have the strength, and as I lie winded on the cold dirty concrete, I start to wish I'd never left the hospital last night.

If I'd taken my time and had more of a plan, I wouldn't have been so distracted and thought coming here was such a good idea. I wouldn't have frozen my arse off hiding and then got caught trespassing or whatever it was the driver yelled at me for doing. Maybe he was just shocked because he almost killed me. I don't know. I don't care. I just wish I weren't here.

They drag me into a booth at the top of the platform. There are three of them, the driver and two guards. The room is small, with one chair. I'm shoved toward it.

"So you're the little wanker putting up posters of yourself, eh? Getting too cocky to cover your face now, are you?" one of them spits.

Oh great. So that's what they think I was doing.

How fucking ironic.

I don't give him the satisfaction of looking at him.

Moving forward, he places a cold heavy hand on my shoulder, squeezes tightly, but someone else pulls him away.

The driver who yelled at me.

"He's just a kid."

"Yeah, and it's not his fucking job on the line if that mess isn't cleared off, is it?"

The door slams as he storms out.

The driver crouches down in front of me.

"We have to call the police, and you're going to have to wait in here while we do."

He has a kind face, and I realize he's just doing his job, but I can also see he's a little angry. What's the point in trying to tell them it wasn't me, when it quite visibly *is* me out there. They've convinced themselves I'm the culprit, and I just don't have the energy it would take to argue with them. What could I say that would make them believe me? I slump back in the chair, completely exhausted. This is turning into a nightmare, and I've had a few too many of those recently.

Always when I'm without Julian. Doesn't that say something? I close my eyes and feel the traitorous prickle of tears. I miss him so much. Everything feels so wrong and empty without him.

I have no idea how I'm going to get out of this one.

But I don't get to feel sorry for myself for long. The pissed-off guard marches in, grabs me (ignoring the protest of the other two), and drags me back out and onto the platform.

He hands me what looks like a wallpaper scraper and a bucket of water and pushes me toward a pillar.

"Looks like you've got some work to do," he sneers.

"John, this is pointless. What do you hope to achieve? Security have called it in."

I just stare at my reflection in the bucket. Can they not see my hands?

"Get on with it."

I don't move. I try to work out how many posters there must be. The platform stretches on and on, and like Pasha said, every upright surface is covered. Some of the posters have been graffitied. My face mocked up or completely blanked out, tagged. I look closer. Several of the posters have a blue tag that looks almost like it could say *Pasha*.

I hear the guard breathing heavily behind me. So close I can feel the heat of his body. He must be twice my size. Where the fuck is the driver now? Can't he see what's going to happen? Can't he see this guy is going to beat the shit out of me, and I'm so fucking exhausted I can't do a thing about it? I can't even run. I drop the bucket and the scraper.

In one smooth movement, his hand grips the back of my skull and mashes my face against the poster of my face on the pillar. If I open my eyes, I can see every pixelated dot. I try not to react, because if I react, he'll see he's scaring me. But I *am* scared. Panic is fluttering madly inside my chest, and when he tightens his grip on my skull, the panic mixed with my exhaustion makes me weak and everything starts to fade out at the edges, as though I've reached some sort of limit.

"Do you know how much work this is every fucking day?" he hisses.

But really, I can't process his words before darkness swallows me, and I black out.

WHEN I come round, I'm lying on a row of chairs in the corner of a different, bigger, room. It looks like a staff room. There are a lot of people in the room. Some of them are police.

A woman in a blue polyester uniform with the logo of one of the train companies on it leans over and checks my pulse.

"My name's Annie. I'm a first aider," she explains. I watch her fingers as they press into my wrist. I feel my heart thumping in my ears. "So you're the mystery boy who puts up all the posters, eh?"

She doesn't sound pissed off. She sounds intrigued. But I guess it's not her job to clean them off.

"Romeo, isn't it?"

I look up sharply.

"How's your head feeling?"

She lets go of my wrist and places a cool hand gently against my forehead. My head feels too heavy to move away.

"There are some officers here to see you. Do you feel up to talking to them?"

When I don't respond, she smiles conspiratorially and whispers, "I won't let them bully you into it."

I mime writing. Puzzled, she reaches into her pocket and hands me a pen and tears a scrap of paper out of a magazine lying on the floor.

How do you know my name? I write, in shaky letters.

She looks at me closely.

"When they checked you for ID, the only thing you had in your pocket was the card of a social worker named Estella King. I called her. She'll be here soon. She said you absconded from hospital."

How could I have been so stupid to keep that card in my pocket? It's as though the forces in the universe are all working against me.

I don't have the energy to respond to Annie and listlessly feel the paper and pencil fall from my fingers, my eyes closing. I don't think I've ever been so unbelievably fucking tired.

"Is he fit to talk?" someone asks, but they sound muffled and far away. Too far away to possibly be talking about me.

"No. You're just going to have to wait for his social worker to arrive." Annie's tone is icy.

If I had the energy, I'd smile at her apparent dislike of the police. It makes me feel safe, and I want her to stay with me. Not that I'd admit that to her. I'm not about to cling to her hand. It's just… I need someone on my side.

Even though I try to fight it, telling myself I should be alert and ready to run, I feel the arms of sleep wrapping around me, pulling me down—in my dreams I see Julian, and I can't resist.

ESTELLA HAS arrived when I wake. I pretend I'm still asleep. I really don't want to face her. She has a short conversation about me with Annie. They all agree I'm in no state to talk to the police, which is a fucking relief. When I open my eyes a slit, I see Crash is with her again too. He really must have nothing better to do and no one better to be with. He spots I'm awake and gives me a tiny smile. I look away.

The room is emptier than before, and the pissed-off guard who slammed my face against the wall is thankfully nowhere to be seen. The driver is here, though, talking to Estella, probably explaining about the posters. I wonder how she's going to make sense out of that one.

Crash moves closer and sits down opposite, staring at his hands and glancing at me every now and then and taking deep breaths.

Please don't be nice to me, I think. I want to be able to lump him in with everyone else here who doesn't understand. But with every little look, he's trying to reach out to me.

I need to use the bathroom, I sign abruptly, getting up.

I don't, but I do need to see if there is any way I can get out of here.

My legs are a little wobbly, and I'm still tired, but I feel mostly okay.

"Hey," Estella calls out and walks over. "You don't get away from me a second time, you know."

She's smiling, as though she doesn't mean it like that, but I know she does.

Bathroom? I sign, looking around.

"Wait a sec." She holds up a hand and breezes over to where Crash is sitting.

I feel like a fucking child.

She signs something to him, and they both walk over.

"He's coming with you," she says, eyebrow raised as if daring me to challenge that.

Great.

The bathroom is small, but large enough for Crash to stand by the door and invade my personal space, watching me as I wash my face in the hand basin. There is only one small window that I don't think I can fit through.

What's your problem with all this? he signs suddenly when I look up into the mirror. I didn't actually expect him to confront me about anything.

I just want to be left alone, I sign back, hoping he'll take the hint.

I wonder how long the corridor we just walked down is. I wish I hadn't been unconscious when they'd carried me up here.

He looks frustrated.

To go back out on the streets? Why? How can you not want something better? It's fucking hell living like that!

I'm surprised and a little shocked at his outburst. I've never seen someone's emotions play out so clearly across their face. It's kind of fascinating. On the streets you learn to become guarded. We stare at each other through the mirror. It's somehow easier to look at him this way, to pretend we are one step removed, and I'm not entranced by how startling his eyes are now I've let myself actually look at him.

I just don't understand, he signs, still looking so completely anguished, which confuses the hell out of me. *My foster parents are the kindest people I've ever met. They care about me. And they would care about you too. I know they would. I don't understand why you won't give them a chance.*

It's not that simple.

Yes, it is. You stay on streets, and after you're eighteen, you really are fucked. Right now, you've got a chance.

Does he think I don't know that? It's the whole reason Julian has no fucking chance.

I never chose to be homeless. And I wouldn't be doing this unless it was absolutely the only way. And I don't care if you run and tell Estella, but wherever she takes me, I will *leave.*

She's not stupid. She knows she can't stop you. But she's only doing this to protect you. What's out there for you?

I can't tell him. If I tell him, I'll have given in, I'll have trusted him, and that's what Estella wants. I can't let that happen. But I want to tell someone. I want to talk about Julian and bring him to life with my words, make him real and not just a memory.

Someone I care about, I sign with my eyes closed. *I have to find them. They're in trouble.*

I take a deep shaky breath, and when I look at him, he gives me this sort of grateful happy look, as if he's pleased I've opened up to him and, against my will, it makes me glad I told him. And I know I'm avoiding the fact that I enjoy looking at him because, I tell myself, it's irrelevant.

What's his name?

I blush, and quickly move toward the window. I don't want him to see I'm embarrassed, but by knowing that I'm gay, he's just confirmed my suspicions that he's gay. I'm usually rubbish at picking up on that; even with Julian I was rubbish. But the glass is opaque, and all I can see is white, so I can't even pretend I'm looking out at the view.

Julian, I sign, turning around, suddenly cold.

What sort of trouble is he in?

I sigh. *Are you going to tell Estella all of this?*

Crash glances at his watch as if he's considering something.

She's going to think something's up if we stay in here much longer.

Crash, I need to get out of here.

What are you going to do once you find him?

I don't know, I sign, not willing to admit my plan to anyone.

We should get back.

Please, I sign, desperately. *If you help me get out of here, I promise once I find him I'll... let them put me in care. Anything.* I hate lying. *Otherwise I'm just going to be looking for opportunities to run.*

Crash stares at the floor. His shiny hair flops over his face. I try and work him out. He dresses like a skater or something… or those kids who jump the railings and somersault off the steps around the city at night, looking so fluid and strong.

If I helped you, where would you go right now?

Tower Hamlets. A friend lives there who might know where he would go.

I don't see the harm in a little bit of truth. Even if he told Estella, Tower Hamlets is pretty huge. They'd have no chance of finding me.

Crash looks straight at me. I have no idea what he's thinking, and I feel uncomfortable for all the wrong reasons.

Okay. I'll help you get out of here, but I'm coming with you.

And even though I don't want to be, I'm so relieved I'm not on my own. With some weirdo out there putting up posters of me, being alone is the worst thing I could possibly be.

POOLS

WHATEVER QUIET, careful escape I imagined, I know without Crash it would never have been as simple as just opening that bathroom door and walking the opposite way down the corridor.

For a fraction of a second, I turn and see the fire of Estella's red hair through the frosted glass in the staff room door. I expect someone to stop us. But Crash holds himself with a quiet confidence and even has the audacity to smile shyly at the two police officers hanging around the doorway that leads out to the concourse.

But however confident he is or is pretending to be, we don't hang around. We pick up our pace as we weave through the crowds and across the busy station. The noise and the freezing air wake me up to the world like cold water splashed in my face.

As soon as we are out on the street, I hear a mobile phone beep, and Crash reaches into his pocket, so I assume it's his, and it must also vibrate or something to alert him to messages.

Some guy paid Julian with a phone once. We played around with it for a bit, but when the battery ran down, we sold it. That's the only time I've ever even held one.

Estella? I ask when Crash looks up from the screen.

He shakes his head and blushes deeply before shoving the phone back in his pocket and looking down at the ground.

A friend, he signs. *I'm supposed to be meeting him.*

I'll be okay, I assure him. *You should go.*

Smiling wryly, he shakes his head, and something about the determined look in his eyes tells me it would be pointless to argue.

Victoria Street is busy, and this close to the station every other building is a sandwich bar or fast-food outlet. The smell is overwhelming. I try not to think about it.

Are you hungry? Crash asks suddenly, as if he can read my mind.

I don't want to, but I nod—not having slept all night and then the whole stress of this morning has left me starving. After being so well fed in hospital, I'm not used to the constant gnawing inside me anymore. It's not something anyone should have to get used to, but Julian taught me ways of dealing with it. Just being with him helped me forget sometimes. Just lying with him in some quiet place trying to shut out the darkness, or when there was no quiet place, just pulling our tarpaulin over our heads and shutting out the world.

I know why I'm thinking about this, and it hurts that I'm trying to ignore him like everyone else is. I don't want to have seen him, but across the road there is a homeless guy wrapped up in a dirty blue sleeping bag, and people are just stepping over him as though he doesn't exist. He's not moving. He could be dead and no one cares.

Without warning the ground seems to shift beneath my feet. I spin around, my chest tight, the crowds a blur. How on earth did we fucking survive it out here?

How is Julian still fucking surviving it?

If….

Crash grasps my arm as the anxiety threatens to overwhelm me and pulls me into a sweet-smelling cafe that sells healthy-looking baguettes stuffed full of salads and beans.

Okay? he signs, eyebrows drawn together, concerned.

I focus on his face, taking one breath after another, and feel everything slow. His eyes are mesmerizing. I wonder disconnectedly if anyone has ever told him how beautiful he is. They must have done. I look away. Nod.

All self-conscious and awkward again, he gestures to the sign above the doorway.

Vegetarian okay?

I don't honestly care what sort of food it is right now. I can't understand why some people won't eat this or won't eat that, really. It seems like a waste.

Kay and Peter are vegetarian, he signs in explanation, as though he understands my thoughts on this too. *My foster parents.*

I glance out the window at the guy in the sleeping bag again and when I look back, Crash is staring out there too.

At the counter he points to some huge sandwiches behind the glass counter and orders three.

Despite being shy and deaf, he doesn't seem at all fazed by this sort of situation. He watches people carefully to work out what they're saying, and either just nods or shakes his head or holds up his hand and, bizarrely, they seem to understand what he wants. I couldn't do that. I don't go anywhere normally without some paper and a pencil. I write *everything* down, but watching Crash just pitch himself into communicating with people shows me how much I hold back, how much I relied on Julian to do the talking. I relied on him too much to deal with a lot of things. And I know he probably didn't mind. He told me many times that he *wanted* to take care of me, but it makes me wonder if all the little things he felt responsible for built up into one huge thing he couldn't deal with anymore, and that was why he chose the drugs to escape and that was why he left me.

Crash's hand waves slowly in front of my eyes, and I realize I zoned out, and I'm stood in the way of people trying to pay for their food. He gently tugs my jumper and pulls me over to the only free table in the cafe.

You should sit down, he signs. *You don't seem okay. What is it?*

I look at the third sandwich. My back is to the window, but I know the guy is still out there in the cold.

I wish I could do more, he signs, looking self-conscious.

But it's more than I see anyone else doing. I give him a tiny smile. I'm thinking too much. He's a good person, caring and thoughtful.

He frowns. *It's not just that, though, is it?*

I want to trust him. I do. But I can't. I'm scared to. You trust people, and they hurt you, in one way or another. Julian is the only person I have ever trusted completely, and I know that he is hurting just as much as I am right now. He has to be.

Outside the window the sunlight slants across the street. Such definite lines of light and shadow.

It's just... I miss him, I sign, after a while.

I miss him so much it hurts, and I don't think it will ever stop.

Crash stares at his hands before signing. *Two years ago I lost someone I cared very much about. I still miss him.* He must catch the way I react to this as he suddenly looks horrified. *I didn't mean....*

It's okay, I sign, but it's not really. That's not something I ever want to think about.

He nods, and the way he stares at the blank screen of his phone makes me think maybe this friend he was supposed to meet is more than just a friend to him.

We should go, I sign. I feel like I'm wasting time sitting down.

Crash picks up the third sandwich, and we're just about ready to leave when his phone goes off again. I don't think he feels it buzz this time, so I touch his arm and point to his pocket.

He shows me the message. It's from Estella. *I trust you, Crash* is all it says.

Out on the street everything glitters in the sunshine. It should be beautiful.

We cross the road, and Crash crouches down and touches the sleeping bag near the guy's head. When he opens his eyes, Crash gives him the sandwich, and we walk away before he can say anything to us.

All the way to Gem's, we don't really communicate. I'm a little disappointed that Crash has completely let up with the curiosity. He appears lost in thought and doesn't even ask for any more details about where we're going. I don't know if I want him to give me so much space, and I glance at him every now and again, hoping he'll get the hint that I want to talk. I want him to ask me questions because I don't even know how to begin.

DEPENDING ON how you look at it, our timing is either spectacularly bad or spectacularly good—we meet Gem in the stairwell of her block on her way out to work. She has a new job dancing at a club. I guess she must need to rehearse in the mornings or something. She looks breathtaking. Crash blushes when I introduce him.

I was hoping to see Joel, Gem's little boy, but instead we walk with Gem out to the bus stop as her bus is due any minute.

I wish I had more time to explain what has happened, but I can only plead that Gem tell me if she knows anywhere Julian might go if he needed to hide, anywhere he might run to, anywhere they used to go as kids.

Please let there be somewhere, I think. I need something to go on. I don't think he would have left London, but the thought of walking this vast city directionless is swallowing me.

Gem stares out across the playing fields opposite and shrugs.

"All the places we used to go are gone now. Demolished, redeveloped. I don't know."

I know she cares. I know this cool act is just self-preservation, but I'm desperate. I grab her hand. Her skin is cool.

Please, I sign. I know she understands that.

"What do you want me to say, Romeo?" she snaps. "What do you think I know that you don't? I'm not the one in a fucking relationship with him."

I hear the bus arriving and scribble, *Please try and think. I don't have anything else to go on.*

"When Julian's dad beat the fuck out of him, we'd go down the rec and sit on the swings and smoke—it's a fucking car park now. The first time we kissed was at the abandoned lido down in Battersea—it's not abandoned anymore! I can't do this, Romeo!"

The bus pulls over. The doors hiss open.

Rarely does Gem appear anything but okay, but for a fleeting second, before she gets on the bus, the pain in her expression reflects my own. And strangely, despite her hopeless words, that comforts me.

And as I watch the bus pick up speed and round the corner, I realize it's more than that. Something about what she said resonates within me like a blinding truth—Julian had a thing about old swimming pools. He loved the architecture, the weird art deco shapes, and the extravagant Victorian embellishments. We didn't do it a lot, but sometimes we'd dream we were rich, and he'd tell me how he'd buy some old swimming pool and restore it and live there with me.

Crash, I sign frantically as the bus disappears. *Can you get the Internet on your phone?*

Deftly, he unlocks the screen and hands it to me, but I pass it back. I've no idea how to use it.

Can you get a list of all the abandoned swimming pools near here?

A few seconds later he shows me the results. There are five disused old pools in a three-mile radius. We work out the nearest one is a fifteen-minute walk away.

We should have got on that bus.

I don't think I remember how good it feels to smile. How light I feel when I do. And I can't explain this certainty I feel, but as we follow the directions on the map, I know I'm walking toward him. I think I could walk forever.

The sun feels warm on my skin. The sky is almost beautiful.

INTO THE DARK

IT'S FOUR o'clock, and already it's dark. Already another day has slipped out of sight. I trail my hand against the bricks as I walk down the side of the building. The concrete bites into my healing skin like sandpaper, my fingertips feel raw and bloody, but I grind my teeth together as I memorize the contours of every brick. I want the pain.

There's no way in, I sign in frustration as I reach the front of the building again. This is the second time I've circled it.

Crash watches my hands, then goes back to staring at the boarded-up frontage as though he is thinking about something.

Above our heads, the sky is a smoky black void. Everything is dark and shadowed; nothing is beautiful.

This is the third swimming pool on the list. The first two were rigged with CCTV and signs were stuck to the metal barricades saying the feed was watched directly by the police. I didn't exactly believe the police would think two abandoned swimming pools were worth watching, but I know Julian wouldn't have risked it—there's hiding in plain sight and there's pushing your luck. And anyway, they just didn't feel right.

When we got here, I felt a tiny spark of hope rekindling itself in my chest. This is just the sort of crumbling old building Julian loved. And it's on a street behind the main road too, so it's tucked away and quiet. But there is just no. Fucking. Way. In.

Come on, I sign irritably. I don't want to waste any more time here. I just want to get on to the next pool.

Crash steps forward and tugs at the drainpipe for the fifteenth time. Everything he does is beginning to piss me off, especially when he now seems to be ignoring me.

Kicking at the ground, I turn on my heel and start to walk back down the street. I don't even know where the next pool is, but if I don't keep moving toward *something*, I'm going to break down.

A warm hand circles my bicep before I've taken ten steps.

Where are you going? Crash mouths puzzled.

He looks at me with more concern than I know I deserve right now.

Why do you care?

Rolling his eyes, he pulls me gently backward into the shadows and folds his arms around me.

Fuck, I think just before I start to drown. I don't deserve this. I don't deserve his concern, his care. It's going to kill me. He strokes my back, and I desperately try to shove all my feelings back down inside myself. If my throat gets any tighter, I'm going to stop breathing. I should never have let him get this close, but I can't quite find the strength to shove him away, because even if he's not Julian, he's here stroking my hair and his warm breath is against my cheek and I don't want to be alone. I don't want to feel alone. God, I hate that I'm imagining the similarities. *Wishing.*

Reluctantly, I let my arms do what they so desperately want to and hold him back.

He's so much taller, and he smells so warm and different, and his heart beats so much faster. There aren't really that many similarities at all, but still it feels like I'm forgetting, or if not quite forgetting, that I'm covering up my memories, and I'd rather never hold anyone in my arms again if it means forgetting what it feels like to hold Julian. *Wouldn't I?* God, it hurts.

After a while I swallow my tears, and the urge to cry goes away. I shift, and awkwardly we break apart. I don't know what just happened really. Crash and I, we just sort of collide.

I think I found a way in, he signs, moving into the light a little.

I swallow hard. *Okay*, I sign and follow him back to the pool.

The street isn't busy, but this is London and the traffic never dies completely. There are a couple of kids watching us curiously from the opposite side of the road. I glance at them warily.

Crash smiles. He smiles too easily. *Wait here*, he signs.

And before I've even realized what he's doing, he runs at the wall, grabs hold of the drainpipe, and scrambles up to the unboarded second-floor window. I barely see him whack the glass with the flat of his hand before the window swings open, and he pulls himself up and tumbles gracefully inside. I am rooted to the spot, wide-eyed and a little amazed. I don't even want to turn around to check if anyone else saw that. I'm pretending those kids just don't exist. I don't want to look suspicious or obvious or to draw any attention at all; breaking and entering is still breaking and entering, however much style you do it with.

The sound of wood being split comes from down the alleyway at the side of the building. I can just about make Crash's silhouette out of the shadows, and I run toward him. He's holding a door off its hinges and carefully leaning it up against the wall.

Want to have a look around? he signs.

We should put the door back. I motion that there were kids watching us outside.

Inside, there is very little light. Crash uses his phone to illuminate the debris-strewn corridor that leads to the changing room and pool, but it wears the battery down quite quickly so he slips the phone back in his pocket, and we make our way slowly and carefully in the dark. I put my hand on his arm and tell him to stop every now and then so I can listen.

I didn't expect the place to be quite so eerie. We're gripping on to one another's sleeves by the time we reach the changing room. There is too much silence. Nowhere is this silent in London. It's as though we're in a vacuum.

As we edge our way through the gutted changing room and out into the large open space of the pool, the air temperature seems to drop, and I shudder involuntarily. The pool is huge and empty, though the room still smells damply of chemicals. In the dull orange gleam of the streetlight that streams in through the glass ceiling, I can see the bottom of the pool is set out like a mini bedsit with a broken sofa and a mattress and various stained-looking cushions and blankets scattered around.

Crash jumps onto the ladder and slides down the metal handrails to the bottom of the pool. The loose tiles crack as he walks across them.

Think this is theirs? he signs, holding up a blanket.

I stare at the dirty, ragged thing, hopelessness coursing through me. I don't know. How am I supposed to know if it's a blanket Julian or Pasha have picked up? I want *him* to be here, curled up beneath that blanket, safe and warm. But he doesn't have belongings; he doesn't leave a trace.

Even if they were here, they're not here now, and that is what counts.

Crash springs up out of the pool and puts a sympathetic hand on my arm. I can't look at his face. He knew this was impossible from the start, and he didn't say anything. He humored me because if he didn't, he knew I would have run. Well, I want to run now. But I don't. My traitorous body leans into his, and I let him take my weight and hold me. I don't protest as he leads me out of the building and into the shivery cold. I know he's going to take me home to his foster parents. I know I'm going to let him.

The windows of the bus are fogged up, and it's warm. I don't even care that it's so busy we have to stand up in the narrow aisle and fall into each other every time the bus stops.

I want to carry on searching, I sign. But my heart's not in it. There's only so much disappointment I can take.

Crash looks at me kindly. *Tomorrow we'll bring a torch*, he signs and absently pats his pocket, frowning.

What is it? I sign.

My phone, it's not here. He checks all his pockets again, and runs his hand anxiously through his hair.

The bus stops and more people pile on, and we're shifted farther up the aisle. It must be coming up for rush hour.

When was the last time you had it? I ask, though I know the answer. We used it as a torch back at the swimming pool. He must have dropped it.

Bizarrely, my heart leaps a little at the thought of going back.

We can go back for it tomorrow. I can tell he's trying to will himself to relax. I can almost see the words he's telling himself circle around his head.

The bus slows, and I grab his sleeve.

Come on, I mouth.

We step out into some cold, unfamiliar street and wait for another bus on the opposite side of the road.

It feels like hours later, but we're back outside the swimming pool again. We sealed the side entrance pretty well, and it doesn't look like anyone else has been there. Crash yanks the door off its hinges and looks at me somewhat apologetically.

You're still going to come back with me after this, aren't you?

I nod. I'm not sure why he thinks looking for his lost phone would change anything.

My foster parents would love to meet you. You'll like them....

I still Crash's hand—there is a sound from deep inside the building. It sounds like tiles cracking on the bottom of an empty pool as someone steps across them.

I freeze, no longer sure I want to find out who is walking around inside, but it might be Julian.

What's wrong? Crash reaches out to me.

There's someone in there, I sign. *In the pool.*

Okay. He shrugs, like this is no big deal, like whoever is in there is not a potential threat and won't mind us intruding on the little hideout they've got going on. *Let's find out who it is, then.*

It's not that simple, I sign.

Yes, it is, he signs and strides past me down the corridor.

I stare after him. How can he do that? He's deaf, for God's sake. Shouldn't he be just a little bit more cautious? How the fucking hell did he survive out on the streets?

I chase his disappearing figure down the corridor, perplexed at how differently he reacts to situations, how given a choice he'd probably pick fight rather than flight. Then again, I think Julian probably would too. He'd rather deal with something head-on than run away from it. Whereas me, I can run for the whole of London.

I hear his voice before I catch up to him. It sounds deep, just like I imagined it would, only he speaks with no inflection, and his words sound clipped and a little muted. He's telling someone it's okay, that he's deaf, and we're just looking for someone. But whoever they are, they're not speaking back to him. I step out of the changing rooms just in time to see a figure scrabbling up the broken ladder on the far side of the pool.

Crash stands awkwardly on the edge in front of me, his hands shoved deep in his pockets. The light is so poor we're all just grainy figures blurring into the darkness. The figure on the far side of the pool reaches the top of the ladder and quickly vanishes into the darkness beyond it. I guess some people are even more scared of confrontation that I am. I always imagine that in situations like this I am going to be challenged or hurt, but maybe most people just want to be left alone, and Crash is right, I'm worrying about nothing.

The blankets that lay scattered on the bottom of the pool are gone. A small black rectangular object lying on the tiles captures my eye, and I clamber gracelessly down the ladder to take a closer look. It's Crash's phone. I'm glad we've found it and that whoever was here didn't take it. I'm about to hold it up to him, but something catches my eye, something I'm sure wasn't scrawled on the bottom of the pool earlier— my gaze flicks toward the other end of the pool and then back to the writing—something I definitely saw scrawled on a poster of my face this morning. Could it have been?

Crash jumps down next to me. *What is it?* He signs, though it is so dark by now I can barely make out his hand movements.

I saw this earlier at the train station. I point to the tag. *I think it says Pasha. He was with Julian.*

Are you sure?

Yes.

Crash takes a picture of the tag with his phone.

Do you think that was Pasha?

We both stare into the silent darkness.

I shrug. *I don't know. I thought he would have stopped if he recognized me.*

Maybe he didn't see you.

I know there is no point running into the dark and chasing him. He's a ghost now, surely long gone. But I think Crash's lack of caution is affecting me, and I grab his hand, pull him toward the other end of the pool, up the ladder and into the dark.

CHANCES II

ALL IS silent, crushingly so, as if this darkness has a solid weight to it, smothering all sound, drowning all light. And even though the pool is just behind us, I feel like this is all there is.

Gripping my hand tightly, Crash holds out his phone and in the faint light it emits, we edge forward into the sooty blackness, every step becoming more and more hesitant and unsure, our shadows looming like specters.

It feels like we're being watched.

The hairs on the back of my neck stand on end, and all the terrifying thoughts I've ever had about the dark, about whatever psychopath has plastered my face all over the train station, about… anything and everything flood my brain. I see shapes I know aren't really there. I feel the gloom solidify and touch my skin. And all hopes of Julian and Pasha being back here seem suddenly ridiculous, as childish as my lack of caution.

Breathing in shallow sips, I try not to make a sound, but the floor is uneven, and I stumble noisily, quickly righting myself as though my life depends upon it. I don't want to go any farther. The darkness is too complete, the tiles underneath my feet too slippery and unsteady. I can't see enough and my panic grows.

Crash bumps into my back as I stop, his warmth knocking me forward until his arm wraps around my waist like a safety harness and pulls me back against his chest. His heart thuds strong and steady, while mine hammers wildly, a bird in a cage.

I turn, half ignoring the fact that Crash's arm is still around me, and search out the streetlights, the glow of London visible through the pool's high glass windows behind us, life. Only when I see them do I feel my chest able to expand a little more freely.

Whomever we followed is gone, I'm sure of it. The sensation of being watched just a result of my paranoia. So when a wide beam of light flicks across the room, hovering over us like a searchlight, I dig my fingers into Crash's arm as he squeezes me tighter and freeze.

"Hello?" Crash calls out.

I notice how his body tenses, and I know he feels me shaking.

Nobody answers. With the light shining on us, I can see we're stood underneath a crumbling archway leading through to several what look like plunge pools. The floor beneath our feet is covered in smashed bricks and tiles.

Covering my eyes a little, I stare up to where the torch light is shining from. There seems to be a low stone balcony just above us, but it's too bright to make anything else out.

"Who are you?" a wavering voice calls out. The evident exhaustion in the speaker's tone lessening my fear a little.

He wants to know who we are, I sign to Crash.

"We're looking for our friends, two boys, one has a Russian accent, have you seen them?" Crash calls out.

"If you're deaf, how can you hear me?"

I sign the question.

"I can't," Crash says, frowning.

The torch beam swings away, highlighting the deep curve of tiles around the domed roof, and back to the ground. The speaker makes his way slowly down the stairs, moving with difficulty, as though he's in pain. He's just a wiry old man with thick, fractured glasses and a ragged tweed coat pulled so tightly around himself I can make out the skeletal ridges of his spine.

"You don't speak, I suppose?" He jabs a finger at me, and mutters something under his breath as though he's talking to someone else we can't see.

I shake my head.

"You kids need a place to sleep? You shouldn't be out in the cold on nights like this."

Again, I shake my head. However desperate I've been, offers of places to sleep from strangers set alarm bells ringing through my head.

"Two boys...," he murmurs. "Thought all they needed was each other...."

Ask him about the two boys, I sign quickly to Crash as the man walks back again toward the pool and climbs down the ladder.

"Were two boys staying here?"

The man stops, a half glazed look on his face. "There are always two," he says softly. And I know with a sinking feeling he's not seeing us or hearing us. He's either living in the past or in his head.

We watch as he picks up a bundle tucked away in a dark corner of the pool. Crash holds me back with a strange apprehensive look on his face. It's only when he suddenly releases his arm from my waist that I realize how tightly he was holding me.

Are you okay? he signs.

I nod.

Want to get out of here?

Disappointment sweeps through me, but again I nod. I said I'd go home with him. I promised. And I will.

The man climbs back up the ladder. He has a bottle concealed in a torn plastic bag. The scent of alcohol fills the air as he twists off the cap and offers it to us.

When neither of us moves to take it from him, he shrugs his bony shoulders and takes a swig.

"You should take care of your heart," he says earnestly to Crash. "Take care of him." He looks pointedly at me, and I feel sick thinking how much I wish it were Julian standing with me right now.

What's he saying? Crash signs.

He's just lonely, I respond, taking his hand and pulling him away around the edge of the pool.

"Won't you stay, my Louis, my Louis, so lost and alone," the man sings quietly as we walk away.

Louis…? It couldn't possibly be the same Louis from the shelter, but my chest tightens painfully all the same as I wonder.

What I thought was Pasha's tag on the bottom of the pool catches my eye, and all at once I realize how foolish I must be to think I will find signs of them everywhere I go. How impossible and futile this all really is. There are ten million people in London, and I want to find just one.

THE BUS is near empty. We sit at the back, and I stare out the window into the passing dark feeling flattened and subdued. That man must have been near sixty. It scares me to think he could have lived all those years with nothing. Was he once like me? Did the days just roll together into years that crushed him to a place too far down to ever return from?

That *loneliness…* how could he have survived it?

Crash's warm fingers brush my hand.

We're here, he signs as the bus pulls over.

We step out into a quiet street, the wind gusting lightly around us. An avenue of tall, straight trees lines the pavements, ancient sentries guarding over all they can see.

Involuntarily, I shiver. This is just the sort of street that Julian and I would avoid. Every house set back away from the road, new cars parked on driveways, curtains drawn against the night and whatever might be lurking out there. The sort of street where people don't hesitate to call the police to report suspicious-looking boys with their dirty blankets and tired, stumbling feet. I can't help the resentment I feel prowling my gut.

Crash bites his lip as he looks at me. He must have felt this too, once.

They're good people, he signs.

I don't care. I can't do this. I don't want *to do this.* And I look away wishing with all that I have, all that I am, that I could take away the last few weeks, scour them from existence, but quietly he waits for my anxiety to pass.

We walk in the same direction the bus took for a little way. I try not to look too closely at the huge houses, each one more extravagant than the last. What I feel is pointless and exhausting.

We stop at the corner. A thick square hedge towers above us, hiding the house behind it almost entirely.

This is it. Crash inclines his head at a small garden gate hidden amongst the greenery. *I should text Estella,* he adds, looking at me expectantly as if wanting my permission.

I pluck a tiny waxy leaf and rub it to mush between my fingers, nervous as fuck and trying to distract my hands from shaking as I shrug.

Maybe she'll give him a pat on the head for doing so well in getting me here, I think darkly as he texts away.

I'm just a pawn that's been maneuvered into place, and now they think they have me. They think my every move will be mapped out, that I'll be like them, and Julian will become just a boy I knew once and lost.

But despite how completely out of place I am here, despite it being the polar opposite of all the places I have ever spent my life, despite how much I want to hate it and for it to hate me so I can carry on believing at some level that people like this are the cause of all our problems, despite the fact that Julian is not with me, despite *everything*, I feel a knee-collapsing weakness as we walk up to the warmly lit front door, little pots of well-tended plants lining our way. And when a middle-aged woman with short blonde hair and messy layers of mismatched clothes answers the door—so unlike everything I had imagined her to be—looks from one to the other of us and then throws her arms around us both without saying a word, I feel so utterly and inexplicably relieved.

Struggling with the tightness that builds in my throat and stings behind my eyes, I let myself be guided inside, out of the cold.

EVERYTHING HURTS

"YOU MUST be Romeo," the Bohemian-looking woman says once we are inside, smiling warmly and signing so naturally she doesn't look like she's even thinking about it as she speaks. "I'm Kay. Crash has told me a lot about you, and I'm so happy to finally meet you. Please come through to the kitchen so you can meet my husband."

The house is painfully colorful and eclectic, decorated by someone with a love of everything around them. Photographs of forests and rivers vie for space with paintings of the same, a large tapestry hangs on the stair, and the dark wooden floors are covered with richly patterned Persian rugs in reds and browns. It feels full, even though it's so huge. Full of life. Of opportunity. Of a sort of freedom so alien to me I can't even imagine what it tastes like.

It's too much. So instead I watch the way my broken trainers gape at the sides with every step, the rubber split across the soles in a thin-lipped smile. I think of how far I've walked in them, how many pointless miles have worn them through. And even though I don't want to, even though they're just stupid trainers and the rest of me isn't fixed up any better, I feel ashamed at how dirty they look compared to everything in here.

Crash catches my fingers as we walk down the hallway and squeezes lightly. If I meet his eyes, I'm not going to be able to hold back. I'm a shivering emotional wreck behind my blank, hopeless expression, and he knows it. He thinks this is how it needs to be. He thinks he can save me.

As we enter the kitchen, the man sitting at the table stands up, a look of surprise on his face.

"Romeo, this is Peter, my husband." Kay's manner is so genuine I wish I could just let go and accept all this for what it is—an offer of help, of hope. But a part of me holds back. A part of me is still waiting outside.

For a moment I think Peter is going to come over and hug me too, and I tense, but he just asks me if I would like a drink or something to eat, tells me that they are vegetarians, and talks in a steady stream as though words really are that easy, making it seem normal that I don't respond, that I sit down and stare at the tabletop as though it's the only thing I can see.

I eat what they give me without really caring what it is. They ask me what foods I like, and I just don't know how to answer. I don't know whether they are just trying to get me to talk or whether they really want to know because they think I'm staying. I catch them looking at one another, some secret communication going on. Crash sits next to me, not saying much, mostly watching, but I'm used to that now.

After we've eaten, he tactfully signs he's going to show me around the house. He can see my brief sense of relief has worn off.

"That's fine," Kay says, smiling kindly. "Romeo, just let Crash know if you're tired, and he'll show you to one of the spare rooms, and we'll talk some more in the morning, okay?"

She pats my arm reassuringly, and I have to swallow and look away, unsure of why such a gesture makes me want to cry.

I follow Crash out of the kitchen.

I just want to go to bed, I sign when we're in the hallway. *I'm exhausted and my hands are hurting.*

Drawing his eyebrows together in a concern that's far too sweet to be meant for me, he asks, *Do you want me to get you some painkillers?*

The irony hurts so badly I want to laugh, because really it's not just exhaustion or physical pain; it's the fact that I feel like I'm breaking apart, and I don't think I have the ability to hold myself together any longer, and I don't think they've got tablets for that.

No. I shake my head.

Still frowning, he leads me up the wide old staircase to a room he says they call the garden room because of its view. It's cozy and warm despite its size, full of solid plain-looking furniture and two windows black with night, a room so much bigger than any of the cold, bare slices of building my mother and I shared so long ago.

My room is opposite, he signs, taking his time and drawing the curtains across for me. *And the bathroom is at the end of the hall.* He hesitates a little, and I want to push him out of the door, I am so desperate for him to go. *If you need anything, just come get me, okay?* And finally he leaves.

As soon as the door shuts, I sink to the floor near the bed, and covering my face with my arms, ride out sobs that silently rack my body. My heart is a shattered, broken mess. I can't take it. I just… can't. *Julian. This loneliness is killing me.* I need him so much. It doesn't matter where or how, but I need him in my life, with me. I need to know he still cares, that he loves me, that he didn't just fuck off and leave me because his feelings changed. How could they have changed? I don't understand. I don't understand anything. All I know is I never want to feel like this again.

There is a knock on the door. Quickly I stand up, hurriedly wiping my eyes and taking a deep breath to calm down. When no one comes into the room, I walk over to the door and open it. On the carpet just outside, there is a little tray with a mug of hot chocolate and a small pile of biscuits.

This kindness undoes me entirely.

Shaking horribly, I pick up the tray and carry it into the room, placing it carefully down on the chest of drawers before I collapse onto my knees and fall apart completely, my tears soaking into the carpet.

It feels like the end.

Eventually I still. Husked out, empty, unable even to take a deep breath without my chest hurting from exertion. With trembling arms, I pull myself up and numbly drink the now cold hot chocolate and work my way slowly though the biscuits. I'm not hungry, but I'll never be able to waste the food in front of me. Even if I lived the rest of my life in comfort, I know there will always be a part of me that doesn't trust the next meal won't be my last.

It's late, but I don't want to be in this room on my own anymore.

Listening out and feeling like an intruder stealing through some family's home, I open the door and creep across the thickly carpeted hall to the room Crash told me was his. I pray that I don't bump into Kay or Peter.

I can hear the sounds of a television chattering away to itself somewhere, the low rumble of it strangely more comforting than silence, but then maybe I'm so used to constant background noise, I now need it.

Crash's room is dark. I think at first he might be asleep, but as my eyes adjust to the gloom I see he is lying on his bed, his phone in his hand.

I must look like crap because as soon as he sees me he flicks the lamp at his side and gets up, signing worriedly, *What's wrong?*

His room is kind of messy—clothes are strewn everywhere, books, a laptop, a skateboard without any wheels, what looks like school books and several posters, which have detached themselves from the walls—and I like it more because of that. I like seeing him like this. I like that he doesn't seem to care about meaningless stuff.

I don't want to be on my own, I reply, picking my way across the floor and sitting down heavily on the end of his bed.

Do you want to talk about it?

I shake my head.

Can I sleep here? My eyes plead with him.

A brief look of apprehension crosses his face, but it's gone in a blink. He nods and starts to clear a space on the floor next to the bed, but I put my hand on his arm and stop him.

I mean with you. I trace the abstract pattern splashed across the duvet. *Just sleep.*

Chewing his lip, he sits back down on the bed. His leg brushes against mine. He doesn't look at me.

Instead he pulls a piece of paper and leaky pen off the nightstand, writes something then hands it to me.

I like you, it says.

A distant warmth squirms in my gut. This is painful but a pain I can deal with better than being alone.

I know, I write back, letting my head fall onto his shoulder. *Could you hold me? Please.*

Immediately his arm comes around me, drawing me close, and I lean into him, closing my eyes and letting his warm scent comfort me.

Do your foster parents know you're gay? I write, not wanting him to get into trouble having me in his room like this.

His fingers close over mine briefly as he takes the pen, and I think I feel his lips brush my hair, but I could just be imagining it. *I'm not,* he writes. *I probably like skinny dark-haired boys more than any girls, though.*

His arm still around me, we shift up the bed so we're leaning against the headboard and Crash pulls the duvet up over our legs.

So who's the person you were supposed to meet today?

Glancing at me, he smiles wryly and writes.

Someone who's never going to feel the same way about me as I feel about them.

Why?

He sighs deeply, and I close my eyes to just feel the way his chest moves against mine. He doesn't feel anything like Julian, but it comforts me all the same. Just this nearness and knowing someone cares soothes the ache inside me to a bearable amount of pain.

We've gotten really close, but he's straight. Sometimes we play-fight, but he pulls back if it goes too far.

I wonder what too far might be and write, *Do you think he knows how you feel?*

Crash shrugs.

We run together sometimes. There's this park most people meet at before going in the city for the bigger jumps and stuff—

Oh, the climbing buildings stuff you do, I sign, remembering the way he scaled the building earlier, how strong and beautiful he was to watch.

Crash rolls his eyes. *Yeah, we call it parkour for short.* He doodles a tower block in the margin before writing. *Sometimes it's just me and him, we have this route we do together near the park, that's just ours. We ran it together last week, and I tried to tell him that I'm not straight, but he doesn't always understand all my sign, and I don't know.... He didn't say anything. He likes this girl anyway. I should probably just give up on him.*

It's not always that easy, I sign, suddenly cold and wishing I was asleep or it was tomorrow and we could get out of here and get searching again.

I watch as he draws a whole constellation of stars above the tower block, and I know he wants to ask me about Julian, or he's waiting for me to tell him, but I can't. It all hurts too much right now.

So I just lie against him, letting him hold me, feeling selfish and untrue but yet so much better than I did earlier.

LIES

I MUST sleep, for a while at least, but it's not even past midnight when I wake again. Crash's arm still pulls me tight against him, his breath quiet and hot against my neck. I panic a little, needing to get out of his bed, away from the claustrophobic heat our bodies have created. I am all too aware of how well we fit together, how my body responds to his, even though I don't want it to. It's like a thousand pieces of glass being pushed into my heart.

Not wanting to disturb him, I ease his arm from around me and slip out of the bed. The bathroom is at the end of the corridor, but I pass so many other doors it feels like I'm in an empty hotel.

I can no longer hear the TV burbling away. Everything is disturbingly quiet—no traffic, no arguing in the street outside. It's like the silence after an explosion. It makes me want to hold my breath.

I drink from the tap and use the toilet without even turning the bathroom light on. I don't want to see how nice the room is. Everything here must remain at arm's length. Detached. Because that's the way it is. My world is the one we're all pretending doesn't exist. And although I'm here, I'm not thinking about what that might mean yet, but I know I can't straddle the divide forever.

Cupping warm water in my hands, I wash my face and try not to look back at the boy in the mirror above the sink. I hardly recognize him anymore—he's changing too traitorously quick to grasp hold of. The glass is cold beneath my palm as I cover his face.

Back in Crash's room, I don't know what to do with myself. I'm too restless to sleep. I glance at the papers and books that are under my feet. School books, homework. Other world stuff.

I sit down at his desk and flick through a couple of them, knowing I'm being nosy as hell but unable to stop myself looking for more of his little doodled illustrations—cityscapes seem to be his favorite, with faceless boys on skateboards riding down stairwells and over barriers. Estella said he was an artist of a sort, and although he's good, and I'm entranced by all the quirky details like the graffiti in the background, I don't think this is what she meant. His magic is in the way he moves. The way his body describes the space around him, the way he tests the limits and boundaries in his movements.

Closing the books, I notice for the first time the name that appears on the front of them is not Crash but... *Christopher*. I say it over in my head. It's as though I have discovered a secret.

I keep glancing at the blank notebook on the side of his desk, pretending I don't feel its pull as I stretch my fingers out, then make a fist, feeling the way my skin tightens against my bones. I'm scared I won't be able to do it anymore, that I've somehow broken that almost mystical connection between my brain and my hand. But I know it's thinking like this that's really going to break the connection.

Carefully, I pick up the notebook and quietly tear out a piece of paper. I fold it over and root around on the floor until I eventually find a pencil and something to lean on. I know what I want to draw. I'm not sure what his reaction to me drawing him sleeping will be, though. Maybe I won't show him. Maybe I'll keep it like the picture I drew of the boys kissing on the bus. A moment, a snapshot, captured and stolen out of time.

THE GRAY morning light filters through the bare branches of the oak outside the window. The ground below is swathed in mist. Wrapped in one of Crash's jumpers, I'm sitting on his windowsill, waiting for the night to fade away completely. I've been sat here for hours now, thinking, trying to make sense of everything. Trying to work out what I should do.

I can't remember ever being able to hear birds sing so clearly—the city drowns out everything but its own song. It's never quiet, like this.

But by seven my patience has evaporated; I've had enough. Lack of sleep has me restless to be gone, and I decide it's not too early to wake Crash. I crouch down in front of him and brush his silky hair out of his eyes, watching as he blinks sleepily at me and stretches languidly, his arms above his head.

I want to go see a friend before I look at the rest of the pools and get my drawings from the hospital, I sign in a rush. *She works at a cafe. She gets there early.*

Cassey saw Julian more than I did in those last few days. Maybe she can help me make sense of things.

You didn't sleep much, did you? he signs, ever perceptive, as he squints at me. *What about talking to Kay and Peter?*

I will, just... later. I know he's just woken up, but I'm ready to leave now.

I can't deny that I'm starting to feel caged in. If I talk to them, they'll try to stop me, try to convince me that my continual searching is not the way to do things, tell me I need to stop and get on with things, my life. My chest feels tight just thinking about it.

They could help.

I shake my head.

They wouldn't understand. How could they?

He sighs. *I need to talk to them before I go anywhere.*

Out in the corridor there is movement; a floorboard creaks near Crash's door. I begin to feel a little desperate.

You don't have to come. It would be better if he didn't. But at the same time, his presence comforts me.

He gives me a lopsided smile. *I want to come. But I can't just go without saying anything.*

Do you need their permission whenever you want to go outside? It pisses me off that he can't seem to do anything without some sort of adult interference.

No, but I want it. He looks at me steadily. *So I've got to talk to them.*

I don't want to wait, I sign irritably. I want to just go, but I don't know where I am, and I have no money for the bus. I walk across the room and stand by the door, frustrated.

With immense casual grace, Crash gets up, picks his clothes off the floor, and pulls them on. He walks over to me and before I know what's happening, pulls me into a hug. I lean into it for a second, then push him away.

I feel like shit, don't be nice to me. I scowl.

Briefly, he searches my eyes and he signs, *Wait here.*

When he returns Kay is with him. She has a sandwich for me. She holds it out like a peace offering—except it's me who should be offering something.

I put the plate on the bed next to me, cast my eyes down, and glower at the carpet.

"Romeo, I know you don't want to talk right now," she says gently. "Crash told me you want to go and see a friend this morning."

I refuse to look up, but I nod.

"Okay." She pauses, and I assume she's signing something to Crash. "I just want you to know that we're here if you need us, and we'd very much like it if you came back later."

If she means that in some way more than just doing her job to make me feel wanted, I can't understand why—I've been nothing but a silent presence that's eaten their food and hidden away in their house. I wonder if Crash was like this, or if he was just so grateful to finally belong somewhere, everything fell easily into place.

But again I nod.

Her feet step lightly across the room, out of sight. I hear the door shut.

Crash dips his head and peers at me until I look back at him.

Sorry, I couldn't stop her. He doesn't look sorry. *No one is going to force you to stay. But given a choice between this and*—he gestures toward the window—*out there, I've never looked back.*

IT'S COLD, he signs as he passes me the fur-lined hooded top I wrapped myself in last night.

It smells of him, and I relax infinitesimally as I slip my arms down the sleeves.

I wait by the door while he searches through his drawers for something.

Here. He hands me a mobile phone. *I'll put some credit on it when we're out.*

I pass it back to him. *I can't.*

For texting. He mimes, like I don't know what that is.

But it's not that I can't use it; it's that I can't take a phone from him. I can't pay him back.

Please. He places it back in my palm, folds his hand over mine over the phone.

My resistance is being worn away, like a city slowly crumbling to dust. I put it in my pocket.

WE STAND at the bus stop down the road, freezing. I pull at the neck of the top to cover my mouth and look around.

Everything is so green out here, wherever we are, whatever middle-class borough we're in. Even though it's winter and it's the frost that flowers in the gutters and across the cracks in the road, there are still thorny hedges and frozen grass and weird-shaped conifers in everyone's gardens. It's all more green than gray, and it makes me feel as though I'm taking a deep breath, a breath I need to take. There is no panicked flood of things happening, there is nothing moving through the stillness, everything is glacier slow, yet the moment is full, peaceful. Another world.

THE BLACK knot in my chest grows heavy as the bus stops on the embankment and we get off. It weighs me down as though it will be my cross to bear. My devastated heart, my loss.

She felt like this too, my mother. I don't know how I know it, but I do. She lost her love, her family—all she had left was me. And it all twisted up bitter and sharp inside her until everything good was gone.

I don't want to be like that.

Like the slow spread of a disease, I'm beginning to hate this city and what it's done to us. To all of us, to everyone I know. I glance at Crash. Maybe I am starting to understand why he wants me to take what's being offered.

I DON'T know where Cassey's sister's cafe is, but I don't want to admit that to Crash after he's come so far with me, so for a while I wander up and down the litter-filled streets near the embankment, trying to look as if I know where I'm going.

We see a newsagents and go in so Crash can put some credit on the phone he gave me and, swallowing whatever fear usually stops me,

I write a note and pass it to the woman behind the counter, asking her where Jackie's cafe is.

"Next left, Old Paradise Street," she says.

It's not far.

It's just a tiny place, smaller than Joe Brown's used to be, with yellow lighting and steamed-up windows that radiate warmth. I stop outside, dreading what I'm about to do.

At the end of the street—the restless gray ribbon of river, the sky like mist above it. Nothing ever black-and-white.

Crash looks at me expectantly, but I won't hold his gaze.

You want to see her on your own, he surprises me by signing what I was just about to.

I bite my lip and nod, my eyes flicking over his.

Will you collect my drawings from the hospital?

I hate that I'm asking him this, and I don't want to hurt him, but I'm here to talk to Cassey about Julian. He was never meant to come.

Will you be here when I get back?

Yes, I mouth.

Is it a lie? I just don't know.

I stand in the doorway and watch him until he disappears. He looks back once, before the corner, and I know he sees me.

WHEN I push open the door, the smell of hot grease and tea brings back a storm of hopeless memories I have to swallow down. Cassey is stood behind the counter serving a young girl with a baby. She nearly drops the plate of toast she is passing to her when she sees me.

"Jesus Christ, Romeo, I've been so worried! The hospital said you'd run away. Come here!"

She pulls me into a hug across the counter, squeezing me so hard my ribs might crack.

"I'll make you a tea," she says, unnecessarily turning away to get a cup so I can wipe my eyes and steady myself again.

"Jackie!" she calls, lifting the counter top. "I'm just taking five."

We sit at one of the empty tables. It's only just past eight, but the first wave of breakfast customers is gone, and there are only a few stragglers left.

I pull out a page from Crash's notebook and pass it to her. Everything I need to know is on that page.

She skims my questions briefly before looking back at me, confused, pitying maybe.

"You haven't heard?"

Blood rushes in my ears, making my head throb. I can't breathe for fear of what she's going to tell me. The world stops when I shake my head.

"Romeo, Pasha isn't with Julian anymore. Pasha's back down the embankment with Roxy."

Before I realize what I'm doing, I'm up and out the door, leaving it wide open behind me.

PASHA

I RUN toward the river, not seeing anything but my destination—the embankment, the sharp concrete steps, the sleeping bodies lying in shelter beneath the concrete sky. There are too many for the police to move on, although they will have tried. Beyond them the underpasses turn into the tunnels.

I am disconnected from my body, unaware, as I weave my way between the sleeping forms and run into the dark. I'm not scared anymore, even though this is the place where I pushed Cricket into the fire and burned my hands, even though Cricket is probably still here somewhere. I don't care. I just need to find Pasha.

There are few fires burning at the center of the tunnels, and it is dark and cold. My footsteps splash through the black water, and the sounds echo on around me as I run through the vast, unlit space. I don't know where I'm going. Pasha will be with Roxy, and Roxy will be… where?

I stop, staring around at all the boxes and blankets and sagging tarpaulin shelters, listening to the sounds of fitful sleep, the coughing, the moans. I can't take it. This is my life, and at the same time, it's not anymore.

Taking myself by surprise, I crouch down and shake the blanket-wrapped body nearest to me.

Do you know Roxy? I mouth.

Dark, tired eyes glare up at me, not even trying to understand. "Fuck off."

I move on to the next body, waking them and wishing I had paper and a pen, wishing I hadn't left everything back at the cafe. But I'm shrugged off and pushed away.

I consider using the phone in my pocket to write out Roxy's name on the screen and show them, but I risk being mugged for it, even though the phone is old and probably not worth the effort.

No one wants to know anyway. Why would they help me when I offer them nothing in return?

The smell of unwashed bodies, piss, and smoke begins to get to me, so I give up and move away.

I skirt around the back wall. It's colder and less populated, but it is a good vantage point. I keep my eyes out for Roxy's black mess of hair, Cricket's dirty blond crew cut.

I don't expect to find Pasha first, but as I pass the far corner, I'm sure I see him. His close-shaved head laid bare against the concrete—his hair so much like mine used to be—his eyes closed, sleeping, blanketless, and cold. He is alone. I can't see Roxy anywhere near him.

It's probably for the best. I'm sure Roxy hates me because of what I did.

As I get closer, I'm struck by how fragile he looks, how young. His wrists are so thin, his skin white as the bones beneath it.

With his face unguarded and expressionless, he appears much younger than I was my first night on the streets, and it tears at me how wrong this is. He's just a child, lost out here in the freezing temperatures, no one giving a fuck if he gets sick or hurt.

A coughing fit that would have me doubled over racks his body, but he sleeps right through it. He stinks of alcohol and there is a dark pool of vomit near his head. But it doesn't matter. I crouch down and put my arms around him, feeling the tremors that run through his body. He's shaking so badly with the cold. I try to sit him up, but he just flops against me, no weight to him at all. The movement doesn't wake him, and it scares me a little, but I tell myself he's just drunk.

Drunk, unconscious, and freezing cold—people die like this out here. But I can help him. I can do something about it, and the alcohol will work its way out of his system.

If it *is* alcohol. If he's overdosed on something else, it could be too late already.

I can't let myself panic. I've got to get him to Cassey's. I've got to get him warm.

Slipping one hand beneath his knees and the other around his back, I lift him up. His head lolls backward over my arm, exposing his pale throat, the dark thumb-sized bruises around his collarbone. His trousers are undone too, barely pulled up, the zip broken. I can see the faint dark line of hair than runs down his pale stomach from his navel to his genitals, and I want so much to cover him up, but I need to get him out of here.

I'm unable to wipe my tears and they fall freely, blurring my way as I stumble through the dark, back the way I came.

Outside, it has started to rain and a bitter wind whips the icy water around us. I have to stop when I reach the steps. I can't carry on; my arms are trembling with the exertion of carrying him just the short distance through the underpass. Gently, I lay him down and take off the top Crash gave me to wrap around him. I'm not cold right now anyway.

It takes all my determination to make it to the top of the steps. I cross the road and walk on in short bursts, stopping every few meters until I feel like my legs are going to give way beneath the weight in my arms. I turn down Old Paradise Street. It's a long road, but I can see the cafe in the distance, its bright sign lit up against the grayness.

The rain is coming down heavily now, plastering my hair to my head and soaking through my thin T-shirt.

I concentrate on putting one foot in front of the other, on taking one step at a time. A figure runs down the road toward us, but I don't pay any attention. My muscles are burning. I focus on what I have to do.

But as the figure gets closer, I realize I know who is running toward us, and the relief makes me weak. My knees give way, and I fall gracelessly down on the unforgiving pavement, taking Pasha's weight in my arms, rocking him back and forth.

Crash skids to a halt in front of me, breathing heavily.

Julian? he signs, eyes wide as he looks from me to the boy in my arms.

I shake my head and mouth, *Pasha.*

Crash reaches down and with great care takes Pasha into his arms. I don't think I've ever felt so grateful to anyone—except maybe Julian when he rushed in and stopped my being beaten to death all those months ago.

"Come on," he says in his careful way, his arms too full to sign. "Get up. It will be okay."

CASSEY IS pacing backward and forward, peering anxiously out the steamed-up cafe window when we push open the door.

"Dear God, are you lot trying to give me a heart attack!" she exclaims when she sees Pasha unconscious in Crash's arms. "Come through to the back."

We follow Cassey through the tiny cafe kitchen to a box room at the back of the building. Extra tables, chairs, and supplies for the cafe are piled high along the walls. The window at the end looks out onto a back alley full of black bin bags. It's not warm, and my teeth chatter as the cold seeps to my bones without Crash's jumper. Cassey rushes to get a heater and something to lay Pasha down on. Her sister, Jackie, looks on, not saying a word.

When Cassey returns with an ancient-looking bar heater and a thick blanket, I help her make a space on the floor so Crash can lay Pasha down. We wrap him tightly and the heater blasts out warm air into the room, but still he doesn't wake.

Bending over him, Cassey places her hand on his forehead.

"I'm going to give him—" Cassey looks at her watch with a fleetingly anxious expression. "—twenty minutes. If he's still like this by then, I'm going to call an ambulance."

I nod and sign Cassey's words to Crash.

"I'll come back in a bit with something hot for you two, alright?"

Cassey leaves us. I lie down next to Pasha, tentatively stroking his head, his arm, his cheek. I thread my fingers through his, wanting to feel him warm with my touch, but instead I feel the cold leach into me. The wet fabric of my T-shirt sticks to my skin unpleasantly, and my feet are so cold and wet I can no longer feel my toes. But none of that matters.

Please wake up, I think. And not just because he can help me find Julian. Right now, I just need him to wake up and be okay.

Folding his long limbs, Crash sits down and watches us, a serious, almost pained expression on his face.

What happened? he signs.

I don't know. I pull myself up wiping at my eyes and feel Crash's fingers brush against mine, against my cheek, warmth radiating through his skin. *He was supposed to be with Julian. I thought he was with Julian. But he's just a kid.*

I feel that by putting so much faith in Pasha staying with Julian, Pasha looking after him even, that I've betrayed him somehow. I had no right to place such hopes on his shoulders, even if he did take them on willingly.

I stroke Pasha's back, rubbing in a constant motion, begging him to wake up.

Shifting closer, Crash places his arm around my shoulders. I tuck my head under his chin and lean against his chest, the strong thump of his heart so comforting, so alive. I feel like I am using him too—though it occurs to me maybe he knows and maybe he's letting me.

WATCH YOUR BACK

FOR A moment there is only the slow tick of the rain against the glass, the rise and fall of Pasha's chest, Crash's heart beating heavy in my ear, and the low whir and click of the heater in the corner. The room is warm, I am no longer shivering, and Pasha's tremors grow less and less.

I don't know what I'll do if he doesn't wake up. I don't want to think about it. Instead I wonder about Pasha's background. What was it that made him come here to London, to England? I wonder that no one cared enough to stop him and if anyone did care, how they will never know how much he's had to go through, where he sleeps at night.

Without meaning to, I picture my mother's face and close my eyes against the pain.

But even more powerful than my memories is an exhaustion so heavy it flattens me, and I can do nothing but give in to it.

THE SUDDEN commotion in the cafe makes me jump, my heart pounding. Beyond the closed door to this small room, tables and chairs are scraped along the floor or are knocked over, and someone is shouting angrily. I tense, prepared to run for it, but then remember where I am, who I'm with, and I know I don't need to run anymore.

Slowly, I pull away from Crash's embrace and sit up, trying to hear what's happening. Crash looks at me bewildered, unaware of the noise. I gently let go of Pasha's limp hand and get up to move closer to the door so I can listen, but by now the shouting has stopped.

A second later the door flies open, nearly knocking me against the wall, and Roxy rushes in, followed by Cassey calling for him to calm down. He glances at me, then at Crash, and crumples on the floor next to Pasha, a low sound coming out of his mouth. It's only when I get closer I realize he's crying.

Roxy, I sign to Crash. *Someone....* I trail off. Someone I used to know.

But someone I now barely recognize, even though it has only been a few weeks since I last saw him. He looks so different, and not in a good way. His messed-up hair is bleached some unnatural white blond, and when I look closer, I can see there are patches of hair missing at the back. The bones of his spine poke out through the fabric of his top, and it reminds me of the old man we saw at the swimming pool, surviving and yet so lost.

The Roxy I once knew is gone, his innocence wasted, his sweetness peeled away bit by bit until there is nothing left of it, until there's nothing but skin covering bones. The thought makes me feel hollow and empty.

If I'd seen him in the underpasses, I wouldn't have known.

"Nononono," he moans, cradling Pasha's head.

Behind him, Cassey looks on unhappily.

Her expression surely reflects my own. Yes, he's here now, but where was he when Pasha was drunk and vulnerable and he needed someone? Where was he when Pasha was being fucking molested?

"I thought he'd been kidnapped," Roxy says in a low voice, eyes narrowed at me. "Someone saw him being taken here. I didn't know it was you."

I desperately look around for something to write on. A fierce anger burns through me, ignited by his words.

Crash realizes what I want and passes me a delivery receipt off the side of one of the boxes, and I pick up a pulverized biro off the floor.

What the fuck did he take? How could you just leave him like that? He was freezing when I found him. People die like that out there! The pen rips through the paper as I write, and my hands shake when I think that he still might not be okay.

I shove it at Roxy. He glances at what I've written and lets go of Pasha to snatch the pen off me.

Fuck you! he scrawls across my words. "He can do what he likes. I'm not his fucking keeper."

So why are you here? I sign, throwing my arms wide, frustrated, knowing Roxy can't understand me but needing to express how I feel. *You can't just care when it suits you. He's just a kid. He's younger than we were!*

As if she can understand the exact meaning of my gestures, Cassey shakes her head at Roxy. "You call that boy your friend, and you just left him like this."

"Fuck it. I'm not staying here to listen to this." Laying Pasha back down, he gets up to leave. "Pasha knows where to find me."

I glare at him. It's so fucking easy to just go. Roxy never had any backbone anyway. It's why we didn't stay together long. I knew from the first that if things went bad, he wouldn't be there for me. Just like he wasn't there for Pasha. I can't let that happen again.

But I can't let myself be like him either. Reluctantly, I reach out and put my hand on his arm to stop him. His clothes are as soaking and cold as mine.

He casts his eyes to the floor and shakes off my touch, but he doesn't leave.

Behind us I hear a cough. Pasha's eyes flicker open and, squinting in the brightness, he groans before throwing up on the floor.

The bonds wound around my heart release a little, and I take a deep, shaky breath. You don't realize how tightly things hold you in until they let you go a little.

"Where'm I?" Pasha slurs, placing his cheek against the carpet, unable to focus on either of us.

He's still intoxicated. And the state he's in still makes me angry.

"You're at Jackie's cafe, Pasha. You came here yesterday with Roxy. What did you take?" Cassey asks him gently, while grabbing a mop and some paper towels from the corner of the room.

"Drunk s'all," he mumbles.

I sink down onto the rough floor tiles to help her clean him and the floor up. She shouldn't have to do this. It was me that brought him here.

Subdued, Roxy bites his fingernails in the doorway, keeping his distance.

Pasha zones out for a second. I put my hand on his face and turn his head until he opens his eyes again.

When Crash crouches down next to me, I want to move closer and be surrounded by his warmth. I want to share with him my relief that Pasha's woken up.

If there is any alcohol still in his stomach he needs to get it out. Get him to drink warm water and throw up until he can't throw up any more, he signs.

He hands me a cup of tepid water he must have got from the little sink in the corner.

Is there a bathroom we can take Pasha to? I write on my torn receipt and hold it out to Cassey.

Cassey nods, and with Crash's help we get Pasha upright. I motion for Roxy to come with us, but he shakes his head, then seems to have second thoughts and picks up the blanket off the floor, drapes it around Pasha's shoulders, and follows us to the bathroom.

It's a tiny room, just enough space for a toilet and sink, but at least it's clean. I kneel down on the floor next to Pasha while Crash and Roxy stand outside.

The toilet is flimsy and the seat slips around as Pasha leans his arms on it and rests his head between them. I rub my hand up and down his back, feeling the skin slip over the bones, the thin layers of muscle. And even though he probably feels like death, the way he leans his body into my touch breaks my heart a little more. When was the last time anyone touched him without wanting something in return?

I do as Crash suggested and get him to drink warm water and throw up. There's not much left inside him, and after a while he just brings up bile and shivers uncontrollably. I wrap him back up in the blanket and help him walk back to the room with the heater.

Crash and Roxy bring in a couple of chairs from the cafe, and Cassey follows behind them with a tray of soup and biscuits, which she sets on top of the boxes.

"I can't send you back out into the rain cold and hungry," she says, glancing worriedly at Pasha, who, although now walking unaided, still looks fairly spaced out and faintly blue with cold. But I know there is only so much she can do. She can't be looking after everyone who steps in through the cafe doors looking a bit worse for wear. She would end up taking care of half of London.

"You need some dry clothes, love," she says.

But that's something we just don't have. The only clothes Pasha has are the ones he's wearing.

Cassey sighs. "Or at least dry those ones."

She leaves us. The cafe is getting busy again as the second wave of commuters call in for breakfast on their way to work.

I motion for Crash to help me undress him. If we hang his clothes in front of the heater, they should be dry in no time.

Pasha doesn't protest, but he wraps his arms around his chest protectively after we've pulled off his T-shirt, his teeth chattering. His chest and neck are black with bruises.

The clothing he has doesn't look too worn, and they are different than the clothes he came to visit me at the hospital in. It's stupid, but it hurts to think of Julian going to the clothing bank with Pasha instead of me and getting these for him.

I pull the blanket up over his shoulders and grip it tightly so he can take his trousers off in privacy. But he can't. They're too wet, and he's shaking too badly, and when Crash moves to pull them from the ankle, tears fill Pasha's eyes that he bites his lip to hold back.

It's okay, I mouth, stroking his cheek with my free hand. He shakes his head and drops to the floor, forcing me to sit down with him. It's not the softest blanket, but we fold it over his body, and he manages to kick off his jeans.

"Julian told him to fuck off and leave," Roxy says behind me, drinking soup and picking at the thin rubber of his shoes. The quiet scrape of his fingernails against the rubber irritates the hell out of me. "But I don't suppose you care now that you've *moved on.*"

I hold Pasha's gaze. His eyes look haunted. Fleetingly, I think I might hate Roxy.

"Remee," Pasha whispers softly, shaking his head.

My chest tightens. Remee is what Julian calls me. No one else. And yet, I know why Pasha is saying that name—Julian must have spoken about me, or maybe he talked in his sleep.

With an anguished expression, Pasha places a cold hand against my face and says quickly in Russian, "He told me to go, to leave him and find Cassey. He didn't want me with him anymore."

When he breathes, it is a sob.

Where is he? I mouth, not sure he can understand me.

Desperately, I gesture at Crash. *Ask him where!*

"I went back to the hospital for you, but your bed was empty. He just wanted to get out of his head. Alone. I'm scared for him."

"Where is he?" Crash asks.

"I don't know. We were on the north bank when he told me to go. He needed money. He didn't want to run anymore. He owed people, but I don't think he cared."

His words rip through me like barbs tearing open old wounds. The north bank is where he used to go to get picked up. The only money he is going to get is by selling himself.

The anger I felt at Roxy is nothing compared to this. I don't know if I'm angry at Julian, myself, or the whole fucking world.

Unsteadily, I get up. I don't feel right. I walk first one way, then another before heading toward the door.

"Romeo?"

I turn around, not really seeing the room anymore.

Where are you going? Crash signs.

Take Pasha to your foster parents, I sign.

What?

Please. Please do this for me.

Where are you going?

I'll come back. I promise. I have to look away from Crash. I can't bear to see what I'm doing to him. I feel as though I'm breaking something fragile and unspoken. Instead I pull the phone he gave me out of my pocket. *I have this.*

They wouldn't let me collect your pictures from the hospital. That's why I was so quick. They would only give them to Estella or you. I thought we could go and pick them up now.

I can live without my pictures. I can do more.

Help him, I plead to Crash. *I know where Julian is. You know I have to do this. I will come back. I just need to find him.*

What if he doesn't want to come with you?

Why does he have to ask me that?

He holds my gaze, and I can't look away without appearing a liar, so I don't. I never want to go back out on those streets again, and I will do anything I can to get Julian away from them.

Please take Pasha back home with you. He's going to get sick if he goes back out there.

I turn away.

"Wait," Pasha calls.

He holds out his hand, and I crouch back down in front of him. "I'm sorry, Remee," he says.

Oh God, I don't want him to be sorry!

I'm sorry too, I mouth, briefly pressing my forehead against his. *None of this is your fault.*

"What's wrong with him?" Pasha asks me quietly, glancing at Crash. "He speaks, but he's like you."

I touch my ears.

"Oh. How do I talk to him?"

I mime writing.

"I can read some, but I can only write in Russian." Pasha looks embarrassed.

Taking his hand in mine, I squeeze it, wanting to hug him, but not wanting to hurt him. *Speak slow so he can read your lips.*

I'm not sure Pasha understands, but I know he will be okay with Crash. I know Crash will look after him.

As I stand up, Crash quickly takes off his jacket and hands it to me.

You can't go out there like that. I want it back, he signs trying to smile, but I can see how much I'm hurting him. He moves his head so hair falls across his eyes, and he doesn't even try to brush it away.

I can't look back, even when Cassey calls out my name. I just shove open the steamed-up cafe door and keep running.

The rain has turned to sleet, and the darkening sky casts everything a deep blue-gray. I pull Crash's hood around my face and slow down, keeping close to the buildings to avoid the worst of the weather, but still the bitter cold makes my hands and face ache dully.

Roxy catches up with me at the end of the street and grabs hold of my arm to stop me. I try to struggle out of his grasp, but he holds on.

"There's something you should know," he says out of breath. "A few days ago, someone was asking around about you down the embankment. A man. He was Russian. He was offering a hot meal to anyone that had information about your whereabouts."

The familiar feeling of dread settles heavily in my stomach, but then I think of Julian and what he's doing right now, and it hardly seems important.

Roxy waits for my reaction, but I don't have one. I want to be somewhere else right now. I need to be somewhere else. I need to find Julian. And whether it's anger or love that's burning brightest through me, it doesn't matter as long as it drives me forward and I find him before he does something I can't help him walk away from.

Letting go of my arm, he shrugs.

"You should watch your back," he shouts, dodging the cars as he runs across the road.

But I don't care about watching my back. Whatever's happening behind me, I can't change. I look out across the river, twisting roughly under the gray-black bridges, and for the first time in my life, I feel a deep conviction that whatever I'm heading toward is the thing I can change.

THERE ARE ALWAYS TWO

ONCE I reach the other side of the river, I can't decide which way to go. If Julian's here, he could be anywhere along this road. I choose the direction the wind is blowing, so the icy rain hits the back of my head instead of my face, and walk along right next to the river, watching how the wind whips the water up into the air and the rain drifts across in great billowing curtains.

There's hardly anyone else around, and the few people I see are hurrying to be somewhere else, somewhere safe and dry. I still don't see myself as one of them, but I don't belong out here anymore either. I don't belong anywhere. The feeling makes me want to carve out my own little world, somewhere I've made safe, somewhere away from all this.

My pace has slowed, and it's not because I'm too tired to run. It's just… however much I try to put Crash's words out of my mind, I can't—what if I find Julian, and he really doesn't want to come with me? Where does that leave me?

I can't force him. I don't want to manipulate him. I want him to *want* to be with me, to want something better for both of us, but what if he just doesn't? What if he wants to self-destruct, to let the streets annihilate all that he is, all that he ever was, and all that we ever were in the process?

I don't let myself consider that if he wanted to still be with me, he would have found me already, because that thought scares me almost as much as not knowing where he is.

So I don't run. Not yet.

I pass the ruins of Joe Brown's cafe—Cassey's cafe—Joe was her husband. I don't look too closely. It's mostly hidden behind a six-foot paneled security fence anyway; only the remains of the collapsed roof are visible, the blackened beams swelling and splitting in the rain. My chest tightens up just being here. I have to force my legs to keep stepping forward before the whole of me seizes up and the memories crush me in place. But still they come. I remember the shock of finding out the fire had destroyed the only place we felt at home, the only place that had *been* our home, albeit only briefly. I remember how distraught Julian was. I remember how he cried as he fucked me. I remember the helplessness I felt as he fell apart, his arms around me.

It was after that that everything changed.

I walk faster.

After today, I vow never to come here again.

The path drops down, away from the river. If the rain wasn't so heavy, I could see the wasteland from here, the arches beyond it, but today I see nothing but a bleak, ghostlike mist.

I walk slowly, the icy puddle water seeping into my shoes until my feet are so cold I can no longer feel them. No one is hanging around. No one is trying to sell themselves. No one is looking. I glance at the time on my phone—it is only midmorning, which might explain the lack of trade.

I see a bus stop a few hundred meters away. I head toward it, wanting only to hide out from the relentless downpour for a moment and gather my resolve.

Unfortunately, I'm not the only one.

"Hi," the girl says, smiling at me hopefully while she tries not to shiver. She needs more clothes on than a Lycra miniskirt and a halter-neck top in this weather. She must be freezing.

There is only one long tippy seat, and she is sat in the middle of it, a painted doll, her makeup too bright in this grayness.

"You look like you could use a bit of distraction. I could give you something that would be very distracting." Her unreal gaze darts down to my groin, then slowly back up, and she smiles again, though it doesn't reach her eyes. It's just business.

I shake my head and sit down, watching the gutter at the roadside overflow with black water. I'm not walking to find another shelter from the rain just because she wants me to pay her to give me a blowjob. She must be desperate, but I guess Crash's expensive coat is covering up most of my poverty.

She sighs, knocking her head against the Perspex behind her, and shimmies her skirt a centimeter farther down her thighs. "I just need one more fucking customer, then I can go back. You know he's made me sit out here in the fucking rain since ten last night?"

I don't know who he is. I don't want to—I hate him already—but I don't want to talk to her or be her friend. I feel sorry for her, I really do, but it's just this whole thing. No one should be reduced to this, used like this. It disgusts me. And when I think of Julian hitting on men in bus shelters or by the side of the road, not enough clothes on for the weather, I start to unravel inside.

"If you're waiting for the bus, it left five minutes ago. You've got a bit of a wait 'til the next one."

Fuck…. I dig my fingernails into my palm. I *am* unraveling inside.

I should be running the length of this road searching for him. Instead I'm sitting in a bus shelter being hit on by a prostitute, waiting for the rain to stop, terrified of what might happen if I do find him, of what might be destroyed. It's pathetic, and right now I feel so powerless. And I can't stand feeling like this anymore.

This morning was so calm, those birds singing in that misty garden so far away from this moment. I can't reconcile it.

I pull out my phone.

I'm looking for a boy. He has blond hair. His name is Julian. I type and show her the screen.

She shrugs dismissively. "You should come later. There are a lot of boys, whatever color hair you want. If you close your eyes, we can pretend." She smirks, and I dig my fingernails in deeper. "You lend us a quid so I can go get a cup of tea?"

Scowling, I put the phone away and glance sidelong at her. Money? I've got no money. I didn't even think that far ahead.

I thrust the phone back in my trousers and ball my frozen hands into fists and shove them in Crash's coat pocket. The back of my fingers brushes against something. A leaden weight settles on my chest as I realize I have Crash's wallet.

He got cash out this morning to top up my phone. He knew it was in here when he gave it to me. He must have. This hurts so fucking much when I think of how I left him. How I gave him no consideration at all. I close my eyes against the rain. Sometimes it's so much easier not to care for anyone.

I stare down the road at the never-ending stream of cars, trying to suppress the hopeless panic I suddenly feel—it's the same way I used to feel as Julian disappeared with some stranger, and I waited for him, imagining I might never see him again. Fuck... where is he? Even if he doesn't want me anymore, I've got to find him and help him see there is more than this, so much more than this dirty, gray, oppressive, fucking city.

I get up and, as an afterthought, blindly root around in the wallet and pull out a note. It's a ten. I hold it out to the girl. I know Crash would want me to give it to her.

She stuffs it into her top and nods in thanks, and I walk back out into the rain. I hear a car pull up behind me, a door slam. I don't know what makes me turn around and look. Maybe I have acquired a sixth sense for trouble, living out here for so long, but when I do, I see the girl pinned up against the back of the shelter by a man in a black hooded top I assume to be her pimp. Her eyes are trained on me, her arm pointing, and when he turns, I know he's going to come after me, and I know I have to run.

Everything happens so quickly. I don't know if it's some sort of scam, if she just waits there to find out if someone is worth mugging, and he dives in hoping the victim is too embarrassed to go to the police to report being robbed by a prostitute, or whether she's just so desperate to get out of the cold right now she told her pimp I hadn't paid her.

It doesn't matter; it doesn't change anything. I'm still going to get robbed if I don't get out of there.

He is only a few meters away. I have no advantage on him at all. And he's fast. I can hear his breathing, his feet splashing against the ground right behind me. Any second I expect his hand to close around Crash's coat and my feet to be jerked from under me, but it doesn't happen.

I feel like an animal caught out in the wilderness, my heart hammering so hard my ribs are going to crack. I spot an alleyway I recognize across the street, and without really looking, I fly out into the road, dodging traffic and praying nothing hits me. A car swerves, and I stumble, but I right myself and carry on. I sprint down the narrow alley, my shoes slipping on the waterlogged cobblestones, the noises echoing all around me. I remember sleeping here once in one of the run-down garages filled with old rubbish and broken pieces of machinery. It wasn't long after I was beaten up, but I remember not caring because Julian always made me feel so safe we could have been anywhere on earth. It's all so familiar, and yet it seems as though I'm remembering scenes from another life.

My legs are burning, but I'm fast. I know I'm fast. I know I can outrun him if I just keep going. Sometimes Julian and I would just run and run, just for the exhilarating hell of it, just to feel free, untethered. It was the only real feeling of freedom we ever got.

I can't tell how close behind me he is anymore. I don't want to look. I take a tiny turning—not even wide enough to stretch my arms out—which leads behind a dilapidated Chinese restaurant. My mouth waters even though I'm in flight. I used to love the smell of this place, but all I see now is how pitiful and dirty it is.

I keep making odd turns and double back until I can no longer hear him behind me, and I'm almost certain I've lost him. I'm running on autopilot, relying on my knowledge of these streets to find me somewhere to lay low for an hour or two before I can go back out there, when it hits me where I am, where I've run to. I stop and hold my aching sides, bending down to get my breath back. Ahead of me is a familiar six-foot security fence. I'm not really surprised; rather I'm filled with a deep sense of resignation. I ran here like we always did, because it was the one place that was safe. Cassey's cafe. I guess even burned out and destroyed, it might still be safe for a short while. Messily, and with none of Crash's strength or grace, I leap and manage to scramble up and over the panel. I drop to the floor on the other side and sink back against the inner fence.

The ruin is pretty unrecognizable as a building now. I suppose that's a good thing. I can pretend I'm somewhere else, at least.

I pick my way carefully across the debris toward an opening. But however cautious I am, shards of broken glass and sharp pieces of metal still pierce the thin soles of my shoes to cut my feet.

I don't intend to go all the way in. I just want a bit of shelter, but the black beams drip relentlessly and the only shelter seems to be much farther inside.

Julian thought people would use this place as a squat, but it's completely uninhabitable even for the desperate. Everything still smells charred and dead. The burnt wood is turning to mush beneath my feet, and I'm afraid to touch anything in case I knock something crucial out of place and the whole thing collapses. I'm considering crouching under the sagging counter for a while—it's not raining under there at least—when I see the only intact door still left in the place is shut. It leads to the room we stayed in while we lived here, the room we lay with one another and fell to pieces in after we found the place like this.

It'll just be full of ghosts, full of fractured and painful echoes of all we were, and I shouldn't want to go in there after everything, but they're my ghosts, mine and Julian's. And maybe they're all I'll ever have.

I stand before it, the rain surrounding me like a shroud.

At first I think it's locked, but it's just stiff, and the wood has swelled up in the frame. I push it hard with my shoulder, putting all my weight into it, and it swings wide so fast I'm sent sprawling across the relatively dry floor, but in such stale darkness, I can't see. I gather myself up onto my knees and wait until my eyes adjust to the quiet gloom. Slowly, I can pick out a few shapes, a cupboard we balanced the old TV set Cassey lent us on, the sink we used to wash the dishes in, the two tiny sunken chairs. The window is boarded up with the warped top of a table from the cafe nailed to the frame, beneath it a lumpy mattress piled with blankets. I stand up, curious. Someone has stayed here in this wretched place. I inch closer and freeze.

Two eyes stare up at me, unblinking.

My heart stops.

There are no blankets on the mattress, just a body layered with too many clothes.

And they are so very, very still.

It can't be. I don't want to, but I know without a doubt.

Julian.

My heart is obliterated, everything.

I can't move. I imagine this is what it is to be shot. The agony utter and inescapable.

Time stops.

My knees give way, and the pain shocks me into moving, into dragging myself toward him. I can't breathe. I'm suffocating. My ears are ringing. *This* is the explosion. The aftermath will never come. Everything has gone. Nothing is left. I am too late. I should have known he would come here. All the time I wasted searching stupid swimming pools. Why didn't I work it out? This was our *home.* My fingers reach out, my arm shaking so violently something will break. I'm going to be sick, but I need to touch him. Oh God, I need to touch him.

He is so cold.

But corpses don't cry, and he blinks, just once, his breath hitching the same time mine does. The world blurs. I still can't fill my lungs, but I don't care. My face is pressed so tightly against him, all I need to feel are his tears soaking into my hair.

NEVER LET ME GO

JULIAN IS in a bad way. Even through the breathless relief I feel to have my arms around him, pushing the both of us against the stinking mattress, I know he's not right.

I'm just trying to ignore it for a few selfish, bright seconds.

I'm just so fucking elated to have found him, I pretend the darkness can't touch me. I am alight and glowing from within. And I desperately want this reprieve to last.

But it doesn't. It can't.

Because apart from blinking and the occasional whisper of breath I feel against my neck, Julian hasn't moved. He doesn't hug me or touch me or even shiver with cold—and he is so, *so* cold—he just lies deathly still, his tears a dark patch on the mattress beneath his head.

My thumb rubs gently across the unshaven coarseness of his cheek as I search his face, trying to hold his gaze and communicate something, *anything* in this gloom, but he seems to have retreated and won't even look at me anymore. And it's this complete desolation that distresses me more than anything, an apathy so crushing I can feel it heavy in the air around me. But how can he feel any other way while he's rotting away in this dingy room?

I can't let my fear or panic take hold. I've got to help him.

Wiping my eyes with the back of my shaking hand, I turn my head in the gloom, looking for something to use as a lever to pry the tabletop away from the window frame. We need some light in here instead of this grimy darkness, though I am terrified of how much worse Julian's condition might be once I can actually see him properly.

I feel around on the debris-strewn floor next to me, searching for something suitable, but there are just bits of glass and nails and—my heart plummets as my fingers trace their cold plastic bodies—needles.

It's not as if I didn't know he was using, I tell myself. So the evidence should come as no great surprise. But it still hurts that this artificial escape is what he chose over me. It still scares me that I don't know how to deal with it.

But I can't focus on that right now. Whether he wants me or not, I'm going to help him. I'm not going to abandon him. Ever. He can push me away all he wants, but I'm going to be there for him.

I move to stand up, but I find that the hem of Crash's coat is caught somewhere. I tug, but it doesn't give. I slide my hand down to feel Julian's fingers griping the soft material. My heart soars at this tiny contact, and I lock my warm hand around his icy one and curl forward, letting my forehead rest against his side, feeling so strong and yet so weak at the same time.

Never let me go, I think desperately, my throat tight as I squeeze his fingers. *Please, never.*

"Remee?" His voice is so fragile and unsure, it's like ice fracturing apart under too much pressure. "Is this real?"

I look up, still not certain if he's seeing me or not, and bring his hand up to the side of my head and nod so he can feel it, tears filling my eyes again.

"I'm so tired," he whispers, and he sounds so far away I don't know if I'll ever be able to reach him.

I know, I sign brokenly, but it's too dark for him to see me.

THE TABLETOP splinters and splits as I rip it away from the frame. For a second I think the whole thing is going to come away in one huge heavy piece, and I drag the mattress into the center of the room out of the way. It takes all my strength to lever the nails out and eventually lift it away in two warped sections.

Rainy gray light spills into the room, making everything look ten times worse than before, when the fire-damaged mess was hidden in the darkness. The melted furniture and bowing black walls are the stuff of nightmares. I kick the glass and needles out of the way and crouch down in front of Julian, intent on slipping my arm under his shoulders to help him up. I couldn't carry him like I carried Pasha. I'm not strong enough, though I would try if I had to.

Come on, I sign. *We're getting out of here.*

His eyes are black and bruised right down to his cheekbones, and he flinches away as my hand reaches out to touch him again.

I recoil as though I've been slapped.

But fuck, I can't act like some hurt kid anymore. I can't fall to pieces every fucking time my heart cracks apart a little more, because if I did, I wouldn't be here. I would be lost out there like Roxy and Cricket and all the others are. I would be as broken as Julian is.

I've got to carry on and keep carrying on, even when it feels too much, the world too heavy.

I hate the way he won't meet my eyes. I don't know if it's the effects of some drug he's still on, or if he's just disappeared so far inside his own head nothing can reach him. Either way, he's not himself. Everything about him is pale and faded.

But despite all that, when I look at him, I know I'm exactly where I should be. All my hopes, all my dreams, all my fucking fantasies lead to him. Still. Even like this. I am his.

Heavy footsteps crunch across the courtyard outside, then stop. Alarmed, I glance at Julian, but he doesn't react as though he's heard anything at all. Tiptoeing over to the end of the room, I peer out of the window, but no one is there. I strain my ears, but only the hushy sounds of the rain hitting the ground fill the silence. Then out in the cafe something is knocked, a voice curses softly, and I hurriedly scan the room for a weapon, something I can use to protect us. I see the bent metal bar that once held the tabletop I've just broken off the window, and I hold it aloft, my heart beating too fast, my breath held, as the door to the room is shoved open.

I exhale shakily. It's not the man who chased me from the bus stop. This guy is maybe twenty and dressed as poorly as we are. He glances behind himself as if checking to see whether this is a trap, then looks from Julian to me. His bleached white hair makes him look like a badly drawn caricature, like he wants to be someone else. I wholly distrust him. I don't know what he wants, but I can see him weighing me up. I shift the bar so I can swing it if I have to and step in front of Julian.

"I've got some business to conduct, kid. Go play outside." His voice is deep and commands attention. His eyes bore into me. I hold my ground. I'm terrified of what he wants with Julian.

"That means *fuck off.*"

Maybe he can see the way the bar is trembling in my hands, but I'm not moving.

All at once he lunges, and I swing, but I'm too late, and I hit the wall, spraying dust and plaster all around us. He laughs coldly, ducking behind me to the other side of the mattress.

"It's alright, Remee. Put it down," Julian says, still sounding so far away and wincing as if it hurts to speak.

No. I shake my head. How can this possibly be all right?

"I don't have enough," Julian whispers, but not to me.

The guy leans in close to him, and I can see the glint of a blade taped to the inside of his jacket.

Fuckfuckfuck. He has a knife. My teeth sink into my lip so hard I can taste blood. I don't know what's going on, but the way this is playing out, so sudden and familiar, is terrifying.

"Well, I'm here now… and you owe me and you know I don't like to leave empty-handed." The guy shrugs indifferently as he speaks, a hardness to his gestures that scares me almost as much as the knife does.

My hands are sweating so much it's hard to grip the bar. My heart is beating louder than any other sound—I don't know how they can't hear it, how they can just both ignore me. I don't know what to do.

"I don't *have* anything to give you, Vic." Julian seems to deflate even further into the mattress, the words hissing out of him like air out of a punctured tire, like he wants to just disappear.

Vic's hand reaches out to grab Julian's shoulder. Maybe he's just going to shake him, but the leer on his face tells me it's more than that, and I don't think about what I'm doing. I just react, shoving the bar into his chest with all my weight behind it and pushing him off. The force knocks the air out of him, and I watch astonished as he flies backward and lies winded among debris underneath the window. I gulp down a lungful of air. I've never hit anyone like that before.

Julian blinks at me, his expression as shocked as my own, a fog clearing from his eyes.

"Run," he gasps.

What?

I can hear Vic scrabbling to get up, but I don't take my eyes off Julian's—they used to be lighter, the color so warm and beautiful it was like the autumn sun. But that light has gone. I've never seen him look so terrified.

And it becomes clear he knows Vic has a knife. He knows because whatever he owes, for whatever reason, he's been threatened with it before.

I shake my head and step over him. However this is going to end, it's not going to be with me running. The past few weeks have been hell, the worst in my life—the fire here, burning my hands, the hospital, finding out about my mother, and above it all, Julian leaving. And today I've had enough. Of everything. I've just found the one person my heart has torn itself apart for these past few weeks, and I've barely gotten over the relief, and now this dick with his ridiculous hair and his fucking sense of being owed thinks he's going to take that away from me. Anger twists around me like vapor. I'm angry at all of them, at everything. But most of all, I'm angry at this fucking concrete wasteland of a city, at people like Vic standing before me, knife in hand, people who think they can just keep taking and taking and destroying everything because they don't have the strength to stop falling. I swing the bar in an awkward blur of movement. I can hardly see. Satisfaction fills me when I feel the bar connect with something, someone, but I have no focus. I'm just striking out in any way I can. Pain bites my side, but it hardly matters, neither does the noise— Julian's near-hysterical voice as I'm being shoved back against the empty mattress, feeling suddenly weak as the rage evaporates and dissolves into the air.

I think he stabbed me.

The thought shocks me back into the moment. I sit up. Julian has the bar in his hands; his shoulders are trembling. Vic is crumpled in a heap at his feet. The knife is on the floor, covered in dust and blood.

I hold my side. There's not much blood. It just stings a bit.

I pull myself up and on wobbly legs walk over to Julian. I don't think he can stand up for much longer. His legs look as though they are going to give way beneath him. He drops the bar and holds on to the wall.

Everything is so very quiet.

The tremors run through my hand as I lay it on his shoulder. I feel him tense, and he turns and glances anxiously at my side.

"He stabbed you."

He looks close to losing it, but at least he's not so far away and unreachable.

I'm alright. It's okay.

"No, no, this is so far from okay…." Julian swallows. He looks like he's going to be sick. Vic isn't moving. "You've got to get out of here."

I know how much effort it is taking for him to stand here like this. I can hear the strain of it in his voice.

We've got to get out of here.

"They found you a family."

It's not a question. I wonder if I look different somehow to him now, and I can't bear the thought if I do.

I shrug. I guess they did, and at the same time, they didn't.

You are my family, I sign.

He drops his head, and I know there are tears in his eyes again.

I can't take it. This is too much.

"*You* need to get out of here, Remee. This is it for me." He sounds so hollow.

No. Not without you.

He starts to sink helplessly down to the floor, his gaze all over the place, and I wonder when the last time he ate was. Vic coughs thickly, his eyes still closed. There is a bloody gash on the side of his head.

Come outside and call him an ambulance. I hold out my phone. *Then let me buy you something to eat, please.*

He makes a sound halfway between a laugh and a sob. "I'm not hungry anymore, baby."

There is a certain point you have to stop arguing with people and just get on with moving forward. I scan the room for anything that might possibly still belong to Julian. Unsurprisingly, there is nothing. Then I grab his arm, settle myself under his shoulder to support him and help him stand up, and start walking.

He doesn't try to stop me. Maybe he can sense the scale of the fight he'd have to put up if he did.

The rain has stopped, and although the air is still sharp with cold, the mist seems to be lifting, the clouds whiter. I pull his weight against me as I dial 999 and hold the phone up to his ear so he can ask for an ambulance. I just want to be close to him.

I have no idea how we are going to get him over this fence. But it turns out I don't have to—of course there is a door. We step out onto the windy embankment. Julian leans heavily against me, but I want this weight.

"Not Cassey's sister," he murmurs.

I know he means the cafe.

Okay, I sign.

I don't look back.

There Is a Light That Never Goes Out

Freezing wind gusts across the choppy water, making me wish we were anywhere but next to this gray stretch of river right now. The bitter cold it brings is so familiar, it hurts to remember all the times I've suffered out here like this. I clutch Julian closer, my arm under his shoulders, holding on to him as much as holding him up. This time is different; it has to be.

Painfully slowly, we cross the bridge and stumble away from the embankment toward Vauxhall.

I don't want to hear the ambulance arrive. I want to be as far away from that place as possible. I want to forget everything that just happened, but Julian is heavy and my side is hurting more than it was ten minutes ago when I dragged him outside. I need to stop somewhere, somewhere out of this cold.

Stuck between a launderette and a charity shop, there is a tiny cafe that I've probably walked past a hundred times but never thought twice about. Not a lot of cafes around here tolerated us—when you've got nowhere else to go, most people just don't want to know. They'd rather you disappeared so they can pretend you don't exist—Cassey's was the only one we knew.

But I'm not that homeless kid anymore.

It catches me then like a sucker punch *how* different everything is—how different everything *will be*—cracks are forming all around me. The world I knew is shattering like colored glass.

I head toward the cafe's brightness.

Blissful warmth envelops us as we step through the door. There are four or five round plastic tables with bright plastic flowers in bright plastic vases. A few workmen sit eating a late breakfast in orange overalls. And although they pay no attention, I know we stand out with our shell-shocked expressions and charcoal-stained clothes, but I don't care. I help Julian sit down at a free table in the corner by the fogged-up window before I make my way up to the counter to order however much toast and bacon and eggs as I can afford with Crash's money. He would want to help, I tell myself as I pull two tens out of his wallet—though it hurts to think about why.

One day I am determined to pay him back for all of this. For everything.

I write my order for two full breakfasts and two teas on a napkin and hand it with my money to the girl behind the counter. It feels strange to order so much, to have this money in my hand and not endlessly go over all the possibilities it could buy us, to just pass it over unthinking. It's as though I have stepped into another life, and it's too big and doesn't quite fit me yet.

The girl is young and disinterested. She doesn't really look at me. She just tells me she'll bring it over when it's ready. I nod, but I wish it was Cassey standing there. I wish she were here to worry and fuss over us, but instead it's just me anxiously wondering what to do to make this right as Julian stares desolately out the window and doesn't talk to me.

My chair scrapes too loudly across the floor as I pull it out and sit down. Wincing, I draw my icy fingers across my side under my clothes, feeling for the damp stain of blood on my T-shirt and noticing dejectedly how the rip goes right through Crash's coat. My whole side aches deeply, and even though warm air is all around us, I feel shivery cold now we've stopped moving.

"Remee?" Julian says gently.

He looks so drawn and ill, and I know it's not just hunger. I know it's more than that, and I want to put my arms around him and somehow show him that we're going to be all right, but I'm not sure how he'd react to that anymore, and I'm not sure I can throw myself in the path of rejection like a leaf trusting itself to the wind. I need a bit more than that.

"Come here, let me see."

I'm alright, I sign, because I don't want him to feel guilty, and I know he does. His eyes give him away. They always did.

Please, he signs back, dipping his head.

And I smile a little despite myself—because, though I know he understands me, he has so rarely ever signed anything himself, sometimes I forget he can.

I move my chair around next to him and lift Crash's coat, sucking in a breath as his cold fingers brush my skin, the weird mix of pleasure and pain making me tremble. I close my eyes to it, not sure if I like the feeling, but not wanting him to stop. His hand cups my side over the wound, the pressure makes me gasp, and he lets up immediately, slipping a napkin against my skin instead. I catch his eye. A few people are staring at us, but he doesn't move his hand.

"It's just a nick."

He looks relieved, though I can see my blood blossoming beneath his fingers, staining the white of the napkin like a slow-moving red tide. And I know I need to clean the cut and dress it properly with something sterile.

I could clean up here—there will be a tiny toilet, these places always have them, but I don't want to leave him. I'm scared he will be gone when I come out. And I know it's stupid to think like that. He could leave anytime he wanted, but I can't bear the thought of him just disappearing out of my life with barely a word like before.

The girl brings over our breakfasts. My phone buzzes as she sets them down on the table, and I think about ignoring it, but how can I after everything? I take it out of my pocket.

Of course it's from Crash.

I'm here if you need me. I'll always be here is all it says.

My throat tightens as I stare at the words, thinking about him. About how much he wants to care. How much he wants to be here. For me. About how I felt when he held me last night, when I thought I'd never see Julian again. I run my hand through my hair.

I don't know whether I want to reply right now. I don't know what to say.

"Your family?" Julian asks quietly, shakily picking up his fork and then glancing at his plate of food as though he has no idea what to do with it.

I wish he wouldn't call them that.

A friend. Crash. He gave me this phone.

"He's worried about you?"

I shrug.

I wish he'd eat, but right now he looks in more turmoil than I am. I hate the way his hands are trembling.

Eat, I plead. Though my own stomach is one huge knot of uncertainty, and I couldn't feel less like eating.

"I can't," he whispers hoarsely.

I reach out, I can't help it, and when he doesn't push me away, I grip his hand.

All at once, his chest and shoulders start to shake as though he's coughing. He tries to cover his mouth to stop the sounds, and I realize with anguish that he's sobbing.

The toilet is through a door next to the counter. It's tiny and dark and smells of piney disinfectant and damp. There is hardly enough room for us both to stand between the little bowl of a sink and the squat white toilet, but I'm too distraught to care, and I press us both inside, holding him tightly and wishing I could tell him it will be all right, but not knowing how to make him believe it.

Maybe I was being naïve earlier, and it's not my old life that's shattering to pieces at all. Maybe it's Julian that's falling to pieces, here, in my arms, and how can I ever be strong enough to hold him together?

Eventually, his breathing becomes steadier, and I feel his lips move warmly against my ear. The sensation is so much what I've missed and craved and ached for—I want to pull him down on top of me, tumble into some netherworld of touch and feeling—that I almost don't hear his words.

"You don't owe me anything, Remee," he murmurs, trying to hide the pain in his voice by speaking quietly. "Please, please just go back to them. You deserve more than this."

I grip him tighter, but I can't stop the words searing whitely, cutting deeper than they should because it feels like he's trying to say good-bye.

How does he think I can leave him like this? Doesn't he realize I think *he* deserves more than this too?

He pulls away to look at me, his hand shaking as his fingers touch my cheek in a single hesitant gesture. I blink back my tears and look away, too upset to try and sort my feelings out, to try and convince him how wrong he is about this right now.

We clean ourselves up as best we can—I don't touch my side. I'll sort that out later—and we go back out into the cafe.

The food is cold, and Julian's words are still echoing around my head, but I sit down and eat methodically, without tasting a thing, until it is gone. Out the corner of my eye, I see Julian slowly eat the toast and then the bacon. But I know that this isn't all that he needs. That his shaking isn't just from hunger.

I don't look at him until he has finished. Instead I text Crash.

I'm coming back, I write, my fingers moving stiffly across the keys, knowing I am forcing a choice I might later regret.

I ask him what bus I need and what stop to get off.

He texts back immediately, and I can sense how happy he feels through his words.

Julian watches from across the table, though he pretends not to—I can tell this hurts him.

I pile our plates together and help him up. He doesn't ask where we're going. And although he doesn't outwardly protest as I lead him to a bus stop on the river, I feel the resistance in him.

The motion of the world outside is a blur I don't recognize anymore. Everything has lost its meaning. The weight I feel threatens to crush it all.

We are not alone at the bus stop, but I don't pay any attention to anyone else. There is just him and me, and I have things I need to say, and my heart aches that he will understand. I push him down into one of the uncomfortable red plastic seats and stand in front of him.

You said I don't owe you anything, but that's a lie, and more than that, you owe me!

His tired eyes widen at the direction I'm going in, and his drawn expression tenses. But I hold my nerve. I can't pretend that beneath my relief to have found him I'm not angry with him, that I don't want him to fucking know that, because I am and I do. And I need to touch the surface of it before it starts to consume me.

You promised me that you'd be there. I shake my head as his hand reaches out to me. I don't even bother to wipe away my tears. *That you'd do anything for me.*

He nods, hurt, and then looks at me, really looks at me for the first time, and I know the traffic, the people, the whole fucking world has vanished for him too.

I don't want him to ever stop looking at me like that.

I'm not getting on this bus, I sign. *Unless you get on it with me and you stay with me tonight. If you want to go in the morning, I won't stop you. After everything, you owe me this much.*

I fold my arms stubbornly, trying to appear as strong as my words, but tears are still rolling down my cheeks. This is it, all I have, and if he doesn't want me….

Julian drops his head, and for one awful second I think he's going to say no, but instead of saying anything, he pulls me into his arms and rests his head against my stomach—so, so careful of my side.

I can't bear the thought of anyone ever knowing me like he does.

The bus comes, and we get on it.

I pull him with me down the aisle, and we tuck ourselves away on the worn back seats, the floor sticky beneath our feet. Closing his eyes, Julian wearily rests his head on my shoulder, and I put my arm around him and pull his skinny frame against my good side. His chest rises and falls shakily but steadily beneath my hand—I don't know where we are with one another, but this, at least, is a start.

London moves slowly beyond the window; the black fumes of the traffic stain the air. If I never saw this place again, I don't think I'd miss it.

Without wanting to, I start to worry about what I have just done. There are no guarantees that Kay and Peter will want to take in yet another homeless kid, even for a night. I don't even know whether Pasha is still with Crash, though I can't imagine Crash letting them turn him away. And I expect Estella will have to be involved.

And even if they do let Julian stay for the night, what then? What becomes of us tomorrow in the cold light of morning? What do I do if he just wants to leave? I said I wouldn't stop him, but they were just tiny words, and the promise I made to myself to always be there for him is much, much bigger.

TAKE MY HAND

EVEN IF Crash weren't standing on the pavement, leaning against the sign indicating the bus stop, I would have remembered it from this morning.

Whatever happens, I will never forget this treelined street, its huge set-back houses, the unreal expanses of green under the endless gray of the sky. I feel calmer and more contained amongst all this green than I have ever felt before in my life. I'm starting to realize maybe I need it in a way I never imagined I would need anything apart from my drawing. Not neat manicured lawns and well-clipped hedges maybe, but wilder places I've never been—forests, copses, woods, glens—the quiet, ancient beauty they contain, more a feeling than a fact, something to banish the dead weight of concrete that has crushed me for so long. Somewhere free.

We pull up alongside the pavement, and Crash anxiously scans both decks of the bus before he sees me and his face relaxes. And all at once I am struck by how very different he is from the boy by my side, how young and full of boundless energy, a force always moving forward, never looking back, strong enough to erase whatever mark the streets left on him. Whereas Julian's energy is more inward, always thoughtful and serious, his warmth a light that has shone in so many dark places, his need to take on the weight of the world his most damaging attribute. And his pain will never be gone. The scars are too deep—like mine.

We step off the bus, gripped at once by the frigid air. Crash smiles brightly—though that brightness dims ever so slightly when he sees Julian pressed against my side, barely able to hold himself up.

Immediately, Crash steps forward to help, hooking his arm around Julian's waist and taking his weight.

I feel Julian tense at his touch and pull himself upright, removing Crash's arm.

"I'm okay," he says quietly, though it takes him some effort, and he can't hide how much he's shaking.

Crash nods, looking embarrassed, and steps away.

This is Julian, I sign.

I guessed, Crash signs back quickly.

They glance warily at one another, and I'm shocked at the slight fizzle of tension, like a crackle of static electricity flickering between them, as though they don't know quite what to make of one another and have to be on their guard.

I didn't expect this.

Reaching out his hand, Julian grips the signpost. I watch him, worried he's going to fall over.

Are you okay? Crash signs at me, frowning.

Fuck, he's staring at his coat.

Yeah... I'm sorry about your coat. I chew my lip, not sure I want to tell him about the knife that went through it.

Don't worry about it, he signs. *Is that blood?*

I shrug uneasily. *How's Pasha?*

Sleeping, back at the house.

"Pasha?" Julian asks, confused.

I nod, not wanting to relive the moment I found him down there in that dark, cavernous room but not being able to stop. It terrifies me how close I thought he was to being gone—though not as much as when I thought Julian *was* gone when I found him. I never want to go through anything like that again.

I found him this morning under the embankment, freezing and sick. I thought he was dying. My gaze flicks out to the road, unable to meet Julian's eye as I sign that word.

Distressed, Julian rakes a shaking hand through his hair. I just want to get him inside.

"Is he okay?"

I think so. Crash brought him here.

I see Crash nod on the edge of my vision, his soft hair falling across his eyes.

"I told him not to go back there. I told him to go to Cassey," Julian mutters, more to the uneven pavement than to us.

But whatever was said, it doesn't matter. What matters is that Pasha is here, safe.

The sky is brightening, but it's still so cold, and Julian's clothes are not warm enough, and he's not well enough for us to be stood out here like this.

Taking a deep trembling breath, I sign to Crash, *Julian needs to stay here too tonight.*

Wide-eyed, Crash looks between us as though he doesn't know what to say.

Nothing is going like I imagined. I thought he would have anticipated me asking this.

Kay called Estella about Pasha. She'll be here soon.

My stomach fills with something heavy and turbulent. He knows I can't ask him again. I look away, afraid he'll see how anxious his words have made me.

When Estella gets here, everything will have to be official and complicated, and I know she's just doing her job, and she wants to find kids like Pasha, like me, somewhere to live, but it's not enough to fill out all the correct paperwork and tick all the fucking boxes. And I know sending Pasha with Crash was a shot in the dark, but I just hoped…

…I don't know what I hoped, just that it'd be simpler than this, that we'd have more time.

Worst of all, she'll probably want to ship Julian off to some shelter too, and that will be it. He will be gone.

I feel helpless.

This is all going wrong.

My side begins to throb painfully, but I grit my teeth. If Estella finds out I'm injured, she'll want to know why.

I take a deep breath of clear, grassy air. There are hardly any cars around. I can hear the birds and the quiet snatches of silence that follow their calls. *It's okay,* I tell myself. Julian catches my eye. I don't know whether he feels nature calling to him like I do, but I want to show him.

No one talks for a while. It's as though we're all finding our equilibrium.

Crash eventually turns to Julian, and I can see he's trying.

"Do you want to come and get cleaned up, then?" he asks in his careful way.

Thank you, Julian signs.

Crash points up the pavement to where I know there is a gate hidden in the dark tangle of hedge.

Briefly, Julian's gaze flicks over mine. Behind the cool front he's trying to show the world, I can see he feels helpless too, only for different reasons than I do, and I want to wrap my arms around him and bury my face in the warm skin of his neck and let him know it will be okay, that *we* will be okay, just as he used to tell me.

But it doesn't always work like that. There is no easy fix, though I wish there were.

We follow Crash up the street and through the garden gate. Julian's movements are stiff and uncoordinated, as though every step hurts. Cautiously, I put my arm around him again, comforted by the fact he doesn't push me away. But also scared by the distance between us that makes me think he might.

The mist and rain have left the garden such a deep, resonant green; it's as though all the music inside me is, for once, in the right key, and the smell of the trees and grasses is so pure it affects all my senses, and I feel I am seeing things clearly for the first time. Nothing like the downpours we have lived through in the city, the gray rain sluicing across the dirty streets, stirring up the griminess but never taking it away.

I know I'm no longer the only one feeling as though I shouldn't be here as Crash pushes open the heavy front door and we step through into the dark-wooded hall. I wonder if I'll ever get used to being in a place like this, ever take all this for granted, if I'll ever not feel out of place, and now Julian is beside me, if I'll ever not long for somewhere that's our own. Just us.

If you both want to go and get cleaned up, I'll talk to Kay. There are towels in an airing cupboard on the landing, Crash signs, barely looking at me, and I'm suddenly scared how this is all going to turn out, but I don't offer to go with him and explain to Kay. Instead I take Julian's cold hand in mine and lead him up the stairs.

I run a bath for him, going through the cupboards looking at all the different bath salts and bubble bath, while Julian sits on the closed lid of the toilet, his head in his hands. They say different scents can make you feel differently, so I pick out a jar of salts that says *invigorate*. I pour them into the water. They smell as fresh and hold as much promise as I imagine the sea does, though I've never seen it. I would love to slip in there, to just lie in all that warm water, suspended, in heaven. Showers are nice but not the same thing at all.

I touch Julian's arm. *Do you want me to leave you alone for a bit?*

I don't want him to say yes, but I sense he wants to do this on his own. I sense there are secrets, things he might be ashamed of, that would be revealed on the map of his skin.

He nods, his eyes glassy, before grabbing my hand.

"I can never tell you how sorry I am for letting you down," he whispers. "I never meant to let you down."

I sink to my knees in front of him, brush away his tears with the pad of my thumb.

I understand, I sign, swallowed by the deep gold of his eyes. And right then, I think I do.

He drags his sleeve across his face, the gesture making him look so much younger, so much more lost, and gives me the saddest of smiles.

I'll see if I can find you some decent clothes, I tell him, thinking of the clothing strewn messily across Crash's floor.

I squeeze his hand and get up and, checking there is no lock, close the door.

I hover around the upstairs corridor, imagining Kay and Crash downstairs, having some silent conversation about all this. I wouldn't be surprised if Kay wished I'd never come here.

I don't intend to go looking for Pasha, but none of the doors are locked.

Most of the rooms are empty shell guest rooms, with neatly made beds and the same arrangement of furniture. On a whim, I push open the door to the guest room I was in briefly last night, the room that looks over the garden. The curtains are still drawn over the tall sash windows, the material thin enough to allow the soft glow of daylight into the room. Pasha is splayed out under the covers of the bed I never slept in, so thin and bruised, but looking completely relaxed and sleeping so much deeper than I'm sure he ever did on the streets.

I don't hear Kay approach from behind me, and I nearly bolt into Pasha's room when she says my name.

"…I'm sorry, I didn't mean to startle you."

I must look terrified. When you've lived as I have, not many people manage to creep up on you for good reason.

Appearing younger than I suspect she is, she hooks a strand of hair behind her ear and smiles sort of sadly at me, though the last thing I want is her pity.

"I'm glad you came back…."

I look down at my hands, but no words come. Have I come back? I've never felt less sure about any decision than the one I made to bring Julian here, and now I'm just going to have to ride it out.

"Your friend is welcome to stay for tonight, but tomorrow we are going to have to sort out something more suitable for him. Estella will be here soon to talk about it."

For a second I'm not sure if she means Pasha or Julian. I don't know what Crash has told her, or whether she even knows Julian is in her bathroom taking a bath. But when she glances into the room behind me at Pasha, concern, worry, and something else in her eyes, I know she means Julian is the one who can't stay.

I nod, resigned. Julian doesn't want to stay here anyway. I knew that from the beginning; I just didn't want to admit it.

A sudden twinge of pain makes me want to grasp my side. Kay is watching me closely.

Is there another bathroom I can get cleaned up in? I sign hurriedly.

And then, because I have to ask. *Do you have any dressings? I think I might have scratched myself.*

"You look as though you're in a bit of pain. Can I see?"

I shake my head a bit too firmly, but she doesn't push it. This is probably the longest conversation we've had.

Instead she leads me into the large room next to Crash's. The window is open, and I can taste the cold green breeze as it billows through the long curtains. There is an en suite in the corner.

"I'll send Crash up with the first aid kit."

I nod reluctantly as I realize I'm going to have to tell him what happened.

Again noticing there is no lock on the door, I close it and slowly ease myself out of Crash's coat and pull my bloodied T-shirt off over my head. But even though I am careful, the movement has me squeezing my eyes shut and gripping the cold porcelain of the sink to ride out the wave of pain that hits me, so sharp and intense I barely hear Crash's knock.

Still reeling, I pull open the door without thinking to cover the wound up.

Oh my God, what happened? Crash stares worriedly at my stomach.

I can feel blood running over my hip. I must have opened the cut up again. I look down at it. The cut is only an inch or two in diameter, but I think it's deeper than I initially thought. Unsteadily, I back away, meaning to sit down on the edge of the bath, but I misjudge and end up on the floor.

I'm going to get Kay. She used to be a nurse.

Don't. I reach out and grab Crash's arm to stop him. *It's okay. I just feel a bit dizzy.*

I put my head between my knees as Crash unzips the first aid kit and I feel a wad of cotton gauze placed in my hand. He guides my hand down my side and places it over the wound. I hiss and gasp at the contact. The cotton must have something astringent on it, and it fucking stings. Crash locks his fingers over mine and sits down next to me, anchoring me until the stinging has worn off, and I feel the world come together around me again.

What happened? Crash signs again, before ripping open a fresh packet of gauze and setting out some dressing strips.

I know he won't let up until I've told him.

Some prick with a knife.

He raises an eyebrow but doesn't stop what he's doing. *Something to do with Julian?*

Not exactly. He wanted something from him. I look away quickly. I can't talk about how Julian being touched by someone else makes me feel.

Crash stands up and washes his hands before carefully watching my expression for any signs of pain, then, gently cleaning the edges of my cut, presses Steri-Strips along the length of it to stop it opening so easily.

Kay will give you a tetanus shot.

Are you angry that I brought him here?

Looking a little unnerved by my question, Crash turns away and washes his hands again.

I just don't want to see you hurt, he signs when he turns back around. But he quickly changes the subject. *Are you hungry? Estella will be here in five minutes.*

No. Could Julian borrow some of your clothes?

Without meeting my eyes, Crash nods.

Estella is downstairs. I can hear her voice. And I know I should just get this over with, but I really don't want to see her right now. I don't need her to remind me I have no control over this situation.

I take Crash's clothes to Julian and wait outside the bathroom for him.

When he comes out, the difference in his appearance is astounding—it has me staring, unable to look away. The hot water has washed away the horror of this morning and left his skin with an echo of the glow that used to be there always. I long to touch him, not just his hand.

Estella is in the hall with Kay, arms full of folders, her flaming hair tied in a loose ponytail. She smiles tightly as she sees me, and I know something is wrong. Dread seeps to every part of my body.

"I'd just like a moment alone with Romeo," she says briskly to Kay.

"You can use the study if you like," Kay replies, a little bewildered, and points to a closed door across the hall.

Instinctively, I take Julian's hand and pull him after me.

Estella sighs as she sees this.

"And you are?" she queries, holding open the door.

"Julian," he answers.

The study is dark, the massive shutters still closed over the windows. Estella flicks a switch and beautiful ornate sconces halfway down the walls fill with light. I feel as though we have been transported back in time.

There is no preamble.

"Romeo, you have been implicated in an assault this morning in a derelict building next to the Thames."

Horrified, I step back, my knees hitting the back of an old leather chesterfield, which catches me with a whoosh of air. Julian remains standing.

Assault? I can't believe Vic would want to bring charges.

"The victim identified you from this." Estella pulls out a much-folded poster from her bag.

The image haunts me.

"Do you know anything about these posters? They were all over the train—"

"Romeo had nothing to do with it. It was me," Julian interrupts, standing tall and speaking more firmly than I've heard him speak for a long time.

"The police have checked the CCTV. He's on it entering the building."

"He was in another room. He didn't see what happened."

I don't know why he's lying. I can't let him take the blame. I won't let him do this.

No. I stand up, putting myself between Estella and Julian. I pull up my top.

He stabbed me, I sign. *Julian was just protecting me.*

"Then you'll have to give a statement to the police. This is in their hands." She pinches the bridge of her nose and shakes her head tiredly. "What were you doing there, Romeo?"

Feeling overwhelmed, I wrap my arms around my chest, unable to take it all.

Looking for Julian.

"You can't just bring everyone here. Kay and Peter are not some open door!"

I wipe my eyes and feel Julian's hand grip the back of my top to pull me back against him. His heart thuds against me so hard it feels like it's beating in my chest. My whole being aches for him; every cell in my body calls his name. I close my eyes and feel his arms twitch loosely by his sides, and I know he wants to put them around me, but he stops himself.

Estella sighs again. "I have other things to sort out with Kay. Given everything that's happened—" She looks pointedly at my side. "—it's in your interest to give a statement as soon as possible. I'll let the police know you're here."

When we move out and into the kitchen, Julian seems agitated. He stands by the French doors that look out onto the garden, watching two small birds flitting about on the lawn, his hand across his mouth.

Kay brings out cakes and tea, and we sit around the long kitchen table—Julian sits next to me, Crash opposite, Kay and Estella at either end. It all seems so innocuous until Estella starts talking.

"Julian, I'm afraid you can't stay here," she says, oblivious as I recoil away from the table. "You're in withdrawal," she continues as if it's an explanation.

Julian nods shakily, his expression pained.

"It'll get worse before it gets better. You should be somewhere with people who can help you through it. Kay and Peter did not sign up to look after addicts. I will find you somewhere more suitable."

Hopeless anger rushes through me so fiercely I can barely hear anyone's words. Kay sees my expression.

"It's okay," she says quietly but firmly. "I told Romeo Julian could stay for tonight."

Raising an eyebrow, Estella scribbles some comments down on a sheet.

"Alright, we'll talk about the younger boy. Pasha, is it?"

Julian gets up. "I'm sorry, I just need a bit of fresh air."

I follow him, aware of the way Crash is looking at me.

With far too much understanding in her kind smile, Kay opens the door out to the garden.

We sit around the side of the house on a shady patio, far away from the voices. This side of the house is sheltered by tall trees, conifers that stretch their branches so wide and high I can hardly see the sky beyond them. I feel safe here, under their protection.

For a while neither of us says anything. But something is still bothering Julian.

How bad does withdrawal get? I sign, wondering if this is what's worrying him.

He shrugs. "I've gone through it before." He closes his eyes so all I can see are the bruises that surround them, so I can't see how much truth there is in his words. If he's gone through it once, maybe he doesn't want to go through it again. Maybe the only thing he wants is temporarily out of reach, and once he's back on the streets, he'll carry on using. But suddenly his eyes open, and I know that's not what he was thinking at all.

"I've been so selfish, Remee," he whispers, his trembling fingers tracing the new shoots of grass poking through the paving stones. "I should have helped you find somewhere like this from the beginning, but I fell in love with you so fucking hard, I thought for a while it was enough."

It was *enough,* I think desperately. Together we burned bright enough to obliterate the darkness. He looks up, and the Julian I knew is still there, warm and sunlike; he's just buried beneath a mountain of heartache. His hand touches my face, and I feel I will dissolve into nothing if he stops touching me. I bring both my hands up and hold him there, my tears filling his palm. "And how I feel will never change. I will always love you like that. Always. But you're better off without me. I hate myself for fucking up so badly and letting you down, and I can't let anything take what you have now away from you…. I need to tell you something…."

I shiver as though the sky has darkened, the day drawn in. The wind moans through the branches like a sad song.

"I didn't owe Vic for drugs, Remee. It was for information. I had to know who was looking for you. I had to know if you were in any danger."

You didn't know where I was, I sign, feeling caught in a current determined to sweep me out to sea.

"I knew you were okay. There are always whispers, baby."

I frown. There *are* always whispers. And I wonder what it means that Julian's ghosts whisper about me.

"Vic mentioned he'd spoken to a man putting up posters of a kid in the train station. He said the guy was foreign and a little desperate. He had your poster. I was surprised Vic didn't recognize you first off, but your hair is longer now, and I guess he wouldn't have expected to find you with me.

"Remee, he said the guy was looking for his son."

I stare at him, stunned. There's not enough air, I can't breathe. The color of everything fades… the world recedes… a wave of nausea threatens to empty me.

The man I saw at the train station.

"He said he was here to find his son and take him home. They can't know, Remee. You're only sixteen. If he has some sort of proof that you are his, this"—he gestures at the house, everything—"is gone. He'll take you back to Russia. You can't give a statement to the police. He'll find you. Please let me tell them it was me."

Like a struck match, my anger flares, and I glare at him, sick of this, at all these fucking people, even Julian, planning out my life, expecting me to stay here as if this is my only fucking choice.

All those ghosts and echoes I thought were my mother… my name on the wind haunting me… she never told me about my father… he never existed for me… he still doesn't… but this exists… this wild moment, this life… this family that I have chosen for myself… Julian….

If you leave, it'd make no difference to you if I was in Russia or not, I sign, feeling my anger shift and disappear into the wind with my words, replaced by a much bigger emotion.

It would, he signs back, tears falling. *Of course it would.*

I want to take his hand again, but I don't.

I never wanted this. I fling my arms out wide, feeling something deep inside me click into place. All around us the wind rushes through the trees like a voice, the leaves whisper, and I know I'm making the right decision. I've felt on the outside for so long, all those years with my mother—my whole life, I realize—that without Julian, the divide is too wide to leap. And though I might survive here, I would rather live.

This isn't me. I don't need these walls! I hit the solid brickwork, feel the sting of it against my palm. *I don't fit in. It's too big and complicated, and without you, it's so fucking empty and hollow and it always will be!*

Anguished, he shakes his head. "Don't follow me back out there… I can't…."

But I've no intention of following him back onto the streets. I shake my head.

Have you got any money?

Hesitantly, he pulls forty pounds out of his sock and holds it out to me. "I owe someone else more than I owed Vic." He won't meet my eyes. He knows it hurts me that he would be willing to give himself away unnecessarily. He could have paid Vic off and none of it would have happened.

But it doesn't matter anymore. That money is enough for our train tickets, at least. I know too Crash would give the money from his wallet to us if I asked him, if I could face his disappointment. He tried so hard. And without him, without all this, I wouldn't be able to do what I'm about to do.

I wouldn't be able to accept the need to make my own choices, the need to have something for myself. For us. Away from all the ghosts.

I'm never going back on the streets, I tell him. I'll never even come back to London. *When I was in hospital, Cassey told me a story that gave her hope. I've thought about it a lot. Do you trust me?*

Now I hold out my hand, closing my eyes against all the doubt, and gripping tight to my hope, that singular bright thread that binds us, that he will take it and come with me.

Away from Everything

I LET my mind wander, anxiety fluttering darkly in my chest. What I've given him is akin to an ultimatum. It's probably the worst thing I could have done. But for one illuminated second I see it. Us. Sunburnt and bare-chested, walking hand in hand across patchwork fields, sun-bleached grass high as our hips swaying in the salty breeze, sky so blue it hurts.

Still he doesn't take my hand. My hope falters.

The vision is so clear, but maybe it's just a dream, insubstantial and flickering, so easy to extinguish in the dark of my mind.

Maybe the reality is too hard to picture. Too bleak and familiar. Or too alien.

I feel myself sink low, my chin on my chest, when sudden warm arms surround me tightly, pulling me close.

"I don't know what the right thing to do is anymore," he whispers into my ear, making all my senses come alive, my skin hyperaware of where his hands rest, his lips against my hair. "Where will we go that's not back on the streets?"

Feeling electrified, I push him away so I can sign. *Somewhere we won't get moved on from, somewhere we can belong and make a home. Somewhere....*

He looks at me strangely, brushing away the stray hairs the wind blows across my face.

"You're so beautiful." He swallows audibly. "It scares me that I feel like this. A few hours with you, and you make me want to believe. But I can't run anymore, Remee."

It's not running. Trust me, I plead. But maybe I am and he shouldn't. A dark figure looms large in my mind, and I can't stop and face my feelings right now.

All around us the March sky is fading. Winter is gone. I can taste change in the air, just out of reach. In a few weeks, spring will burst out of nothing, and the sleepy world will ignite with life.

Estella is going to let the police know I'm ready to make a statement, but after what Julian has told me, I can't do it. As far as I'm concerned, Vic got what he deserved, and the police are hardly going to chase me or Julian across the country. I'm not worried about that. But I am worried about Julian. He's exhausted and weak, and withdrawal is going to wreck him if we have to keep going right now, but if we don't go now, there might not be another chance.

We move out from under the shadow of the trees, grass clinging damply to our feet. It reminds me I need some different shoes. Some that will survive the miles we're going to walk.

Stopping out of the view of the French doors, I wonder what to do. Estella's voice is audible through the glass, though I can't make out what she is saying.

It occurs to me we could just walk around the other side of the house and out of the garden gate I've seen there. In a way it would be easier if I don't see Crash before I leave, but I don't think I could bear that. Even if he tries to talk me out of it, I need him to know.

I need to talk to Crash, I sign.

I'll wait around there, Julian signs, gesturing back the way we came.

I shake my head. I still don't understand what it is between them.

Standing in front of the doors, I try to catch Crash's attention. Eventually he comes.

Are you okay? he signs.

I steel myself, but when I look into those eyes that see more than he ever lets on, so honest and true, I no longer know what to say.

Instead, I touch his hand and step back onto the grass.

We'll come back inside in a minute. Julian just feels a bit sick, I lie, frustrated and wanting him to see right through it to the truth, wanting him to see how I really feel, how sorry I am.

If this is good-bye, I think, I never want to say good-bye to anyone ever again. It feels so hopeless, so wasted, so wrong.

Okay. He nods, frowning a little, but then going back inside.

I glance at Julian leaning against the wall, watching me.

Come on, I sign, walking away, trying to swallow the pain inside me.

WE STEP out of the garden without looking back. We have nothing but one another. We are so light we might just rise up, drift away.

Slowly, we walk in the opposite direction to the bus stop—we don't have enough money for the bus, but we need to find a train station. I'm still wearing Crash's coat, though I gave him his wallet back. I pull it closer around me as I cautiously hold on to Julian's hand. I could sell my phone, I think, if we need more money, but that would mean my last link with Crash would be severed. And I don't want to do that.

Once we reach the busy main road, we stop and try and work out where we are.

It will be dark soon.

No doubts, I tell myself. It will be okay. We are heading toward something better, aren't we? We are making something better for ourselves. Julian leans into me, and we sit down on a low wall that surrounds a children's playground for a moment. We're not hungry, we have money for our train tickets, and we have a plan, a sure direction—which is more than we've ever had before. I don't regret leaving. I don't regret that I will never call that house my home, that Kay will think my leaving was a failure on her part... or maybe I do, a little... but it's not saying good-bye that makes me feel guiltiest, not explaining....

I'm so deep in my thoughts, I'm unprepared for the hooded figure running down the road to skid to a halt in front of me and swing his arm around me and hug me hard.

I thought I'd never find you, Crash signs when he pulls away. *I thought I was too late!*

He's not angry. He looks scared more than anything.

The police arrived to take your statement, but no one could find you. I knew—

I'm not going back, I sign, begging him not to try and talk me round, wishing he hadn't found me... and yet....

Where are you going? He wipes his eyes. I don't realize up until that moment how upset he is.

Don't worry. I reach out, my fingers tangling in the soft material of his top. *We're not going back out on the streets.*

So where? He holds his arms out wide, bewildered.

Cornwall.

What? Where are you going to stay?

There's a caravan in a field down there, miles from anywhere. We'll be okay.

Crash shakes his head, looking like he'd rather shake me. *Please don't do this. You can't survive on nothing! What are you going to do for money?*

We have enough for our train tickets. We'll ask around the farms for work, and it'll be summer soon, we can pick strawberries.

And in the meantime? Fuck. He runs his hands through his hair and stares up at the sky.

He's scaring me a little bit.

Don't run from this, Romeo. Please. You can't run forever. You've got to stop sometime. You're not thinking it through! You can't just concentrate on what's going to happen tomorrow or next week! I know that's what being on the street does to you, but you've got to think further. You've got to give yourself a proper chance. And this isn't just some day job to Kay. She really cares. My real mum couldn't give a shit what happened to me, where I was at night. I thought I'd never have someone.... He stops and looks out over at the park, close to breaking down. *I know she would want to talk to you before you go. She won't try to stop you if this is what you really want. Please.*

I'm not going back, I sign again, making the words as small as I can.

Julian is so quiet behind me.

Crash glances at him. *And I can't make you,* he signs, deflating before my eyes.

I shake my head as he pulls his cash card out of his pocket and signs me the pin number. *No.*

But he ignores me.

Take all the money in there. The 53 bus goes to the Richmond train station. There is a cash machine there. You'll need shelter, so buy a tent you can carry in a backpack, and a camping stove and sleeping bags and water and food. Promise me you'll keep the phone and buy a charger for it, and contact me when you can.

I promise.

Without warning he leans forward and kisses me, his lips against mine so briefly I wonder if I imagined it—Julian's expression tells me I didn't—and he's gone, like a thief who's stolen a piece of my heart, running swiftly and soundlessly back the way he came. It doesn't feel like good-bye.

The cash card flexes between my fingers as I squeeze it. So easy to break. But I don't.

Julian watches me closely as we get on the bus. He thinks I'm making a mistake. He thinks I'll regret it, but I won't. This is the only route I can take that won't break my heart completely.

COLLAPSING STARS

THE STREETLAMPS flicker restlessly, the last of the daylight now just a narrow band beneath the dark gray clouds. The bus pulls up outside a small quaint train station—all dark green woodwork, baskets of flowers hanging from the eaves of its low roof—and we get off.

We're still in London, but it's not a London I've ever known.

I put Crash's card in the cash machine outside the station foyer and follow the illuminated instructions on the screen. I try to pretend I've done this a hundred times before, but my fingers hover uncertainly, afraid I'll press something wrong. Julian stands next to me, warily watching my back, even though we're the ones who look suspicious. Maybe we always will.

I check the balance because I can't help it, and take a sharp breath of cold air when I see how much money is in the account—fuck.

I'm no longer living in the world I knew, and it terrifies me.

One day I will pay him back.

Still, I don't take out much, just enough to buy us a bottle of water each, a squashed overpriced sandwich, and some paracetemol for Julian from the tiny off-license across the road.

We wander slowly back toward the station. I eat the sandwich, but Julian listlessly shakes his head when I offer it to him and swallows some paracetemol instead.

It doesn't escape me that we're not talking, that Julian looks pale and tired and in pain. He doesn't complain. He's not the type, but I know he just wants to curl up in some dark corner and sleep. It makes me wonder if he only agreed to come with me because he feels responsible for my reaction after telling me about my father, if he thinks his words were some sort of catalyst to my leaving—and maybe they were—but it doesn't matter. What matters is that we're together. That's the only thing I'm certain of in this whole mess.

I brush my knuckles against his, enjoying his proximity, even if we're not as close as I want right now.

Everything will be more hopeful in the morning when we're free of this place, free of the past, free of the ghosts. I look around. When we wake up tomorrow all this will be gone, its very existence just a painful memory.

STANDING IN front of the train timetable on the wall outside the station, I try and work out if we can somehow bypass London and get on a train direct to Cornwall from here, but the station names are like places from dreams, and the lack of light is making my head hurt.

Out the corner of my eye I see a small red car bounce up the curb and stop, but I don't pay attention to it until Julian touches my arm, his expression unreadable, and inclines his head toward the worried-looking woman who climbs out of it.

Kay.

Of course Crash would have told her where we were going.

I take a deep breath, expecting to have to fight off the urge to disappear into the stream of people coming out of the station behind me, expecting my chest to tighten with anxiety and dread, but strangely I feel none of those things.

She tries to smile, but her eyes are too pained to pull it off.

"I'm going to sit down." Julian points to the row of metal benches inside the station foyer.

I turn toward the car, knowing I can't just walk away. I don't even think I want to.

"Romeo, I'm not here to stop you," Kay says in a low voice as I approach. "I just wondered if I could talk to you before you go?"

She gestures that I get in the car.

I look around, making sure it's not a trap, that Estella and a comic horde of police cars aren't waiting around the corner to whisk me away, and reluctantly open the door and slip into the front seat.

The car is warm, and when I breathe in, all I can smell is Crash when he hugged me, all warm skin and fabric softener. Like pressure on a bruise, it hurts. I watch Julian through the windscreen, awkwardly curled up on one of the hard benches, his eyes closed. I doubt he's sleeping. *He'd just probably rather not see this*, I think miserably.

Kay assumes it's her that's making me uncomfortable, and she starts to speak quickly.

"Romeo, I know this isn't easy for you. I know so much has happened and it feels like running away is the only option you've got, but I want you to know it's not."

Her words are just an echo of Crash's.

I'd be arrested if I went back with you. I can't be arrested, I sign distractedly, not touching on the real reason we're at the train station, though the sight of him fills my vision.

As if he can sense me, Julian opens his eyes. Even worn so thin, his light buried so deep, he still shines brighter than anyone else I've ever known. Just being with him is stepping out of the shade into sunlight. And I don't want to be sat in this car while he's out there, so separate and unreachable, yet here I am.

I turn away, feeling as though this is a tiny betrayal, knowing we can't take many more of those.

All that's left of the daylight is a thin, bright line that threatens to vanish every time I blink. Inside the station people hurry to and fro, the glaring artificial light making them seem more substantial and solid than we are.

Kay shakes her head. "I spoke to the police, and the charges against you will most likely be dropped. You do need to give a statement, though. Crash told me about your cut... what really happened, Romeo?"

She's so concerned, and I'm so tired, too tired to keep everything bottled inside anymore, so I tell her how Vic stabbed me. But my fogged-up brain doesn't know where to stop and words keep pouring out of me. And before I know what's happening I'm telling her about Julian. About how I came to be on the streets, my mother, the posters, the man looking for me, how he might be my father, and how he wants to take me back to Russia.

She listens quietly. She doesn't touch me when I break down. She knows I'm not ready, that this is the closest to me she will get right now.

"Whether he is your father or not, he has no legal rights over you," she says carefully, obviously disquieted by what I've said but trying not to show it. "I've seen your papers. He's not named on them. He can't make you go anywhere you don't want to." She watches for my reaction. "Do you want to meet him?"

No.

"Maybe in time you might. And it's okay, either way, it's okay."

A train rumbles into the station, brakes screeching like birds.

"I don't suppose Crash ever told you what happened when he first came to live with us?" Kay gives me a small wry smile. "He didn't find it easy after being on the streets, and the second night he was here, he graffitied the outside of our house and the next five houses down the street with all the names and tags of the people he knew. It took weeks to clean off. But he needed to get it out of his system before he could move on. I think he felt like he was betraying them, that he had somehow left them behind."

I look away.

Estella once told me Crash was an artist of a sort. I realize now this is what she meant.

"I can see why you think you need to do this, Romeo. After having to figure life out on your own for so long, I understand why you think it has to be this way. But whatever happens, I want you to remember we are here. And if you need me, I will be there for you."

I hear the sincerity of her words, but I don't let myself really think about what she's saying. In the distance, the echoey Tannoy on the platform announces the destination of the next train. I have a desire to be on it.

Are you going to take care of Pasha?

"I hope so," she says simply, smiling that sad smile again. "But there will always be a place for you with us."

Suddenly she frowns and asks, "You're not doing this because you think he needs a home more than you, are you?"

I shake my head. I wish I were that selfless.

Thank you, I sign. *I have to go now.*

My limbs are heavy as I get out of the car.

I don't say good-bye.

I'm scared he's not going to come back. Kay's words drift to me through the open car window. I wish the noise of the station had somehow drowned her out. She's talking to someone on the phone. I see her reflected clearly in the dark glass of a shop window. I reach Julian in the foyer and pull him up and with me around the corner, out of sight, before I crumple. I don't know why it hurts so much.

Gathering me up, Julian puts his trembling arm around me, and we find a seat on one of the curved metal benches along the platform.

We board the next train.

THERE IS a sleeper from Paddington to Penzance that leaves at 10:00 p.m. I'm reluctant to go back into the city, but it's the only way. I half expect fate to have placed a final obstacle in our way—I half expect the man whose shadow has loomed across London to finally darken our path—but we make it onto the sleeper without even a ghost or a whisper.

We buy tickets for a narrow cabin on the train, and with one last push of energy, we pull the thin mattresses off the bunks and lay them out on the floor. Fraught with longing, I curl my body around Julian's, and in between the warmth we create and the constant movement of the train, I finally lose my grip on the day and let the blackness take me.

All night, Julian sleeps fitfully, one moment drenched in sweat, the next shivering and gripping onto me as though I am the only thing holding him out of the abyss. Too tired to wake fully, his restlessness infiltrates my dreams, making them wild and unsettling, full of images I can't decipher, until dawn comes and he clumsily untangles himself to be sick in the miniature sink.

Sleepily, I pull myself upright, certain I fell asleep wearing a T-shirt but unable to locate it now.

Are you okay? I sign.

"Do I look okay?" he snaps.

I flinch, his words stinging.

"Baby, I'm sorry," he groans immediately, rubbing his hands across his face. His skin is pasty and covered in a light sheen of sweat. "I feel like shit. I don't mean to take it out on you."

Gripping his stomach, he heaves into the sink once more. "I wish this fucking train would stop moving," he murmurs.

I search through my pockets for the paracetamol and hand the packet to him, but he shakes his head. "I'm just going to throw them up."

Beyond the palm-sized cabin window, the rushing night is fading. The train is due to stop at a couple of stations outside of Penzance before 7:00 a.m.

We'll get off at the next stop, I sign, certain a few miles won't make much difference. We've walked much farther before.

I find my T-shirt tangled underneath me and pick up the mattresses and pillows while Julian kneels down, his face against the sink, cold water running over his hands.

A BLOODRED sun stains the eastern sky as we step off the train. The air is cold and green, the birds whistling. There is no station as such, just a long empty platform and a few benches. Julian grabs my hand and pulls me off the low edge onto the nettle-thick ground beneath and crouches sickly in the grass. The ground vibrates around us as the train leaves.

My head is spinning, he signs crookedly, unable to speak.

I'm aching to hold him tightly, to lock our bodies together so close I can feel what he feels and take it away somehow. But instead I sit down, my arm loosely around him, so afraid of being rejected, of stretching our current limits too far, but prepared to wait for him, however long it takes.

It must be around nine o'clock by the time we move, the sun shining weakly, the sky fragile as porcelain. A man in a florescent jacket patrols the station car park, just walking up and down, absently brushing his hand against the cars. Remembering how easily Crash communicates with people without writing down or speaking, I take a deep breath and decide to try and ask him where the nearest shops are. Julian squeezes my hand, and though he doesn't know it, that gentle reassurance is all I need. I'm ridiculously elated when the man understands me and directs us to a superstore a mile down the road.

Like tourists in a foreign land, we navigate the narrow country lanes, stopping often to rest beneath the occasional trees—their waxy leaves shyly uncurling toward the light—or to lean against the bramble-covered stone walls that separate the wandering roads from the fields.

Every few hundred yards, Julian sinks to his knees and heaves, but nothing comes up. He's getting weaker and weaker, and the sight of him retching into the grass fills me with a deep fear I try to keep hold of.

Is this just the withdrawal? I sign when I can't take it any longer. If it's some other sickness, I need to get help. I can't watch him getting worse and worse and do nothing.

Wiping his mouth with a shaking hand, he shrugs. *I just... I need to stop. I'm sorry,* he signs helplessly. *I can't....*

The dark bruises around his eyes stand out in stark contrast to his skin as he squeezes his eyes shut and rocks back and forth on his knees.

Crouching down, I rest my head against his shoulder and take his weight. He's burning up and shivering.

It's going to be okay. I press my lips against his ear and will him to hear the words I can't utter.

FOR HOURS we rest at the roadside. Abstractedly, I stroke Julian's hair as he sleeps, his head in my lap, the sun arcing across the sky above us. A thick-branched tree shades us from the brightness and casts strange elongated shadows across the road. I stare off at the close dark copses and sprawling woods beyond the fields, longing to explore their cobwebbed depths, knowing that's where I want to go once we have the provisions Crash suggested. We'll lose ourselves in there, in the dark amongst the trees. And that's what I want, isn't it?

I no longer know.

Everything is so silent and yet at the same time it's not—the low hum of electricity in the wires above our heads, the *puckpuckpuck* of a tractor somewhere, birds calling, the wind and its whispers. All of it is quiet, all of it peaceful.

But I didn't think I would feel this way.

Only two cars have passed us all morning. Trying not to disturb Julian, I pull the phone out of my pocket, but I don't turn it on. I wish I could call Cassey or Crash just to hear their voices, but I'm keeping it charged for an emergency.

The sun is right overhead when a beat-up truck ambles slowly down the road and pulls over beside us. Instinctively I tense.

"Need a lift?" a man's voice calls from inside the truck. I'm too low down to see his face.

In the city it's so easy to just walk away.

Julian stirs and blinks at me blankly, his beautiful eyes dark with discomfort.

My legs feel dead, but I help him up.

Yeah, we need a lift.

The superstore is not far. When the driver of the truck works out I can't speak, he gives up trying to communicate with me and, with a genuinely puzzled look on his face, drops us right outside the entrance. He doesn't seem to expect anything for this simple act of kindness.

I use the cash machine in the football-field-sized car park, taking out so much money it makes me feel a little ill. I have the perverse urge to throw the wad of notes up in the air and watch them flutter away on the wind. But of course I don't.

I focus on the things Crash said we should buy. I sign them to Julian, and we step inside, our new life like a limb we haven't worked out how to use yet.

AT THE END OF EVERYTHING

EXHAUSTED, WE finally make it to a small copse nearby with our new possessions—a tiny, impossible tent and two sleeping bags. I will have to go back for food and water, and I intend to set the tent up for Julian before I do, but my patience has evaporated, and in the end I leave Julian tucked up in a sleeping bag, the tent useless on the ground beside him.

It takes longer than I want. I am daunted by the vastness of the shop, my head spinning, but Julian is still asleep by the time I get back, and without unpacking anything I curl up on the loamy ground beside him and sleep to the sound of rain falling through the branches above.

"BABY. WAKE up."

Although I'm shivering and soaked, it takes me a minute for the world to solidify around me.

It's already near dark, everything grainy and disappearing fast as birds darting between the trees.

In what light remains, I see Julian is sitting up, submerged in the wet sleeping bag, his body shaking fiercely as he rocks back and forth, teeth chattering hard enough to crack. I just want to hold him until he stops. Fuck.

I gather myself and pick up the stupidly complicated tent. I wish to God I'd tried harder to figure this out earlier.

Hardly able to see what I'm doing, I unwrap all the poles and lay out the dark fabric. By touch alone I work out there is a thin channel along the tent that I need to feed the poles through. It doesn't take long. And all at once I have a tent in front of me. A shelter I have made. Closing my eyes, I breathe the feeling deep.

After pushing a peg into the soft ground to secure each corner, I unzip the entrance. The whole thing is contained, floor, walls, roof, all one, all waterproof. I help Julian out of the soaked sleeping bag and into the tent, thankful the sleeping bag I didn't use is still wrapped in plastic and dry.

I'm not quite sure what to do with our wet clothes, but in the end I strip mine off and lay them along the entrance. In the dark I help Julian do the same, before numbly ripping open the sleeping bag, lying down, and covering us both.

With his skin against mine, I'm in a sick sort of heaven. I know he's not right and doesn't want me to touch him—he wants to crawl out of his own skin, and he shifts and moans restlessly. But I can't be this close to him and not remember. I can't be this close to him and not want to lose myself. In him. We have lain together like this so very few times. At Cassey's, on those nights where we couldn't sate the need to know one another inside and out, those nights we fucked so deep I can still feel it. Him. Inside me. I can't forget. I don't want to, and yet. I don't know if it will ever be like that again.

He's freezing. We both are. I force my hands to flatten out and press them to his trembling chest, pulling him back against me. There is nothing sexual in my touch. I want him to know I understand, or at least I'm trying to.

I fall asleep still locked in thought, the rain beating tiny drums against the tent.

My dreams are the emptiest I've ever had.

When I wake, Julian is gone.

A familiar tightness grows in my chest. My breathing catches as though there is not enough oxygen in the air. I unzip the tent, hoping he's just gone to piss behind a tree. Ghostly flickers of sunlight stream through the branches onto the floor of the wood. My clothes are neatly hung over a fallen tree trunk a few meters away.

Julian is nowhere to be seen.

Get a grip. I close my eyes. He wouldn't just leave me here, not after coming all this way. I'm being stupid. I'm missing something, some clue, a vague recollection just out of reach. He was sick, maybe delirious. *Where would he go?*

A twig snaps close by. I dart inside the tent and grab the sleeping bag, before standing up and looking around.

Out of breath and unsteady, Julian steps into the clearing carrying a box and several bags. He carefully puts everything down on the ground, looking ready to fall over.

Where did you go? I sign, shocked by the change in him. For the first time since I found him, he's more than just an echo of the boy I knew.

"We needed something to cook with and some more clothes." He hesitates, looking uncomfortable. "I used some of the money."

I don't care about the money.

I thought you'd gone! I sign, distressed, unable to stop myself.

The knot of fear that he *will* just go, he *will* leave me, is not something I can just undo and erase.

He closes the gap between us. His skin is still wan and pale, but as he flicks his gaze over me, there is something in his eyes that wasn't there yesterday, something I remember. Warmth pools deep inside me. I lean toward him, his clean, soapy toothpaste smell mixing with the green of the wood. He must have washed up in the sinks at the shop.

"I couldn't bear to wake you," he murmurs softly, trailing his hand through my hair, his touch lighter than the wind. "You'd have come with me and after everything you did for me yesterday, I thought you needed to rest."

I lean in closer. We're almost touching. He swallows.

"I brought you something." He pulls a small pad and a pencil out of his pocket. "It's all they had," he shrugs apologetically.

I slump down, sitting just inside the tent with the pad. *You look better,* I sign, feeling a wave of exhaustion take all my strength despite Julian saying I slept well.

"I brought you some breakfast." He opens the box and shakily hands me a Styrofoam cup of hot chocolate. "I bought a cooker too."

I nod. It's stuff we need.

"I'm sorry you thought I was gone." He sits next to me, arms hugging his knees. "I wouldn't leave you." He tries to meet my eyes.

I'm going to lie down, I sign.

"You were crying in your sleep."

I nod tightly. I know.

DAYS PASS. Mostly we sleep. There is nothing to disturb us. The weather is cool but not cold, the bright sky hidden by a web of dark branches. Sometimes I remember the dreams I have, but I'd rather not. They always start with a dark figure standing on a platform at a train station, but however hard I try to reach him, he remains just out of reach.

Nearly a week has gone by when we finally move on. Julian is more himself, though he's still weak. Packing our belongings fairly between us, we follow the windy roads, the signposts to Penzance.

But after two days of walking, we realize we're lost. There are roads, but they're narrow and unmarked. The air has changed too, the wind sharper, as though it has a purpose, the distant trees sparse and bent toward the ground. And even though I have never been there, I know we are heading toward the sea.

I think Julian feels it too. Our pace picks up, as if we're being pulled onward by a greater force than we have ever known, and we head straight across newly furrowed fields and down into a wooded valley. At the bottom of the valley, Julian catches me as I stumble across a metal rail—a railway track long disused and hidden by the undergrowth. We follow it, walking between the rails as the valley stretches up around us. We pass a tiny dark-eyed house I can't help looking back for long after it is out of sight. There were vines and bushes growing out the windows and through the roof. They were ruining it beautifully. I want to go back and draw it. I want to sleep inside.

But later.

Young trees just coming into green line our way, and sometimes block it completely—but we climb over their branches, sometimes pushing aside the vicious tangle of thorn bushes, tripping on sticks and vines, as if we do this every day in our hurry to get somewhere.

Up ahead, the train line stops as abruptly as the trees, as though we have reached our final destination—a massive landslide is barring the path, a dirty mound of mud and vegetation higher than a house.

Taking off our backpacks, we climb up onto the top of the slip, and there, unrelenting and blue-gray as forever, is the sea.

Blindly, Julian's hand finds mine, but I can't look away—I am transfixed. All the land has dropped away, a scattering of rocks into the sea, and I feel as though I am standing at the end of everything. At the end of all I have ever known.

Eventually, we scramble back for our bags and head closer, struggling across the sand dunes, razor grass cutting our legs through our jeans. Julian halts suddenly in front of me, and we crash together. And when he turns there is a wildness in his eyes, a flicker of heat and fire I don't understand the reason for.

We start to unpack the tent, blinded by the blowing sand—still it doesn't take long. We've grown pretty adept over these past few days. We weigh it down with a few well-placed stones so it doesn't blow away. And then we sit just inside, barely shielded from the battery of wind, staring out at the sea.

I don't know why, but it seems as though our whole journey has led us to this point. There is no farther we can go now. All that's happened to us seems so small, our lives so small in the face of this— we are insignificant, unimportant, and yet that only makes me want to burn all the brighter.

I don't know how long we sit like that, lost in our thoughts. I don't know if Julian feels as raw as I do—the surface of me scratched away and exposed by the salty wind, dissolving in the sea spray.

If he asked me right now what I would change, I would sign without thinking. *Everything.* Then I would look at him, and I would realize.

I would change nothing.

In my back pocket weighing me down, Crash's face, the picture I drew. I take it out, unfold it, watching how it flutters in the wind before I open my fingers, and let it go—the paper racing fast as a kite out to sea.

"He has a piece of your heart, doesn't he?" Julian asks bleakly.

You have the rest, I sign.

It puzzles me how he can think I'd ever feel this way about anyone else. Crash is my friend. It's not the same.

He has no right to ask me what he wants to ask me, and he knows it, even though the sea is drawing all the truth out of me—I can't see how it would make any difference how close he thinks Crash and I got, whether or not we fucked. After everything, he must at least understand that.

But I'm not going to lie about how I feel. *I miss him.*

"I know… it's okay." Julian's body language betrays him. "You want to go back… it's okay."

I don't want to go back. I put my head in the circle of my arms and stare at the dark space of sand beneath me. The wind is like cold fingers on the base of my skull.

"But maybe you need to… for a while…."

I look up, and Julian is staring out over the waves, his eyes as gray as the sea.

Does he want me to go?

The resigned slump of his shoulders tells me *no* more powerfully than any words could. But then, all at once it hits me: even if it's not what he wants, he's letting go his hold on me because he has to, because we have to trust that we'll come back to one another, or this is not going to work.

He's telling me I have to let go of him too. Somehow.

"This is nothing to do with leaving one another," he says quietly, as if he can read my mind.

He gives me a sad, lopsided smile that breaks my heart a little bit.

"I'm yours and I always will be. I will wait for you here. I promise."

I turn away, biting my lip. I don't understand how I can be homesick for a home I never had, a city I hate, a man I never knew. But Julian can't run anymore, and I can't either.

It tends to rain here early afternoons. Right on cue, a fine mist descends, and I shift deeper inside the tent, wanting Julian to come lie down with me, wanting to forget about everything, wanting to put my arms around him and settle into his warmth as the clouds break apart above us. Instead he stands up and looks at me, really looks, intensely, before pulling his jumper off over his head and impatiently wrestling with his shoes and socks. Bemused, I can't help but smile. It's all pretty comical until I see the bruises down his spine as his T-shirt rides up, the dark purple bloom over the front of his hip that disappears into his trousers. He sees me looking and stops pulling at his sock; instead he slowly brings the T-shirt up and off, his eyes on mine, his expression open but unsure, waiting for my reaction.

I'm slow on the uptake, but I realize suddenly he's stripping for me.

It feels strange, I suppose, as if our roles have been reversed somehow, and I'm not sure how I'm supposed to react, but I don't want him to stop. With casual grace he lifts his arms above his head, his fingers pointing at the sky. It's like a dance.

I scan the beach, half-afraid I'll see some dog walker wandering toward us, but there is no one.

"That's not doing a lot for my self-confidence," he murmurs, catching my wandering eyes.

His awkwardness is turning me on, more in fact than the stripping. Maybe because he's doing this even though he feels vulnerable, maybe because he's doing this to prove something.

No one else gets to watch, I sign, still a little dazed at his behavior but focusing my attention on him fully.

I could look at him all day—the rain against his skin, the perfect hollow of his collarbone, the pinprick of scars on his arms, the bruised skinny arch of his ribs, that fascinating line of fine hairs that runs from his navel to beneath the top of his jeans, the sharp defined ridge of his hips. Any and every bit of him.

Hands skimming his sides, he unbuttons and drops his trousers and stands shivering in his underwear. I try not to stare at his crotch.

"Come swimming with me?" he whispers conspiratorially, a shaking arm hugging his chest.

I sit up. I don't know quite what's got into him. Or me.

I look out at the wild gray weather, the wind whipping up the surf, and unceremoniously drag off my clothes.

I grip his hand as he steps out of his underwear and we run naked across the sinking sands to the sea.

It takes my breath like nothing else. I choke down laughter, salt water, kisses, as we tumble into the waves. Everything unfamiliar but him. Always him.

Later, we lie together in the half dark, no longer cold, no longer awkward. The torch is dimming as the wind billows against the fabric of the tent, noisy and heavy with spray from the sea, but nothing can touch us in here, no force of nature but time. I trace the bruises on his chest as he talks.

"I will be waiting for you here. I will never leave you," he whispers. "I love you for always." Over and over.

When I can stand it no longer, I let my fingers become my tongue.

He watches through slitted eyes as I stroke him to hardness, pulling me up and kissing me before I can take him into my mouth.

"I want you to fuck me, Remee. Make me come, then fuck me."

I've never—

"I know. It's okay. I just… I need you this way…. And it's safer for you too."

I bought condoms, I sign indignantly.

And he laughs, the sound resonating through me like a million brilliant lights, like sparks of a fire that will never die.

Please, he signs.

MY EPILOGUE

MY NAME is Remee Lavelle. And I am no longer running. My ghosts are gone with the wind blowing in from the sea, their whispers lost in the trees.

There is a man I still dream of, a shadow, but now also a reality too. His name is Roman Danilov. My father. He wants to make a difference in my life, to change things for me. It's been a year, but I'm still not sure yet. We have a long way to go, and I no longer make my decisions on a whim. I still won't see him without Julian, or Kay, or Crash, by my side, but strangely he doesn't mind.

The boy I love has a gift for making things grow. He still wonders at it, that he never knew before now. I tell him it's the light inside him. Things can't help but be drawn to it. And although it can't take away the darkness, I know it brings him peace when nothing else can or ever will.

This is our second summer in our two-room home. It's a signaler's cottage. The same house I saw that day, near lost to the green by the side of those narrow railway tracks, that long-out-of-use line that leads down to the sea. It belongs to the farm Julian worked at before they realized he'd be better landscaping gardens than shifting bales of hay. We rent it off them for next to nothing, showing it off proudly when people come to stay. And they do. Even though it has no running water or electricity. But there is an old well in the garden, and I bought a little generator that runs off petrol with the money from the first drawing I sold.

I deal with London in small doses. But I can't pretend I have two homes. My heart will always be here, with him.

The first night I was back after being away that first time, Julian walked me to the railway house. I didn't know it was ours then. It was still damp and full of vines. But he sat me in the garden he had cleared and wove me a crown from the leaves all around. He had made one for both of us—and with the garden as our church, we made a thousand promises without saying a word.

SUKI FLEET currently lives in the heart of England. Her childhood was quite unconventional and she spent some time living on a boat and travelling at sea with her family. Since she was very small she has always dreamed of writing for a living, but though she has written original fiction online for years and encouraged many new writers to keep going and follow their author dreams, it is only recently she got the courage to make her own dream a reality and actually send something off to a publisher.

By day she runs her own business selling fabric (her second love) and juggling family commitments, by night she weaves the stories that the characters in her head dictate. These stories often start with pain or longing but always end with love.

http://sukifleet.tumblr.com/

https://www.goodreads.com/author/show/7919609.Suki_Fleet

https://www.facebook.com/suki.fleet.3?ref=tn_tnmn

http://sukifleet.wordpress.com/

SPECIAL
EFFECT

RUSSELL J.
SANDERS